Keith Moore now lives, with [text obscured]
East Devon, but the twenty [text obscured]
spent in a town on the ou[tskirts of ...] [text obscured]
the action in this murder mystery, The Man in the [...],
takes place. Widely travelled, and with a past career
predominantly in military aviation, Keith now lists writing,
walking and eating-out with friends among his most favoured
occupations.

Were it not for the last words of a dying man to his eldest son, the body of a man in a grey suit would not have been discovered in a lay-by near the city of Bristol. Even when it was, there was nothing to suggest that the ensuing investigation would be anything other than routine, but the initial pathologist's report soon put paid to that assumption. The cause of death is clear, but very little else about the man in the grey suit is, and the investigation to determine his identity and that of his killer unearths duplicity, intrigue and a dark secret in a side street of Bristol, before it comes to a climax one evening, over a hundred miles away, in London.

Acknowledgements

That this book ever came into being is down to an idle idea shared with friends over a glass of wine in the summer of 2015. The fact that it developed from there owes much to the patience of my wife, Gill, who heard very little from me for the remainder of that year as my head stayed buried in my laptop, the kind attention of 'Jonah' for specialist advice on scene of crime procedures, the time spent by Tom Lowes, who scoured the final draft for errors, and the creative efforts of 'Team Everett', Eddie, Julie and Joe, who took a break from their chickens, donkeys and goats on the ranch in Texas to help produce the cover.

The Man in the Grey Suit

by

Keith Moore

PART ONE

Chapter 1

The body was discovered by a man out walking his dog. He was taking the footbridge over the Long Ashton by-pass, otherwise known as the A370 or 'Weston Road'. The footbridge linked the town of Long Ashton on the outskirts of Bristol with common land – fields, trees and a myriad of footpaths – that the man and his dog knew well. Returning home, the man glanced down just before he left the bridge, as something at the edge of the lay-by beneath him caught his eye.

It was early on the last Sunday in May. It had rained during the night, but the sun was now already up and rising in a clear sky, and traffic was light. Whatever it was, partly obscured by the bushes at the edge of the lay-by, hadn't been there the day before. He was sure of that. People left all sorts of things in the lay-by; usually rubbish associated with take-away food and drink, and there had even been a child's cot mattress on one occasion! It was a constant source of irritation to him and to others who used the footbridge regularly.

The man gently tugged on his dog's lead, and the animal came to a halt with a quizzical expression on its face. He leaned across as far as he safely could, focussing on the object that had caught his attention, and wondering if what he could see was the bottom half of someone. The longer he stared, the more certain he became. There was certainly the lower half of a leg; the trouser leg was partly ridden up towards the knee exposing the white skin of the calf, and there was possibly a sock over the foot and what looked like a shoe, on its side, a short distance away. The other leg was discernible but not immediately recognisable as such because it was twisted and bent in what would be a very uncomfortable way if the person, if that's what it was, was conscious or even asleep.

The man tied the end of the dog lead to the railing and, with a sharp 'Sit!' left the footbridge and scrambled down to the lay-by beneath. He stepped cautiously towards the shape that had caught his attention. It was definitely a leg. He stopped, bent forward and peered beyond the leaves, twigs and branches that had partly obscured his view before. It was a man, and it was pretty clear, even to an untrained eye, that he was no longer alive. He was very still. He was wearing a light blue shirt and dark tie with a light grey suit that would once have appeared quite smart but was now soiled and dishevelled. He was on his side, but his head was at an abnormal angle, his face appearing to be looking back over his left shoulder in a way that just wasn't natural. In an attempt to be sure, the dog-walker stretched the toe of his boot tentatively forward and nudged the man's ankle. 'Hello!' he said, in a loud voice. Each time he pushed, the ankle yielded but fell back into its previous position when he took his foot away, and there was no answer, either by word or gesture, to his brief exploratory greeting. There was nothing for it but to call the police, but first it was necessary to retrieve his dog, which was still sitting patiently on the footbridge above, and to telephone his wife to warn her that he wouldn't be home for a while.

He found his way back up the cutting, having almost to go down on all fours at times to prevent his slipping down again, and his dog wagged its tail expectantly as he reached the footbridge again. He wondered if he should go down to the lay-by with the dog until the police arrived, but he decided against it. He could keep watch just as well from the footbridge; he could keep the dog away from the traffic and, anyway, his mobile phone reception would be better. He fumbled in his pocket for his mobile and pressed the quick-dial key for his home number. He was automatically put through to his answer-phone. 'She's probably in the shower', he thought, so he left a brief message warning his wife that he might be late, and then he dialled 999.

He had never dialled 999 before, but he knew what to expect. A woman's voice answered with the question, 'Emergency. Which service do you require?' He answered 'police' and then, as objectively and concisely as he could, he described who he was, where he was, and what he had found. Then, when he had said all he could, he was asked to wait where he was, and he did.

Even though the traffic was still light, he heard the police car before he saw it, as, with its siren blaring, it sped towards him up the hill from Bristol. It passed him on the opposite carriageway, left the by-pass at a junction half a mile up the road, and, having then re-joined the southbound carriageway, it returned and pulled sharply in to the lay-by. 'I'm the man who telephoned,' he shouted to the first policeman to emerge. 'You'll find the body over there.' He pointed to the shape that had caught his attention earlier, a shape which the second policeman had already spotted and was walking towards, one hand on the radio pinned to the body-armour on his chest.

The ambulance followed a few minutes later, but much more quietly, and by the time it, too, pulled in to the lay-by, the uniformed police had used tape to cordon off a generous area around the body. No-one would be permitted beyond the cordon without protective clothing, and they would keep a record of all who visited the crime scene until the body had been recovered and the area forensically searched. A few minutes' later two unmarked police cars arrived containing the first Scene of Crime Officers. They left their cars on the road because, by then, traffic into Bristol was already being diverted through the village. They put on their white suits and shoe covers before crossing the cordon, and the body was soon hidden from view by a white tent they erected. The dog-walker, who had been asked to stay until the Senior Investigating Officer arrived, watched and wondered about the man in the grey suit. Who was he? How had he met his fate? Behind the walls of the tent attempts would soon be made to gather evidence that would help to answer those very questions.

Chapter 2

Detective Inspector Trevor Knight, on duty to respond to over the weekend, had come straight from home. He had been alerted by telephone, and the journey had taken no more than 20 minutes. He wished the roads were always as clear of traffic as they were early on Sunday mornings! He climbed out of his car beneath the footbridge shortly before 9.00 am, identified himself to the uniformed police, donned his protective clothing, lifted the tape and walked across to the white tent that protected the body from the elements. The ambulance had already left to attend to the needs of the living and would soon be replaced by a more appropriate vehicle for the corpse's journey to the mortuary, but where it had been parked a woman in her early thirties in black leathers was climbing into a protective suit beside a parked BMW motor cycle. She was a senior forensic pathologist, and he had worked with her before. He nodded to her before entering the tent and then ducked inside. He would find out whether there was anything to add to the brief details he had already received by telephone at home and by radio on his way, but he would do so after he had seen the body. It was important, in his view, to maintain objectivity. He had learned to trust his own judgement, and he valued the opportunity to gain a first impression of a crime scene as unsullied by the opinions of others as possible. He accepted that time was often precious in situations such as this, and that it was best practice to allow the pathologist access to the body as early as possible because bodies cooled from their normal temperature of 37.5 degrees Celsius to match ambient temperature at a rate of 1.5 degrees per hour. The rectal temperature could therefore often provide valuable guidance as to how long a person had been dead. He wouldn't be long.

He stood as far back as the tent would allow, and he looked carefully at the body that lay in front of him. He noted the angle of the head. The neck was almost certainly broken, but whether that was the cause of the man's death or a post-mortem injury incurred when the body had been dumped in the lay-by would be for others to determine. There was no sign of bleeding either on or near the body, neither was there any obvious bruising on the face. But there was something odd about the pallor and condition of the skin, and DI Knight couldn't quite think what it was.

The man was white and, perhaps, in his forties. He was neither remarkably tall nor short, probably around 5ft 9ins, and he looked about eleven and a half stone. His suit suggested he was an office worker. You didn't have to be Sherlock Holmes to draw that conclusion, but he could have been a manual worker dressed for a party or a wedding. Knight bent forward, lifted the man's forearm and felt the palm of his right hand; it was soft and smooth through the thin latex. More likely to be the hand of an office worker than a brick-layer! Interestingly, there was no sign of rigor mortis in the muscles of the arm, and the eyelids moved freely under pressure of Knight's gloved thumb. Rigor mortis sets in usually in the smaller muscles first and does so from

Between two and six hours after death, and yet the body was cold to the touch and sufficiently discoloured not to look fresh. Odd! Knight straightened up and looked at the shoe which lay on its side a yard or so from the body. He picked it up and looked at the sole. It was good leather, and there was still sufficient trace of the manufacturer's name on the arch to offer a reasonable expectation of positively identifying the source. 'Every little helps,' he thought. Bending forward again, he gently lifted one pocket of the suit jacket in an attempt to reveal the suit lining and, hopefully, a maker's label, but there was nothing on that side, and the other side of the jacket was tucked beneath the body. Knight stepped out of the tent and raised his eyebrows in the direction of the white-robed photographer who was now standing at the cordon with the two uniformed policemen. He said, 'I'll need to turn the body over after you've taken the initial photographs.' The photographer took that, correctly, as an encouragement to get on with the job. He nodded and walked across to the tent. Knight then made his way over to the footbridge and looked up at the man and his dog looking down. 'Good morning, sir,' he said. 'I understand it was you who discovered the body?' 'Yes, I did' was the reply. 'Thank you for reporting it and for remaining behind. You'll be asked to make a statement before you go, but can I just ask you a few questions? I'm DI Knight,' he said, holding his badge up for the man to see, 'and I'll be leading the investigation.' 'No problem at all,' the man replied. 'Thank you,' Knight responded. 'May I assume you saw the body from where you're standing?' 'That's correct,' said the man, 'I was walking back towards home with my dog.' Knight nodded. 'And did you see anyone in the vicinity of the body?' he asked. 'No,' came the answer; 'there have been a few cars going past, but that's all.' 'And, finally, did you or your dog disturb the body at all?' Knight asked. 'I left the dog on the footbridge and went down myself to make sure it was what I thought it was,' the man replied. 'All I did then was to give the ankle a nudge with the toe of my shoe in case he was asleep, but he looked pretty dead and I telephoned immediately.' Knight nodded and was thanking the man again when one of the uniformed officers came across to say that the initial photography had been completed. 'Is someone going to take this gentleman's statement so that he and his dog can go back home for breakfast?' Knight asked as he made his way back and into the tent.

With great care, Knight bent down and gripped the grey jacket by its collar and the trousers by the belt with gloved hands and rotated the torso through 90 degrees, and he looked for any sign of injury or damage. Nothing unusual presented itself. Holding it in position with one hand, he patted the hip trouser pocket with the other. It was empty. He allowed the body to return to its original position and felt in the jacket breast pocket, but that was empty, too. 'No wallet,' he mused aloud and, looking at the man's wrists, 'no watch.' Either someone had got to the corpse before it was found, or someone had done their best to make the identification of the body more difficult. Nothing was impossible, of course, but identifying the dead from fingerprinting, blood-typing and DNA-matching all took time and each had its weakness. Some people were never reported missing, some had never had cause to be fingerprinted or have their DNA recorded, and the hunt through dental records without some idea of where the deceased lived could be particularly time-consuming because there was no centralised dental data base. Knight used his thumb to lift the nearside cheek of the dead man's face and expose his molars. Yes, he had a filling or two. Again, every little would help, as would the label he had spotted on the outside of the inside breast pocket.

Outside the tent again, Knight asked whether anything other than the shoe had been found, and the answer was 'No.' 'OK,' he said, looking at the forensic pathologist, 'when you're finished, the body can be moved, but', turning to the uniformed officers, 'I want this lay-by searching before the road is opened again, and I want the verge walked for a half mile in the direction of travel. If anything else was chucked out of whatever vehicle was used to bring this man's body here, I need to know about it. If you need extra manpower, ask for it. It needs to be done in the light!'

With that, Knight got back into his car and drove quickly away down the hill toward Bristol. There was little more he could do today other than put a short report together while his mind was still fresh, and, unless anything else blew up, he could be home for lunch. His instinct told him that the patrol officers had been right to be suspicious about the circumstances surrounding the body and to initiate a request for CID attendance because there was more to this than met the eye. He was still puzzled by the presentation of the corpse, and he looked forward very much to learning what conclusions the pathologist reached as to cause and likely time of death.

Chapter 3

Less than two weeks earlier, on a Wednesday, a funeral cortege had wound its way up the road from Pill, on the southern side of the Avon Gorge, west of Bristol, its destination being Canford Crematorium. Instead of turning left for Bristol once at the junction with the A369, the hearse and the following vehicles turned right because the crematorium was situated in Westbury-on-Trym, on the other side of the gorge, and it was shorter and quicker to travel north on the M5 to cross the Avon.

The deceased, Mr Harry Davis, had died of a heart attack at the age of 67 on Thursday 5th May 2011, almost two weeks before. He was survived by his wife, Gloria, and their two sons, Tyler and Terry. Harry and Gloria and Harry's father and grandfather before him had lived in Pill all their lives, and had earned their living from piloting commercial vessels up and down the Avon Gorge between the Severn Estuary and the Bristol docks. Sail had given way to steam over the course of their lives and had posed their own problems, but the construction of the deep dock at the Port of Bristol on the mouth of the Avon in the 1970's had virtually eliminated the commercial traffic and, almost overnight, had taken the living from the men of Pill who had competed for work on the water of the Avon since the early 19th century. Nevertheless, the canny ones among them, the ones who had recognised the inevitability of what would happen, had since found other ways to turn their talents to income without moving away from their roots.

Among other activities, Harry had managed to accumulate some property in Bristol, which generated a very helpful income, and he and his wife were directors of the property company they had formed. It was a simple portfolio. There were three flats in Hotwells and a bank of five lockable garages in an obscure side road in Bedminster. With the help of his sons and, where necessary, a friend or two in the building trade, Harry had modified the flats for use primarily by university students, but that wasn't an essential criterion, and there was seldom a vacancy. Two of the garages were individually rented by each of the boys, but two of the remaining three were rented to people with addresses in Bedminster with only on-road parking.

There had been much talk of plans to redevelop and smarten up parts of Bedminster over the years, and, in Harry's view, the garages represented not only a helpful source of income but also a potential capital investment. Six months before, Bristol City Council had finalised their plans and issued Compulsory Purchase Orders for the garages and surrounding buildings. Sadly, although Harry had lived long enough to negotiate, with the aid of Gordon Long, a solicitor in Pill who had become a good family friend over the years, and who had assisted him and the boys out of many scrapes that their eye for a quick profit and characteristic lack of deference to authority had landed them in, he died before completion date. Between them, Harry and Gordon had made a very good case for adequate compensation. The generous rent the boys were 'paying' for garages No 4 and

No 5 had helped, of course, but then so had the revenue generated by the other three garages, particularly garage No 2, which hadn't changed hands for some six years.

On the way to the crematorium, the older boy, Tyler, was thinking about the garages. He had been with his Dad when the heart attack struck him down and had accompanied him in the ambulance to Bristol Royal Infirmary. Harry had initially been conscious and had managed to say a few words to him, motioning his head down to level with the pillow and making himself heard through the oxygen mask before the attendant intervened. 'Look after your Ma.' Tyler had heard, and then, with some urgency, 'Garage No 2. Get rid of everything from No 2!'

Tyler wasn't sure what was in garage No 2. It had always been locked as far as he could remember, and he had no idea who rented it. His Dad had personally done the deal years before, and a very good deal it had turned out to be. Whoever rented that garage had been content to pay double the market rate provided that he could control entry to it in all circumstances, and Harry had been happy to agree. There had never been any problem with the rent, it was paid in cash, six months in advance, and it was adjusted every year in line with inflation as agreed. It was, as they say, 'a nice little earner'.

As with the garages that had been used by the boys, Harry had never questioned what might be going in or out of the other garages. Provided the rent was paid on time, he was happy and although he might have wondered from time to time, particularly about No 2, he had never asked. If Harry was floating around in the spirit world right now, he might just take a peek, Tyler thought. If so, he'd have found a consignment of flat-screen TV's in Tyler's lock-up, and he'd have found a substantial number of packets of cigarettes in Terry's, but he would probably chuckle. He'd have to be quick, however, because the ownership of the garages would transfer to Bristol Town Council at the end of the month, and both Tyler and Terry were already looking round for other places to store their contraband. He had expected that the tenants of the other three garages would have been notified, but it was too late to ask Dad why the tenant of No 2 couldn't look after the contents of the garage he rented because Harry had been dead on arrival, despite the best efforts of the paramedic. It looked like he and Terry would now have to attend to garage No 2 and shift whatever it was that had been exercising his Dad so much, and they had about a week and a half to do so. Terry resolved to get Gordon, the solicitor, in a corner during the wake that would follow the cremation. He would have to do so before too much alcohol had been served, but if anyone would know why his Dad had been so agitated about garage No 2, it was him.

∞∞∞∞∞∞∞

The wake at the home of Gloria and the late Harry Davis in Pill was well under way when Tyler motioned to his brother, Terry, with his head and made his way across to the corner of the lounge where the family solicitor, Gordon Long was sitting by the wall, trying to balance a plate of food on his knee while drinking from a bottle of lager.

He looked up and raised his eyebrows as the two brothers approached him. 'Gordon, we need to talk about the garages,' said Tyler. 'Can we do so in here or should we go outside?' 'Well, I'd like to finish what's on my plate,' said Gordon. 'What is it you want to know?' Tyler took a sip from his glass. 'We knew about the Compulsory Purchase Order,' he replied, 'and we'll have our stuff out by the end of the month, but what about the other garages? 'Well,' said Gordon,' garages No1 and No3 shouldn't be a problem. I've been in touch with the guys who've been using them, and they know what the deadline is. They'll clear them and let me have their keys before the end of the month. Your Dad was handling No 2 himself, and I don't know what he did about it, so that might create a problem.' 'Who rents No2?' asked Tyler, 'I've never seen anyone in it in all the years I've been going to mine. Have you Terry?' 'No,' said Terry, shaking his head. 'It's always been locked when I've gone past.' Gordon motioned the two brothers further into the corner and lowered his voice. 'I've never ever met whoever rents No 2. It was a deal made five or six years ago by your Dad. I know from the case we made for compensation that whoever has that garage is happy to pay twice the going rate for it, and I suspect part of the agreement was for the tenant to fit their own lock. For twice the rent, your Dad was happy to go along with that, but the deal was done by a shake of the hand. The rent is paid six months in advance, and it's paid in cash.' 'So, are you saying you don't know who the tenant is and what is behind that padlocked door?' asked Tyler. 'That's right,' replied Gordon, 'I'm just hoping that whoever it is will read of your Dad's death in the paper and make contact before completion, otherwise the Council will simply take bolt-cutters to the padlock and charge us for disposal of whatever might be inside, and there's nothing we can do to stop them.' He paused and then went on. 'I asked your Ma for Harry's mobile phone, and I'll hang on to it if you're happy, just in case whoever rents No 2 rings in.'

The two brothers moved away to talk to other mourners, but Tyler's mind, at least, was not wholly focussed on the conversation. After all the goodbyes had been said and before Terry and his partner began to show signs of leaving, Tyler went up to him and said, 'Brother, we have to speak. I'm going to need your help. I didn't mention it to Gordon, but the last thing Dad told me in the ambulance before he died was to get rid of everything in Garage No 2. He didn't say why, but it was obviously very important to him. We need to see what's inside, and we need to do so soon. If there's anything dodgy in there, it'll attract the police, and they might want to take a look in your garage and mine, before we've cleared them out.' 'OK,' said Terry, 'but I've got a driveway to tarmac in Westbury-on-Trym tomorrow, and some roofing work on Friday and Saturday, weather permitting, so let's meet at the garage on Sunday.' 'Right,' replied Tyler, who also had one or two commitments in the following week and wanted to call in to see his Ma a couple of times as well. 'I'll bring my bolt-cutter and a new padlock, just in case, but we will only have a week to move whatever is inside. I'll go on Sunday afternoon. I'll give you a ring before I leave.'

∞∞∞∞∞∞∞∞

Across the road from the five garages, in one of the upstairs flat of a tenement block, an elderly lady was looking through the net curtain at a view of the side street that would soon be gone if the Council had their way. It wasn't a particularly pretty scene (that part of Bedminster had undeniably become very run-down), but it was a scene that had come to fascinate her. She had been more active in the early days of her tenancy and had got out a lot more during the day, but for the past two or three years she found enjoyment in sitting at her window, watching the comings and goings across the road and allowing her imagination to entertain her with thoughts of what might be going in and what might be coming out of the garages, particularly when visits took place at night. Fortunately, it was never completely dark because the side street was partly illuminated by a street lamp across the road. Curiously, the second garage in the row hadn't attracted any activity for years and was well and truly locked. She had no idea how much the rent was. Some people seemed to have money to burn!

Chapter 4

Tyler visited garage No 2 twice in what remained of the week after Harry's cremation. On both occasions he was visiting his own garage to transfer as much of its contents to storage in a lock-up he had found in St Paul's. He wasn't very happy with the area in which his new storage was sited, but he had left things a little late and, in any case, his Dad's sudden death and all that followed had left him with much less time than he had expected. On the first occasion, with his white van fully loaded and his own garage somewhat less full than it had been, he had locked it and walked over to garage No 2 to inspect the padlock. It was a serious padlock! Whoever had chosen it wanted to protect the contents of the garage at all costs and wouldn't have baulked at the price tag. They had purchased a lock made by a highly reputable maker of products optimised for marine environments – expensive yachts (and their contents) that were out in all weathers. The lock was key-operated, but there simply wasn't the time to even consider asking the maker for a duplicate. The padlock was rust-proof. It had an aluminium-alloy body and a stainless steel shackle, and the shackle was protected by an integrated shackle guard that made access by a bolt cropper very difficult. 'Difficult, but not impossible,' thought Tyler, who had yet to meet a lock that was a match for the bolt cropper he carried in his van.

On the second occasion, he visited his garage in the evening. He preferred to do so under cover of darkness on this occasion because the plasma TVs he was shifting were difficult to disguise, and even with his van backed up against the open door of his garage, there remained a risk of the load being spotted by idle and curious eyes. He didn't want any complications; the week had been busy enough as it was. He locked his almost empty garage, climbed into the driver's seat of his van and made to drive away to St Paul's, but he stopped at the entrance to garage No 2 on the way, and looked across at the padlock he had inspected a day or so before. It was still there, securing the door as it had done for years. Whatever it was protecting, whatever lay behind the door, would soon be known to him and Terry. In a way he was looking forward to the discovery they would make on Sunday, but in another way he was a little nervous. He'd felt nervous ever since his Dad had asked him to deal with the contents of garage No 2. How could the contents of a garage be so important as to feature in a man's dying words? Tyler sighed, engaged gear and pulled out onto the road.

∞∞∞∞∞∞∞

The elderly lady in the flat across the road was intrigued. She'd recognised Tyler, not by name but by his van and then, on closer inspection, by his build and clothes, as the man who had used one of the further garages periodically in recent years. Sometimes he came by day, but more often he visited at night and always in the white van. She was fascinated by what it might be that went into his garage from the van and came out again, but she was never able to see much because he was so careful. That made her even more curious. She had been watching in the afternoon earlier in the week, when Tyler had inspected the padlock on the second garage. She decided she ought to keep an even more watchful eye on events across the road.

Chapter 5

Harry's mobile phone lay on the corner of Gordon Long's desk. It was a simple and relatively old Vodafone model with no web connectivity, but that was all Harry had wanted. All calls received and made from the phone earlier than two months before his death had been deleted. The same went for the record of text messages. There would be a record somewhere, but as Harry's was a 'pay-as-you-go' contract, it wouldn't be easy to obtain that sort of data now that Harry had died even though Gordon was co-executor of his will (with Gloria).

Gordon had kept the mobile phone on his desk since sending a text message to the number he'd found on Harry's contact list, a number without a corresponding name but with the reference 'Garage Two'. There had been no record of any calls to or from this number among those still showing on the phone register, which could mean that Harry had not warned the tenant of Garage No 2 of the impending transfer of ownership. Alternatively, it could simply mean that Harry had deleted all record of such calls even before all the others made in the same period. Of course, Harry might have used other means of communication. Gordon was unsure but hoped soon to find out.

His text message had been brief. He hadn't offered any detail of the events of the past few weeks but had simply asked the recipient to make early contact, using either the mobile number or his office number.

Gordon had thought long and hard about Garage No 2 since his conversation with Tyler and Terry. He had always felt uneasy about the arrangement Harry had made with the tenant of the garage over six years ago, and although the rent had always arrived on time, and there had been no fuss or difficulty that he was aware of, his unease had never entirely left him. He still wasn't sure if Harry had been completely honest with him, and the old worry had resurfaced when Tyler and Terry had raised the subject with him at Harry's wake. Something had happened or been said to spark their interest, and he didn't know what it was. His instinct told him to maintain a professional distance from the affairs relating to the rental of Garage No 2, but with a week and a half to the end of the month and the deadline imposed by the forthcoming compulsory purchase, he needed to do all he could to ensure that the tenant, whoever he may be, was aware. Gordon had no name and no address for the tenant. As far as he was aware, there never had been any paperwork, whereas written rental agreements had been prepared for the tenants of the first and third garages. All he had now was the mobile phone number. He'd sent the text shortly after coming to work that Thursday morning, but it was now 12.15 pm and the phone remained silent.

It remained silent throughout the day, but fifteen minutes after Gordon left the office that Thursday afternoon the office telephone rang, and it was answered by Stephanie, his PA cum receptionist. 'Gordon Long, Solicitor,' she had chanted into the mouthpiece, 'Stephanie speaking; how may

I help you?' She listened, but after a short silence, the line went dead. 'Wrong number,' she thought, 'but at least they could have apologised!' Then she put the handset back on its cradle.

Had Stephanie immediately dialled 1471, she would have learned the caller's number, although she may not have recognised it as the number that Gordon had sent his short text message to.

Chapter 6

For the elderly lady in the flat across the road from the garages, keeping an eye from her window on the comings and goings was generally more fun at weekends. That said, Saturday had been relatively quiet, but, after all, she had been round to the 'Co-op' to do some shopping in the morning. Now it was Sunday; always a very quiet day for her, particularly now that she had fallen out of the habit of going to church in the morning. Nearly all the people at church she had known as a younger woman had passed on, and those who were left weren't what she might call 'friends'. It had to be said that all the effort at her church seemed to be directed towards attracting young families, and she wasn't alone in feeling that the needs of the elderly were no longer considered important. Of course, there was a traditional service at 8.30 on a Sunday morning, but that was too early for her, now, and the main service at 10.30 am no longer bore any resemblance to the services she had grown up with. She hadn't been to church on a Sunday for over five years and no longer missed it. She would meet her maker one day, she knew that, but she was sure he would understand.

She'd made herself a small sandwich for lunch and settled herself behind the net curtain with a cup of tea and the newspaper. She found that if she sat obliquely she could read her paper but still be alerted by movements across the road seen in her peripheral vision. She had not been sitting there for fifteen minutes when the white van she had seen visit one of the garages at the far end of the row in the past turned up. This time it parked outside the second garage in from the road, and two men got out. She recognised both as men she'd seen coming and going further up the row before, sometimes in the night. She recognised the taller and more thick-set of the two as the man who'd inspected the padlock of the second garage earlier on in the week, and she watched with interest as they inspected the padlock again before opening the back door of the van and extracting what she took to be bolt croppers.

There followed five minutes of fiddling as the taller of the two tried to get some purchase on the padlock, but apparently without success. The pair then turned to the use of a crow bar before returning to the bolt croppers and, with obvious satisfaction, released the padlock's hold on the door. The men replaced the tools in the van and tossed the padlock in afterwards before returning the few paces to stand at the door. Having got this far, they looked almost reluctant to open the door. They looked over their shoulders and all around them, pausing while a boy pushed a bicycle across the access road, then the taller of the two turned the handle and lifted the door high enough to allow them both in. The door closed behind them, and the elderly lady was left only with her imagination. She took advantage of the opportunity to return her empty plate and mug to the kitchenette and place them in the washing-up bowl before returning in time to see the garage door open again and the younger of the two men, bent double, emerge as though in a great hurry. As it turned out, he was bent double for two reasons: first, to allow him to navigate through the partly open garage door and, second, because he was about to be sick. She watched as he managed to get round the corner and onto the grass verge bordering the first garage before allowing the contents of his stomach to be propelled onto the grass. As he stood retching, hands on knees, the taller man emerged from the garage, closed the door behind him and went across to his van. He returned with a different padlock - one that looked all shiny - fitted it and motioned the other man into the van. They remained in the van for ten or fifteen minutes, and then they drove away.

∞∞∞∞∞∞∞

The elderly lady chuckled to herself. 'Better than television,' she muttered.

Chapter 7

It had been harder than he had imagined to dislodge the expensive padlock because the shackle guard had done what it was designed to do, prevent easy purchase around the shackle. They had been forced to cut through the additional hasp, which had been welded to the door specifically to take the new padlock. The padlock had remained intact and was in the back of the van but was no further use to anybody without its key. They'd be able to fit a new padlock to the original hasp, but neither the hasp nor the new padlock would offer serious resistance to someone determined to gain access. The sooner the contents of the garage were removed to obscure any connection with the garages and the family property company, the better.

When they'd ducked under the half open garage door and stood up inside, there was enough light to see that there was a light switch to hand on the wall. Terry operated the switch and a single neon tube flickered into life in the centre of the roof. Much of the light it generated was obscured behind years' worth of dust and cobwebs, but there was enough light to see that the garage was bare except for a once white but now dust-covered chest freezer at the far end. They stood looking at it, both surprised by the initial revelation – neither knowing what they had been expecting, but knowing that they hadn't been expecting a freezer, and one that the both couldn't help but be intrigued by because the red pilot light on the front of it was glowing. The freezer was on.

They looked across at each other and then walked slowly the length of the garage to stand, side by side, looking down at the lid. Tyler placed the tips of the fingers of his right hand on the underside edge of the lid about half way along its length, paused, and leaning back slightly in unconscious anticipation of what might be revealed, lifted the lid. Wiping the dust from his fingertips along the seam of his jeans, he gazed down. The internal light had come on, but neither he nor Terry was immediately able to grasp what it was they were looking at. It was only once Terry had leaned forward and attempted tentatively to brush the frost from the shape inside the freezer that the truth suddenly dawned. Below them, seated on the floor of the freezer with back bent forward, legs bent, and head between the knees was the clothed body of a man. At that point of realisation, Terry had bolted for the door, his eyes wide and his hand over his mouth, but Tyler had remained standing, almost in shock at what their intrusion had revealed. He looked around the garage again, seeing nothing that he had not already noticed with the exception of the dust-covered electrical cable that connected the open freezer to the plug and socket on the wall. Just then, the thermostat sensed the warmer air of the garage, and the freezer motor purred into life. That was too much for Tyler; he closed the lid, again wiped the dust off his hand, and ducked out of the half-open door. Closing it behind him, and checking to see that Terry was alright, he moved over to the van to get the substitute padlock. 'What the bloody hell have we got ourselves into? What the bloody hell did Dad get himself into?' Tyler sat in the driver's seat of

34

his van gripping the steering wheel with both hands and looking straight ahead at the wall with its clumsy graffiti facing him. 'Shit, shit, shit!' he exclaimed. Terry, looking very pale, was sitting in the passenger seat wiping the sides of his mouth and drying his eyes on his sleeve.

'I wasn't ready for that,' said Terry. 'I just couldn't help being sick. I'm sorry'. 'No worries,' replied Tyler, 'I wasn't far off, myself. This changes everything. We've got to think this through. I think Dad knew what was in that garage, and I think he must have been involved somehow. He was really fired up in the back of the ambulance. He didn't want what we've just seen to be found here. He wanted it got rid of, and we're going to have to do it - the sooner the better.'

'Should we tell Gordon?' pondered Terry. 'We need to think about that,' answered Tyler. 'I'm not sure he wouldn't want to tell the police. For the moment we act on our own, and we tell absolutely no-one. Agreed?' 'Agreed,' his brother answered. He'd got into a few scrapes over the years, and Gordon had always been there for him, but he was a straight man, an honest man, and Terry told himself that even though he and Tyler had done no more than open someone else's garage, it would kill Ma if she believed Dad had been involved in what had gone on in that garage five or six years ago. He agreed it would be too risky to bring Gordon in on their discovery now.

What the hell are we going to do?' asked Terry.

Although their first instinct was to go to a pub and examine their options over a pint of beer, the two of them were still sitting in Tyler's van. The pub idea was attractive, and both felt they needed a drink, but they could talk in the van without risk of being overheard. Still shaken by what he had seen in the garage, Tyler forced himself to get a grip and to think rationally. 'We have to get rid of the body and the bloody freezer before midnight on Sunday, and we have to do it in such a way that we aren't incriminated. I think we also have to do so without the two being linked. We can't use your van because it's smaller, and we can't use my flat truck because even if the freezer was covered, there would still be a risk of the shape giving it away. So, we'll have to use this van. It's too high to reverse into the garage, but we can reverse it right up to the door, and if we do it at night and shift it quickly, we should be OK.' 'Where are we going to take it?' asked Terry, 'We can't go to a legit scrap-merchant because they'll have your registration plate on their CCTV and, in any case, we'll probably have to do some paperwork. It's not as easy to get rid of old freezers any more. If we take it to old Gerry on the Weston Road and slip him a tenner or so, we might be able to cut out the paperwork, but that means trusting him to keep his mouth shut, and it means that someone else is involved.' 'You're so bloody right,' answered Tyler. 'I wouldn't trust him as far as I could chuck him. I think we'll have to do it 'on the fly'. There's a place I've used once before. It's tucked away in the trees between the Weston road and the airport. I'll drive up there tomorrow and take a look.' 'We'll have to be sure we don't leave any prints on it,' said Terry, nodding his head. He was no stranger to fly-tipping; it was something he'd done many times before after building and paving jobs. It saved the cost of using a recycling centre, even though the trusting customer had paid for it.

'And what about the body?' asked Terry. 'Even with the two of us, it's not going to be easy to move a frozen stiff.' 'We don't if we want to break any link between it and the freezer,' answered Tyler. 'We let it thaw. It might take three or four days, but we move it when it's thawed out and before it starts to stink. It'll be easier to move and easier to dump.' 'We could put it in the river,' suggested Terry, thinking of the Avon at high water. Tyler nodded. 'We could, but we'd have to get onto the bank because there are cameras everywhere.' 'We could bury it,' went on Terry. 'Yes, but digging a grave takes bloody hours,' said Tyler, 'and there's always the risk of us being seen. I must say, I'm all for tipping him into the bushes quick and easy at the side of a country road. He'll be found eventually, but by that time we'll be long gone, the freezer will be rusting away somewhere else, and there'll be nothing to link us with any of this. But let me think about it.'

'The sooner we do it, the better, then,' said Terry, happy to follow his elder brother's lead, 'but does that mean we should switch the freezer off now so that we can get rid of the body on Thursday night?' 'We could do,' mused Tyler, 'but I'd like a day or two more thinking time. If we switch the freezer off and leave him in it, he'll take much longer to thaw out. I'd rather we simply tip him onto the garage floor to thaw, and once we've done that, we'll have three or four days to get rid of the freezer. I'd like to know exactly where we're going to tip it before we do anything more, and I'm going to have to go out in between jobs. I'll phone you, but let's plan to be here for 10.00 on Wednesday night. I'll pick you up.'

With a nod from Terry, the conversation was over. Both brothers felt better now that they had a plan even though it was a plan dreamed up under the stress of their recent discovery and was not without its weaknesses. Tyler started the van, reversed to his left and, with one glance at the newly-fitted padlock, engaged forward gear and pulled into the side road and drove away.

∞∞∞∞∞∞∞∞

A hundred and twenty miles east of Bristol, in a suburb of South West London, a soberly dressed young man in a suit and tie, somewhere around the age of 35, was sitting alone in a pub nursing a pint of lager and trying to formulate a plan for himself. His was a much more difficult problem: how to protect himself from developments in Bristol, developments that threatened completely to destroy the illusion he had created, the illusion that was his life.

Chapter 8

The weekend had passed, and Gordon Long was back at his desk on Monday 23rd of May. Harry's old Vodafone, which had remained on since Gordon had left the office on the previous Thursday but which had remained stubbornly mute, was again on the far left corner of the desk. If no attempt was made by whoever was listed under 'Garage Two' to establish contact with him by the end of the day, Gordon had resolved to consult Gloria, the sole remaining director of the property company, and to seek her authority to gain access to the garage. In the absence of the tenant, all attempts to serve notice having been fruitless, the responsibility would fall to her to have the garage empty and unlocked in time for the transfer of ownership to the Council. He would telephone her the next day.

Tyler had hoped he would have the chance to drive out towards Weston-super-Mare on the Monday afternoon, but that had not, after all, been possible. He resolved to get up early on the Tuesday and drive the 13 miles or so to take a look at the site he had in mind for disposing of the freezer. He sat in his van before going into his home for his evening meal with Gayle, his wife, and sent a short text message to Terry. He needed to invent an excuse for his early departure the following morning, but that wouldn't be a problem. Gayle had worked as a nursing assistant at Bristol General Hospital for some years and came and went at odd hours, herself. Sadly, the hospital was due to close its doors to those needing rehabilitation from accidents and illnesses in a matter of months, and she would have to go all the way to Bristol Royal Infirmary to work in future. However, since the two children had moved out, she and Tyler had far more flexibility about their comings and goings, and they had grown to enjoy their relative independence. Sending the text message to Terry reminded Tyler that he hadn't talked to his mother since the previous Friday; he should ring Gloria, too.

For his part, Terry was still perfectly happy for Tyler to take all the decisions. Thinking wasn't his most favoured occupation or his strongest point. When he received Tyler's text message, he was in The Brewer's Arms, his local pub. He was doing a deal with a builder he knew, who had been asked if he would carry out drive repairs to a property he was working on. The job would involve digging the old surface out, preparing the site and laying fresh tarmac. The builder was happy to get one of his lads to do the labouring, but he didn't have the resources to lay the tarmac. Terry, however, had contacts that worked with tarmac who could often spare enough on an opportunity basis as long as Terry did the work and the requisite cash changed hands. Terry read the text message, shivered slightly as he was it reminded of what he and Tyler had seen in that garage on the Sunday, but then reached for his drink and gave the matter no further thought as he continued his negotiation. Life, for Terry, was straightforward. As long as he had enough cash in his pocket, and his basic needs were satisfied, he was happy. He always seemed to be able to drum up enough work to generate the wherewithal to pay the bills and indulge his simple pleasures,

And, between the two of them, Karla, who worked as a hairdresser and manicurist, and himself, they seemed to survive.

∞∞∞∞∞∞∞∞

At the window of the flat across the road from the garages, the elderly lady had seen no activity all day and had nodded-off with her newspaper on her lap and a half-empty cup of tea making a ring around the inside of her cup as it cooled on the floor beside her. She woke with a start at about 7.15 pm, wondering if she had missed anything.

Chapter 9

Gordon Long's attempts to contact Gloria by telephone on the Tuesday morning had failed. He had deliberately not telephoned too early, but when he had done so for the first time at about 10.30 am, he had been greeted by the answer-phone, but he left no message as he intended to ring back. An hour later, when his second call again rang eight times before switching to the answerphone, he left a brief message asking Gloria to ring him but didn't say why. Then, just to make sure all was well, he rang Tyler on his mobile and discovered that Gayle had the day off and had taken Gloria shopping. It was something that had been arranged only the evening before. Gordon didn't say why he wanted to speak with Gloria, and Tyler hadn't asked, assuming it was simply something to do with the winding-up of Harry's estate, but he suggested that they'd be back by mid-afternoon.

For his part, Tyler had got to work a little later than planned, having had mixed results with his early morning reconnaissance. He'd found the dirt track that led off into the trees from the lay-by at the bend in the road that linked the Weston road with the A38 at Bristol Airport, but he hadn't been able to drive very far up it because there was a pole barrier across it, and the pole was secured by a padlock. He'd inspected the padlock and decided that, unlike the premium model that had secured the door of the garage, it would prove no obstacle at all to his bolt-croppers were he and Terry to go ahead with the plan to dump the freezer in the forest beyond. The problem was that by taking such a step they would effectively be signalling the possible date on which the freezer was left in the undergrowth there. Even if it wasn't found for ages, someone might connect the two events when, eventually, it was. He went back to his van and decided to explore another possibility. A mile or so further up the A370 to Weston it was possible to turn left onto a minor road that led up through sparsely populated forested land and down to the small village of Wrington. He had a feeling that there would be places within easy reach of the road up there in which a freezer might go unnoticed for some time, and it turned out that his hunch was right. He stopped twice along the minor road to inspect possible sites he and Terry might easily find at night, before continuing along the road to Wrington and, from there, making his way to the A38 and back into Bristol. Freezers were dumped in the countryside all the time, especially so since the new rules about their disposal had made the job for re-cycling centres and scrap metal merchants more onerous and expensive. When they were discovered, the find was usually reported to the local council and to them would fall the task of recovery and disposal. By the time that occurred, Tyler was certain there would be nothing to link the freezer with Garage No 2 or with the body that had been stored in it for over five years.

By the time Gayle had returned her mother in law to her home in Pill and they had shared a cup of tea before returning to Bedminster in her little Fiat 500, it was mid-afternoon, and Gloria simply wanted to do no more than take forty winks in her favourite chair. She was discovering, as so many widows had discovered before her, how quiet it became and how lonely she felt now that the funeral was over and all who had promised to keep in touch with her had reverted to their daily lives. Tyler was a good boy, and he did try, and Gayle was almost like a daughter to her. She would like to hear more from Terry, but she could really do without Karla because she simply didn't understand what she was 'on about', and they had little in common. By the time she had woken from her nap and discovered that the light on the answer-phone was flashing, it was gone 5.00 pm. She resolved to telephone Gordon the following morning.

∞∞∞∞∞∞∞

When Gordon Long had not heard from Gloria by 10.15 on the Wednesday morning, he decided to take the initiative and telephone her again. Time was marching on, and Harry's old mobile phone still remained resolutely silent. Without knowing what was in the garage, it was impossible to gauge how long it would take to empty, and the last thing Gordon wanted was to leave it to the last minute.

The telephone was answered after four rings. 'Hello,' said Gloria with a slight uplift to the tone of her voice. 'Good morning, Gloria,' replied Gordon, slightly relieved, 'It's Gordon Long; I hope I haven't disturbed you,' he continued. 'Oh, hello Gordon,' said Gloria in a noticeably more confident tone, 'I'm sorry I didn't phone back yesterday. I was out shopping and although I got back in good time, I hadn't noticed the answer-phone flashing until it was too late. I was just about to ring you this morning, but you beat me to it. How can I help?' 'Well, it's about the garages,' said Gordon, 'you know they've all got to be cleared by midnight on Sunday otherwise we're liable to the council for the cost of them having to do it?' It was hopefully a rhetorical question, but Gordon wasn't sure how much detail Harry had shared with his wife, and so it was a good place to start. 'Yes, I think I knew that, Gordon,' she replied not overly convincingly 'but I thought that was all under control. I know the boys have already found somewhere else for their stuff, and I thought you and Harry had told the other three tenants.' 'That's almost the case, Gloria,' Gordon replied. 'I'm going to ring the boys and the two who've been renting garages 1 and 3 later today to make sure that there are no last-minute hitches, and I'll probably ask Tyler, if you don't mind, to take a look around tomorrow,' said Gordon, 'but it's not those four garages that I'm really 'phoning about; it's Garage No 2.' Gordon deliberately paused at that point. He was hoping that Gloria might know something of the special arrangement that Harry had with the tenant of Garage No 2, but he was disappointed. 'Go on,' said Gloria, 'what's the problem with Garage No 2?'

'Well,' continued Gordon, 'I haven't managed to contact the tenant. I don't know who he or she is because I don't have any paperwork whatsoever. If you can't cast any light on it, it seems the only person who would have known is Harry because he was the one who did the deal some five or six years ago. There aren't any bank details because the rent was always paid to Harry in cash, and by post, as long as I can remember. All I have is a mobile number, and I've tried it but without success. I will try one more time today, but if I'm still not successful, my advice to you in your capacity as a director of Davis Properties Ltd is that you exercise your right to see what's inside and, if necessary remove it. It will cost a lot more to leave the council to do it.' Gloria gave an audible sigh, and Gordon felt she might be close to tears. Her loss of Harry had come as a complete surprise, and he felt she was beginning to realise how much she had depended on him to conduct all the rental business. In many ways, she had seemed relieved and delighted when the compulsory purchase order had been issued. That was true, and Gloria had been even happier to think of the windfall that would come their way. She had even hoped she and Harry might be able to go on a cruise, but that would never happen now.

'Please do what you need to do, Gordon,' she said. 'I wish I could be more help, but I can't, but please have a word with Tyler first. I'm sure he and Terry will be able to clear whatever's in Garage No 2 along with their own stuff, even if they have to store it together with theirs for the time being. I didn't used to open Harry's letters, but I'm doing so now, obviously, and if anything comes from whoever's renting the garage, I'll let you know straightaway.'

Having ended the call to Gloria, Gordon decided to 'take the bull by the horns' and try once more to make contact with whoever's number was listed on Harry's mobile as 'Garage Two'. He picked the mobile up from where it lay on the corner of his desk, found the number and pressed the call button. Holding the small machine to his ear, he waited, but all he heard was the tone that told him the number was unobtainable. The text message had been sent successfully on Friday, but it seemed that the response of whoever had received it was to disenable their mobile. Had it simply been switched off, Gordon's call would have gone to voicemail, but it seemed that the sim card had been removed and the phone had been completely disconnected.

Chapter 10

'Steph, will you see if you can get hold of Tyler Davis for me, please,' shouted Gordon. 'No problem,' her reply came back, 'I'm just getting you a coffee.' While he waited, Gordon looked pensively at the Vodafone in the palm of his hand and then switched it off and dropped it in his top drawer where it joined a bottle of ink, a couple of AA batteries and some paperclips.

He heard Stephanie talking next door, and then his desk phone gave a short ring to summon his attention. He picked it up to find Tyler on the line, just as Stephanie came in and placed a steaming mug of coffee, black and unsweetened, on the mat in front of him. He returned her smile and mouthed his thanks.

'I'm sorry to intrude, Tyler,' he said, 'but do you have a couple of minutes to talk?' 'Yes,' said Tyler, 'What's the problem?' Gordon told him that he had just finished talking to his mother and went over much the same ground as he had done with Gloria. 'I have just tried again to telephone the contact on your Dad's mobile phone, but now it's been completely disconnected. You and Terry are far more familiar with the garages than I am,' he continued, 'do you think that between the two of you it might be possible to open Garage No 2, see what's in it and, if necessary, re-secure it pending clearance?' There was a pause on the other end of the line. 'You still there, Tyler?' asked Gordon. 'Yeah, yeah,' acknowledged Tyler, thinking fast and trying not to show it.

48

'Terry and me, we'll be doing some tidying up there this evening. I'm pretty sure there's a serious padlock on No 2, but we'll see what we can do, and I'll let you know what we've found by tomorrow morning. Is everything alright, otherwise?' 'I think so,' answered Gordon, 'I'm really grateful to you, and I'll be much happier, for your mother's sake as much as anything, when Monday comes and all has been sorted out.' 'So will I,' replied Tyler, but for very different reasons.

∞∞∞∞∞∞∞∞

The elderly lady in the flat across the road from the garages was already in her nightie and dressing gown and was just doing some last minute tidying up before getting into bed when she caught sight of headlights below her and the white transit van pulling into the area in front of the garages. She stepped away from the window, switched off the light and returned to her customary vantage point in time to see the two men she'd watched on Sunday get out and go over to the second of the five garages. The taller of the two opened the lock, lifted the door half up while the other man, a rolled up sheet or travelling rug under his arm, looked warily around. Then the two of them ducked inside and closed the door behind them. She drew up her chair, sat down and waited.

It seemed a long time, but it would only have been eight or nine minutes, she reckoned, before the door opened again, more tentatively this time. The taller man came out first, looked left and right and walked to the van. The other man followed him out, but then shut the garage door and stood by it while his colleague got in the driver's seat, started the van and reversed, positioning it in line with the long axis of the garage. The man by the door then opened it fully and signalled the driver back until it was a couple of paces away then, signalling him to stop, he opened the two rear doors of the transit van. With the doors open, the driver then carefully reversed the van until the top of the garage door, which jutted out about a foot, was almost touching the rear of the van. Leaving the engine idling, the driver got quickly out of the van and, following the other man, squeezed between the van and the door and into the garage.

Thirty seconds later, the lady saw movement from her lofty position, movement that would have been largely obscured by the van doors from any casual observer at street level. Something fairly large was being lifted and pushed lengthways into the van from within the garage. It was difficult to see what it might be - a table or chest of drawers or something like that. It looked as though it had been covered by a sheet or some such. She saw the head and back of the man nearest to her and the head and face of the man on the other side of the garage as both pushed the object firmly the final foot or so into the van. Quickly, the driver got back into his seat and eased the van away from the garage sufficiently to allow his colleague to close the van doors, close the garage doors, fit the padlock to the latter and jump into the passenger seat. They then drove quickly away.

On the way up the A370, Tyler was careful to stick strictly to the speed limit and to drive in such a way that he wouldn't attract the unwanted attention of a police patrol car, marked or unmarked. It wasn't even 10.30 pm, and that, he felt, was good. White vans were more likely to be considered worth following in the early hours of the morning. All had gone well thus far. All that was in the van, anyway, was an innocuous chest freezer, and one in working order, to boot. That said, Tyler wanted no-one to be able to link what still remained in the garage with him or with his brother. It was already linked somehow with Harry, their Dad, and although he was past earthly retribution, Gloria had to be protected at all costs.

Getting the frozen corpse out of the freezer hadn't been too difficult, after all. They'd removed the electric plug from the socket, positioned a folded decorator's sheet on the floor a yard or so in front of the freezer, put on gloves, and slowly turned the freezer on its long side, lifting the lid as they did so. The frozen body remained stuck to the floor of the freezer, initially, but with assistance from the two men it had been possible to rock it free and assist it forward to the lip of the freezer. Then, they'd taken each end of the freezer and lifted it up, inverting it above the body as they did. The body was left, rocking slightly, part on and part off the folded sheet on the floor. It was then a simple task to manoeuvre the solid mass, still lying on its side, onto the centre of the folded material (which would hopefully absorb water as the body thawed), position the freezer for loading on the van, rub down the parts of it they'd previously touched without the protection of gloves, and cover it with the other sheet they had brought. They then opened the garage door and, lifting and pushing quickly and smoothly, manoeuvred it into the open van. They'd left the body to thaw, lying on its side like some ancient statue that had fallen from its plinth, neglected and bearing silent witness to the crime that had been committed some five years before.

∞∞∞∞∞∞∞∞

The elderly lady was having trouble getting to sleep as it was, so excited had she been by the clandestine goings on she had witnessed from her window. How much more distant the onset of sleep might have been had she known what was left behind on the floor of the garage across the road.

Chapter 11

Tyler and Terry turned off the Weston Road without incident and drove up the minor road that meandered its way uphill. After about a mile, Tyler slowed and checked his mirror for headlights. There weren't any behind or ahead, but he knew they would have to act fast when they did stop because the bends in the road meant they wouldn't get much notice of oncoming traffic in either direction. Nearing the crest of the hill, Tyler slowed to a crawl and edged off the road into a clearing in the trees at its side. He went as far into the lightly forested area as he could with any degree of safety and stopped, immediately switching his lights off. This was a critical stage. All they needed was for some nosey local driver to stop or simply to make a note of the van registration and the whole exercise would be 'blown'. He told Terry to stay where he was for the moment while he got out and draped pieces of old rag across each of the registration plates, tucking them into the gaps between the plates and the body of the van and temporarily obscuring the numbers. Then he indicated to Terry with his thumb that he should join him at the rear of the van.

'Right,' he said, 'we'll open the doors, get the freezer out and put it on the ground on the other side of the van, with the dust-sheet still on it. Then we'll close the doors and move it further into the trees. We ought to be able to go in at least thirty or forty yards by which time we'll be invisible. If anyone stops, I'll pretend I've stopped to use my mobile. We can get this done in about four minutes. Are you ready?'

'Let's get it over with,' replied Terry, who was beginning to wish that Tyler had found a better site, one hidden from the road, but he didn't say anything more. Tyler reached for the door handle just as a headlight beam broke through the trees a couple of hundred yards down the road along which they'd already come. 'Shit!' he said through gritted teeth, moving quickly to join Terry who was already standing with his back flat against the off-side of the van. The car drove past without slowing or stopping, and they watched for the tell-tale sign of brake-lights coming on, but the car soon disappeared around the next tree-lined bend. They quickly opened the doors and eased the freezer out, taking progressively more of its weight. An empty freezer is remarkably light. After all, it's only a thin metal case with insulation and an electric heat exchanger. It was a simple job to extract it and to place it parallel to the far side of the van. Tyler quickly closed the van doors and moved round to lift the end nearest to him; Terry was already at the other end. With his back to the freezer, with hands reversed and with the light of a half-moon and the fresh memory of the exploration of the previous day Tyler led the way further into the undergrowth before calling Terry to a halt. 'It'll go in this hollow,' he said and gently put his end down on the ground. 'We'll leave it on its side with the underside facing towards the road,' he continued, 'that way it'll be even harder to spot.' As they tipped the freezer over on its long side, the lid fell open and something fell out onto it. 'What the bloody hell's that?' asked Terry. 'It's a shoe,' replied Tyler, bending over and retrieving it. 'That's lucky. I'll take it back to the garage later.' Before leaving the freezer and returning to the van with the dust-sheet and the shoe, Tyler knelt down and felt quickly around the interior in the dark for any other bits and pieces that they might have missed, but he found nothing. The pair quickly but cautiously made their way back to the van, pausing before emerging from the trees to make sure the coast was clear, climbed aboard and retraced their route back to Bristol. It was only when they stopped outside Terry's terraced house and Terry got out and walked round the front of the van that he noticed that they'd forgotten to remove the rags obscuring the number plate, and the front one was still in position. He plucked it free and passed it through the driver's window with a lift of his eyebrows before going to the rear, which he found all clear; the rag having fallen off somewhere. 'That's the second bit of good luck we've had tonight, brother,'' he said with a wry grin. 'When do we do the next trip?' 'Saturday night,' replied Tyler. 'I'll call you.'

Back on the hillside, in the hollow surrounded by trees and bushes and in the light of a half-moon, the freezer lay on its side looking as out of place as a guest in top hat and tails at a picnic. By the time Tyler and Terry were back in Bristol it had virtually completely defrosted, and a little water trickled out and onto the ground on which it lay. There was no-one there to see it or hear the very faint rustle as a damp white envelope fell from the side to which it had been pressed by the frozen left shoulder of the man in the grey suit, the side was now the upper surface of the freezer. It fell to the other side, which was now effectively the floor.

Chapter 12

Hello Steph,' said Tyler when his telephone call to the solicitor's office was answered, 'is Gordon in?' 'Hello Tyler,' Stephanie responded, 'good to hear your voice. Yes he is in and he doesn't have anyone with him so I'll pass you through.' 'It's Tyler for you, Gordon,' she said out loud as she pressed the Call Transfer button and waited for Gordon to pick up. 'Hello Tyler,' said Gordon, 'I hope you have good news for me, do you?' 'I think so,' replied Tyler. 'I took a look in Garage No 2. The padlock was a bit of a problem. I couldn't get in to cut the shackle, and I had to cut the hasp that seems to have been specially welded to the door for it, but I got the door open, and there's absolutely nothing inside.' There was no point in telling more lies than were absolutely necessary, and so far Tyler had only told one. He continued. 'Although it's completely empty, I put one of my own padlocks on the old hasp, but I can take it off when I remove the lock on my own on Saturday or Sunday.' Gordon felt that a load had been lifted from his shoulders. Somehow, he had been expecting complications that he simply didn't want as the deadline for transfer of ownership got so very near, but he was relieved by what Tyler had told him, and had no reason to doubt the veracity of Tyler's report. Had there been something valuable in the garage or if it had been full of personal possessions, for example, he might have felt obliged to inspect the garage himself, but as it was empty, he saw no reason to do so. 'I'm very grateful to you, Tyler.' he said. 'Nothing inside; that really is good news! Yes, please take the padlock off when you vacate yours. I presume Terry is almost clear of his, too?' 'I'm fairly sure he is,' replied Tyler, 'but we both plan to go down on Saturday night, and I'll make sure everything is as it should be. Will you tell Ma, or would you like me to?' 'If you're going to see her or speak with her before the weekend,' answered Gordon, 'you may as well. I don't want her to worry about it.' 'Fine,' said Tyler, 'I will'. 'Thanks again,' said Gordon, 'cheers for now.' He replaced the receiver. 'I'll have that coffee if you're making one, Steph,' he said, loud enough to be heard in the adjoining room, 'and if you have any of those chocolate biscuits left, I'll have one of those, too!' It was a simple pleasure, but he felt the occasion warranted it.

Back in his van, Tyler, too, was relieved. He hadn't really had a 'Plan B' if Gordon had insisted on inspecting the garage personally, but he felt he had read Gordon right; no 'Plan B' was necessary, and he patted himself on the back for that. He would tell Ma there was nothing to worry about when he chatted to her on Friday evening. He would have planned to do so earlier if he felt she was worrying unduly, but he doubted that she had given the problem much thought since putting it in his hands. He visualised the corpse he and Terry had left behind on a folded dust-sheet in the garage the previous evening. It would be beginning to thaw now. He didn't particularly relish going back in before it was absolutely necessary - and that would be late Saturday night – but he realised he would have to, particularly if there was any risk of melt water seeping out under the garage door and attracting attention. The dust-sheet should absorb a good amount, but he had no idea how much water a frozen adult male human being would generate as it thawed, and not many other people would! On the other hand, every time the garage door was opened, even briefly, there was a risk of compromise, and he wouldn't know how to deal with the situation that might develop if someone walking past the garage were to get a glimpse inside. He settled on a visit that night, Thursday, preferably with Terry, and, depending on what they found, perhaps a further visit 24 hours later. Darkness offered some protection from prying eyes.

'What are you doing tonight?' Tyler asked when Terry replied to his mobile call with a brief 'Hello'. 'It's darts night,' replied Terry, 'why?' 'We need to check on our mate in the garage,' answered Tyler. 'He ain't goin' anywhere,' responded Terry, 'not tonight, anyway.' 'No,' replied Tyler, 'but he might be leaking more than we thought, and we don't want anyone getting nosey about water trickling under the door, do we?' 'Suppose not,' said Terry, 'but it'll have to be after darts, and you'll have to pick me up at the pub because I'll have had a few beers.' 'What about Karla?' asked Tyler. 'She can jump in, too,' suggested Terry, 'but maybe you can drop her off at home on the way and take me back there after we're done in the garage'. 'OK,' answered Tyler, 'it shouldn't take long, but don't you go getting so pissed you're a liability! There's too much at stake, and if you've had too much I'd rather do it alone.' That was not entirely true. The last thing Tyler wanted was to pay the garage a visit on his own, but he felt the need to make the point to his younger brother. 'Don't get your knickers in a twist,' replied Terry, 'I'll be OK. See you at the Brewer's Arms at 10.30.'

Chapter 13

Tyler had had plenty of time to decide where to dispose of the body on Saturday night and, rather than simply dump it at the side of a country road, had decided on a place about ten miles south west of Bristol. There was a pub on the North Somerset Levels west of Nailsea, which he had frequented on Friday afternoons in the past with a couple of his mates. It wasn't anything to write home about, in fact it looked shabby and neglected both inside and out, but it was a genuine rustic man's drinking hole and seldom closed its doors while there were those willing to exchange money for its wares. The pub lay on the lane that linked Nailsea - a mile or so to the east - with Clevedon three miles or so west. As it ran on towards Clevedon, never more than about fifteen feet above sea level, the lane ran parallel initially with the river on its left, until this branched off to the south-west. It did so at a junction with a lane that ran south across the moor towards the village of Yatton, carrying vehicles over the river by a small hump-back bridge less than a quarter of a mile from the junction. With the body pre-positioned midway in the van, he had decided it would be a quick and simple job to stop the van on the bridge and push the body out of the sliding door on the passenger side. It would fall over the low stone parapet and into the river. It would be dark and deserted, and there wouldn't be a CCTV camera within five miles. The body would not remain undiscovered forever, but that wasn't the point. It would go undiscovered for long enough to sever all connection with the freezer, already rusting gently in a wood many miles to the west, the garage and, of course, the family property business. Once the thawing process made it possible to empty the jacket and trouser pockets, that's exactly what Tyler felt he should do, and reminded himself not to leave the shoe in the back of his van.

∞∞∞∞∞∞∞

Gayle was sitting in her favourite spot on the sofa in the front room of the home she shared with Tyler watching television. She felt she would be glad when the end of the month came and the Davis garages had been sold. Tyler had been spending too much of his time clearing his out and transferring the contents to the new place he had found. While she didn't mind the occasional night on her own, she didn't want to make a habit of it. He'd got home nice and early tonight, but he'd just had to leave to pick Terry up so that they could do some last-minute removal work. He'd promised that it wouldn't take long, but, at the same time he'd let it slip that they would have to do something similar on Friday and Saturday nights. She'd made him promise to take her out for a curry one night the following week, and he must have felt guilty about leaving her so much this week because he'd readily agreed. She would hold him to it!

At much the same time, Tyler, having left his van at the side of the road under a street lamp, was walking the fifty yards or so to The Brewer's Arms. He paused after entering the crowded bar, acknowledged one or two familiar faces, and looked around until he spotted Terry and Karla sitting round a table near the old fireplace. There was no need for a fire; there was sufficient body heat and hot air being generated by the fifty or so drinkers in the room to keep the whole premises warm. He didn't really want to get into conversation with any of the people at the table because he was stone cold sober and because he didn't want to have to make up some story as to why he was picking Terry and Karla up as he didn't know what fiction Terry might already have concocted. He tried to catch Terry's eye but unsuccessfully; so he elbowed his way through those standing between them, nodding and smiling as he did so, until he was at the rear of Karla's chair. Terry, breaking off his conversation with the man on his right, looked up, looked down at his wrist watch and acknowledged him. 'Karla, babe,' he said across the table, 'our chauffeur's here. You just about ready?' Karla got to her feet, turning to face Tyler and holding out her arms as she did so. She let out a long 'Ty..l..er. How nice of you to run us home. Come here. Let me give you a hug.' Tyler acknowledged her greeting as warmly as he could. She'd obviously had one or two vodka and lemonades too many, but she was harmless. 'No problem,' he said, 'I'm glad you've had a good time. I'm parked about fifty yards down the road under the street light,' he said, addressing them both, 'and if you want a couple more minutes to drink up, that's fine; I'll be in the van.' 'No need for that,' answered Terry standing up, 'we're all done. We'll be right behind you.' Saying their farewells, the couple downed what remained in their glasses and followed Tyler out into the night.

It took no more than ten minutes to take Karla home, watch her fumble for her front door key and, slightly unsteadily, let herself in. Ten minutes after that they were following what had become their customary practice of parking the van opposite the door of Garage No 2, looking carefully around, unlocking the padlock, lifting the door only half way, ducking in, closing the garage door behind them, feeling for the light switch and turning the internal light on.

Nothing much had changed. Perhaps the shape under the dust-sheet didn't look quite as angular, quite as solid as it originally did, but neither Tyler nor Terry were quite sure. The thawing process had certainly begun because the folded sheet on which the shape rested looked wet. Terry stepped into the centre of the garage and tentatively lifted a corner of the covering sheet. He reached across with his left hand and felt the lapel of the suit jacket. It was pliable whereas twenty four hours previously he was sure the jacket had been frozen stiff. However, it wasn't anywhere thawed enough to permit a search of the pockets. That would need to wait. 'I think we should take the sheet off,' said Tyler in a low voice, almost a whisper. 'It might be stopping the air from getting to it.' He looked at Terry, who wasn't looking all that well, again, but he replied with a nod. Tyler took the sheet, folded it and put it on the floor to one side of the still, mute, partly frozen corpse. 'We'll come back tomorrow,' he said, 'and then we'll move it out on Saturday night. You gonna be OK?' 'Yeah.' said Terry unconvincingly. 'If there's nothing more to do, let's go.'

∞∞∞∞∞∞∞∞

Across the road, the elderly lady was fast asleep in bed. She hadn't seen them arrive and didn't see them go.

Chapter 14

It was just after 5.00 pm on the Friday afternoon. The M4 at its eastern end was fairly busy, but traffic was flowing steadily in both directions. The rented transit van that was heading away from London was one of possibly hundreds on the motorway between Bristol and London at the time, but this one was different in that it bore the name and logo of a London firm that specialised in the hire of refrigerated vehicles. It had been rented in West London that afternoon by a youngish man in his late thirties, who had paid with a credit card in the name of Simon Lee, and it was the same man, in jeans and t-shirt, who was at the wheel as the van passed north of Heathrow.

It had been a difficult week for him, a week full of uncertainty and suspicion as events he had been successful in controlling for years had suddenly assumed control of him. He knew he really should have taken action long before, but that didn't make it any easier – quite the contrary. He had certainly intended to do so, but he had procrastinated despite the risk of leaving things as they were. Now he had been forced to act, and he hoped he was not too late.

His arrangement with Harry Davis had seemed near perfect. He, on his part, had been meticulous in keeping his side of the bargain. He'd always paid the rent, generous as it was, six months in advance, and Harry had been more than happy to forego the access to the garage that was his by right in return for the cash that was mailed to him every six months. Every man had his price. He hadn't always posted the envelopes in London. He had taken the precaution of posting them as far north as Norwich and as far south as Brighton on occasion, and he was sure that Harry hadn't the faintest clue where he was living. He had been reassured, lulled into a false sense of security perhaps, by the knowledge that only he had access to the garage and that the marine padlock that had cost him a fortune was more than a match for the curious. There was only one key to the padlock, and it was in his pocket.

Communication from Harry over the years had been confined to short text messages confirming receipt of the envelopes containing the rent, and the silence that had reigned in between the six-monthly payments had been reassuring in itself: no news was good news. But, of course, nothing on this world is perfect. Out of the blue a text message had come from Harry's mobile asking him to telephone the mobile or a landline number he didn't recognise. No reason had been given, and, more importantly, the message hadn't been signed off with the customary 'H'. He had been instantly wary, and his concern had grown more acute when he had discovered, without giving himself away, that the landline number was that of a solicitor. With the realisation dawning that something had happened to Harry, he had then turned to his computer and accessed back copies of the Bristol Evening Post, and it did not take him long to discover that Mr Harry Davis, of 24 Shore Road, Pill had died suddenly a couple of weeks before.

As he drove west towards Bristol that evening, he remonstrated with himself time and time, again. He should have had the balls to deal with the situation as soon as he'd got established in London. He should not have allowed himself to get into the fix he was now in. He would be in Bristol within a couple of hours, and he hoped he would be in time to rescue the situation. The first thing he would do would be to park the van, and then he would reconnoitre the side road and garage on foot. If he was sure it was not under observation and that it was safe under cover of darkness to do so, he would return with the van, open up the garage, reverse the van in (he had chosen one with adequate headroom) and transfer the contents of the freezer to it. It wouldn't be easy, particularly as it was something he would obviously have to do alone, but he had a ramp used by delivery men, and he was confident it was achievable. Afterwards, he would leave the freezer behind, with or without the photograph in the envelope he had placed in it over five years before. The envelope probably didn't matter as much now that Harry had died. Its existence had helped to secure Harry's loyalty over the years, but it would be tidier to leave no trace now that Harry was dead. Before leaving, he thought he would put the expensive padlock back on again, but he would throw the key away.

If all went well, he could be back in London before midnight, and the present occupant of the freezer in Garage No 2 would be safely tucked away in the new chest freezer he had installed in the small garage that came with his apartment in

Clapham. He recognised it as an interim, rather than final, solution, but it was one that no longer depended on a third party, and it would give him the time he needed to plan the final, and hopefully complete, disposal of the corpse that represented a real and ever-present danger to him.

Chapter 15

While it may have been dry further east, it was a wet Friday night in Bristol, although the rain was easing as the weight of homebound traffic reached its peak around 6.00 pm. The roads, however, remained wet, the windscreen wipers remained on, and pedestrians remained wary of the roadside edges of pavements lest they be splashed by passing cars and buses.

Tyler was thankful for the rain in one respect: while the pavements and roads remained wet, it would be impossible to detect any melt-water that might be draining from Garage No 2. The prospect of the second visit to inspect the progress of the thaw that was taking place inside the garage had weighed on his mind all day, and, as far as he was concerned, the sooner it was done, the better. He realised that the more the inanimate block they had tipped from the freezer thawed out, the more it would look like what it really was, a body. He hadn't enjoyed the earlier visits, and he wasn't looking forward to the next 24 to 36 hours. As far as Friday night was concerned, the last thing he wanted to have to do was to come out again on a night like this, and he was sure Karen wouldn't be all that happy about it, either. She had been very patient, but he could detect that she was struggling to accept the lame reasons he was concocting to explain the need for his and Terry's repeated night visits to the garages. She didn't ask too many questions, but there was a limit, and he felt she was getting close to it.

At 6.00 pm he was sitting in the driver's seat of his van in the car park of the firm he worked for in Avonmouth. Taking account of the weather and the traffic (which would largely be coming in the opposite direction) he estimated he could be at the garage by 6.45, so he decided to give Terry a call. He took out his mobile phone and speed-dialled. 'Yo!' said his younger brother on accepting the call. 'Hey, mate' responded Tyler, 'can we take a look at the garage tonight earlier than we planned? I don't know about you, but I don't really want to have to come out again. I'd rather get it done early and put my feet up at home, particularly as we'll be out late tomorrow night whatever happens. How are you placed?' 'Yeah, I could be there earlier,' replied Terry, 'but don't you want to wait until dark?' 'It'll need to be dark for the business we have to do tomorrow,' was Tyler's answer, 'but we know the ropes now and provided we're in and out 'smartish', I don't think light is a problem. The rain's going to keep most people inside whether it's dark or light, and we have to close the door and turn the light on inside in any case. At least the light under the door won't be giving the game away that there's someone inside. I could be there between 6.45 and 7.00; how about you?' 'Sounds good to me,' said Terry, 'but I'm just finishing-off a driveway in Fishponds, so could we aim for 7.15?' 'Can you lay tarmac in the rain?' asked Tyler. 'If we couldn't, we'd never lay any tarmac roads in this country,' responded Terry with the sort of spontaneity that suggested he'd been asked that question before. 'Are we going to need some more sheets?' he continued. 'Good question,' acknowledged Tyler realising he might have to get to the garage via home after all and would need the extra time. 'I'll collect some on the way. See you there.'

∞∞∞∞∞∞∞∞

The refrigerated van was leaving the M4 and joining the southbound M32. The windscreen wipers were on 'continuous', as they had been since passing south of Swindon half an hour earlier, and the headlights of the van and the tail lights of the traffic ahead reflected in the wet surface of the motorway. The clock showed 6.30 pm and the indicator on the dashboard showed that the temperature inside the refrigerated section of the van had reached 4 degrees Centigrade. Considering that it had started off at 20 degrees C when he'd collected the van at 4.00 pm, the driver felt the rate of cooling was encouraging, and he was confident that the desired freezing point would be reached by the time he left Bristol bound for home. He hadn't been back to Bristol since he had left for London and a new start in life four years before, but he'd been pretty familiar with it then, and he didn't expect to find that it had changed very much. He planned to avoid the city centre, bearing left with Bond Street into Temple Way, and then, from the giant roundabout, to go right to pick up Redcliffe Street. The home-bound traffic would be easing, and Bedminster was only a few minutes south from there. He would look for a car park in Bedminster that was far enough away from the garage to be discreet but within walking distance of it. Having checked it out and ascertained that all was as it should be, he would return to the van, drive to the garage and do what he had set out to do. Getting the fresh corpse into the freezer singlehanded had been relatively easy five years before, but he knew that the task of getting a frozen body, unyielding and bent double, out of the freezer and into his van would be a lot more difficult.

Chapter 16

The elderly lady in the upstairs flat stood at her window with a cup of tea in her hand looking down at the garages across the road. She found the rain depressing. The only people she saw walking past did so quickly with umbrellas over their heads, and there had been no activity around the garages for two days as far as she was concerned. She imagined that the garages would all have been cleared by now because she had read that the Council was taking them over at the end of the month and that the bull-dozers would soon follow. She would be sad to see the garages go, but it would be interesting to watch the demolition and the rebuilding. She'd have a bird's eye view!

She was just about to turn away when a small van pulled into the side-road and parked facing the opposite wall. She couldn't see who was in it, but she had seen the van before, although it had usually parked a little further up. No one got out, so she drew up her chair and waited. Five minutes later the larger van with which she was now very familiar arrived and parked alongside the other van. Its windscreen wipers stopped, and the taller of the two men she'd seen before got out wearing a blue boiler suit and carrying a roll of fabric under one arm. He was quickly joined by the driver of the smaller van, who she also recognised. The last time she'd seen him, he'd been retching by the side of the garage, but from what she could see of him in the light rain, he looked alright now.

The two men made their way quickly over to the second garage, unlocked it and ducked inside the half-open door as she had seen them do a couple of nights before. They were inside together and out of sight for about ten minutes before re-emerging. Judging by the way he held it, the fabric the taller man had taken in under his arm was now wringing wet, and the lady concluded they had probably had to contend with a leaking roof. The taller man dropped it onto the concrete while he re-fixed the padlock; then, with a brief exchange they each returned to their respective vans and drove away, one after another. 'Oh well' thought the elderly lady as she turned away from the window and took her empty tea cup to the sink, 'that looks like that.'

What the elderly lady did not see was the man who had walked past on her side of the road. He was below her window and outside of her line of sight. He was wearing jeans and a t-shirt under a plastic waterproof, his head protected from the rain by an integral hood. He had walked from her left to her right as she had been staring in thought from her window. He had slowed his pace as he had come abreast the garages and almost paused before continuing for about fifty yards up the road. Then he had stopped, patted his pockets in an exaggerated sort of way, turned round and walked back. He was just about under her window when the first of the two vans pulled in and parked, and he continued walking to the corner of the road, where he stood in a doorway looking intently at his newspaper. He was still in the doorway when the second van arrived. He waited a moment and then started slowly walking back again. He saw the occupants get out of the vans through the corner of his eye, and, feigning disinterest, he half inclined, looking as though he was preparing to cross the road when the garage door slammed shut behind them. He turned back, quickened his pace, rounded the corner and walked briskly away.

Some minutes later, the man in the plastic waterproof turned into the car park he had chosen less than half an hour before, strode to the refrigerated van and, having unlocked it remotely, shrugged off his waterproof topcoat and climbed into the driver's seat. He sat perfectly still with his hands on his lap and tried to pull himself together. He was distressed by the possible implications of what he had just witnessed, but he was also curious and confused.

∞∞∞∞∞∞∞

Before the neon light flickered into life in the garage, both men became aware that the atmosphere had changed. It was difficult to define, but there was a musty sort of smell in the air that gripped at the pits of their stomachs and made them want to breathe in through their mouths, rather than their nostrils. In the light of the single neon tube, they could see that the scene in the garage had not changed dramatically, but it was already apparent to Tyler and to Terry that the rate of thaw was definitely accelerating. The body was now slumped and somehow more spread out than it had been the previous night. It was so much more a 'dead body in a grey suit' than the rigid almost impersonal block of ice they had dealt with before, and Terry felt he would be happy to get the visit over as soon as possible. There was also much more water. The folded dust-sheet on which the body rested, on its side with one arm behind and the other, bent at the elbow, lying in front of where the head would have pointed had the neck not been broken, was clearly wet-through, but fortunately no water had yet begun to drain away towards the door.

Tyler stepped forward three paces and carefully placed the fresh dust-sheet, folded into an oblong cushion, slightly to the side of the body with its longer side aligned with the corpse's length. 'Come on,' he said to Terry, 'we're going to have to lift him off the wet cloth and onto the dry.' Terry walked round to the head, his face betraying his discomfort, and as Tyler bent to take hold of the ankles he inserted a forearm under each of the armpits. 'Keep your eyes on me, old son.' advised Tyler. 'On three! One, two, three!' In a single manoeuvre, the two men raised the body about six inches and lowered it carefully onto the fresh pad that Tyler had pre-positioned. Terry stepped back, his nostrils flaring and his mouth open and turned down at the edges, and he stepped towards the door as if to position himself for a swift departure. Tyler picked up the sodden sheet by one corner and followed Terry, dragging it behind him. On a nod from Tyler, Terry half-opened the door and escaped into the fresh outside air; Tyler immediately followed, closed and locked the door and slung the dripping dust-sheet into the rear of the van. 'You OK?' he asked, 'Better now,' answered Terry, but I'll be glad when this is all over, mate.' 'Me, too,' was Terry's reply. 'I'll bring a blanket tomorrow night. That'll make it a bit easier. Let's be here for 11.00 o'clock. I'll pick you up at 10.40 if that's OK. Make sure you've got some food in your stomach.' 'Yeah,' said Terry, 'see you!'

Chapter 17

The man in the refrigerated van shook his head. It seemed impossible to make any sense of the events of the past fifteen minutes, and without a clear understanding of what had transpired it was impossible to decide how to react. He had been horrified to see, on his first walk-past the garage, that his padlock and the hasp he had arranged to be welded to the top of the door had both been removed and that another padlock, shinier and certainly inferior, had been inserted into the custom hasp half way down the door. The implications of that single observation were enormous and had been like a blow to his stomach, leaving him temporarily short of breath. He had no idea when the change of locks had taken place, but that was almost irrelevant. What really mattered was that his careful security arrangements had been breached, and his secret, the secret on which his newfound respectability and financial security depended, was now known. It had to be known because it followed that whoever had removed the original padlock would undoubtedly have done so in order to gain access to the garage and in order to discover what it contained. Having found nothing more than a freezer, it was unthinkable to imagine that they wouldn't lift the unlocked lid and look inside. Their discovery should have made the national, let alone local, news; yet there had been no press reports at all - no headlines, nothing! Who were the two men and why, having discovered the body, had they not reported it? Maybe they had. Maybe there had been a news blackout. Maybe the police had the garage under surveillance and were waiting for him, the tenant, to turn up. But that didn't make any sense. With a new padlock so obviously in place, the returning tenant was hardly likely to walk up to the door and try his padlock key! Perhaps they had cameras on the side-street? If so, he wondered if he had revealed himself by walking backwards and forwards past the garages, as he had?

From his initial dealings with Harry Davis, he knew there were two sons, but he had never met them and he therefore could not be sure it was them he had seen unlock and enter the garage that evening. Regardless of who they were, he couldn't understand what might have happened since they had first changed the padlock and gained entry to Garage No 2. The freezer and its contents would have still been inside because only he had the key to the original padlock! The more he turned the problem over in his mind, the more uncertain, perplexed and fearful he became. Either the contents of the garage were still as he had left them or the two men had hidden or disposed of them and they hadn't been discovered yet.

He now felt completely helpless and at the mercy of events he couldn't even understand, let alone influence or control. Should he remain in Bristol for the night? Preposterous! Every minute he stayed in Bristol he increased the danger of being recognised by someone who knew him from the 'old days', and that could be almost as much a disaster as what had taken place at the garage. He was now Simon Lee. He had left his Bristol persona behind when he had migrated to London, and any hint that he wasn't now who he once was might cause people to speculate. While Harry had been alive, in addition to supplying a financial incentive of regular cash payments well beyond the market norm for garage rent in an area like Bedminster, he'd also applied some leverage to keep Harry true to his side of the bargain, but that leverage had effectively been nullified by his death. You can't put pressure on a dead man by publicly impugning his reputation with a handful of photographs of him entering and leaving a massage parlour in St Philips, where he obviously regularly spent some of the rental money! But if the two men were the sons, after all, they would only know about their father's penchant for a weekly massage if they'd also discovered the copies of the photographs in the envelope he'd left alongside the body in the freezer. Perhaps they had. Perhaps the need to protect Harry's name and to protect their mother from the revelation, had been enough to encourage them to perpetuate the deception. Whatever the truth was, there was absolutely nothing he could do to further his own advantage by remaining in Bristol any longer. He decided that he should leave for London immediately, although he would definitely stop for coffee and something to eat at the first motorway services he came to.

Having started the engine, he turned on his headlights but turned off the refrigeration unit before pulling out of the car park and heading north for the M32. Little did he know how close to the truth he had come in his desperate thinking and how soon at least one of the questions he had asked himself would be answered.

Chapter 18

It was raining again when the man who called himself Simon Lee returned the refrigerated van to the company he had hired it from the following morning and caught a bus to the nearest tube station from which he would eventually find himself on the Northern Line heading for Clapham South. It was only a ten minute walk from there to his two bedroom apartment in an area that was rapidly shedding its poor and rundown image and becoming very middle class. Since he had purchased his apartment four years earlier with the help of a sizeable deposit and correspondingly manageable mortgage, its value had already risen by a third, and if events in Bristol meant that he would have to start all over again somewhere else, he knew he would have no difficulty selling. He wasn't going to act rashly, but he didn't want to be caught napping, either. He would need to review his options, make contingency plans and remain alert.

In Bristol, by contrast, the sun rose in a clear blue sky, but a deterioration was forecast later in the day. Tyler and Gayle took the opportunity to go shopping together after breakfast and would visit Tyler's mother for tea in the afternoon. Terry and Karla, on the other hand, got up late and went to an open air café in Bristol Docks for a full all-day English breakfast. It was too early in the year for football, and Terry wouldn't be able to join his mates at Ashton Gate on a Saturday afternoon for a couple more months. He wasn't sure what he would find to do, but Karla could be relied upon to come up with something. Both women noticed reluctance in their menfolk to engage in conversation that morning. They seemed curiously preoccupied, but in Terry's case his mood did not impair his appetite.

DI Trevor Knight also indulged in a cooked breakfast, but did so at home at the breakfast table in the kitchen with his wife and their twelve year old son. He was on call again this weekend but so far all had been quiet. Even the portfolio of investigations under his management was pretty much under control and not demanding of weekend working. He had put in enough fifty-hour working weeks in his time as a detective inspector to take full advantage of more normal working hours whenever the opportunities presented themselves because everyone needed rest and usually performed so much better after it. Anyway, the patience of Molly, his wife, had been tested far too many times by the absurd working routines that often went with investigations of major crimes. 'What shall we do this afternoon?' Knight asked across the breakfast table, and he waited for an answer.

On the driveway of a three bedroom semi not far from the centre of the village of Yatton, some twelve miles south west of Bristol, a young man had breakfasted early and was servicing his ten year old VW Golf GTi with the help of a Haynes Manual. He'd changed the oil, renewed the spark plugs, cleaned the carburettor air filter with a stiff brush and topped-up the coolant and the windscreen washer bottle. Now it was time to renew the brake fluid, something he hadn't done before, but he was armed not only with the manual but also with a special kit designed for the purpose.

He'd borrowed it from a friend. It had a receptacle for the old brake fluid and a rubber tube and integral non-return valve. Without the kit, changing the brake fluid would involve two people, one depressing the brake pedal to expel the old fluid through a bleed nipple in each of the four wheels in turn with the other attending to each of the bleed nipples, loosening each before pressure was applied to the brake pedal and tightening each when the brake was held flat against the floor. However, the special kit made it possible for the job to be done by one person. All the young man would need to do would be to fit the rubber tube to the bleed nipple of each wheel hub, loosen it, operate the brake pedal a couple of times, tighten it and then move on to the next until all four had been serviced. In between, it was necessary to inspect the brake fluid level in the reservoir under the bonnet, and top it up with fresh new fluid because the level would fall as the old fluid was expelled. Whether conducted by one operator or two, it was important to maintain a positive pressure in the braking system whenever a bleed nipple was loosened to avoid air being introduced into the braking system. Air, unlike brake fluid, is compressible, and air in the braking system impairs the braking operation. It is usually recommended that the bleed-kits are used only once, but it was generally the view among the young man's friends and others he'd talked to that the manufacturers were only concerned with profit and with protecting themselves from litigation.

Chapter 19

The afternoon and the evening that followed passed desperately slowly for Tyler and his brother, Terry. When they'd heard of the men's intentions to go out to the garages together that night neither Gayle nor Karla had been particularly happy, and they'd made it known as only wives and girlfriends can. What puzzled and irritated them both was their refusal to offer any good reason for their night-time expedition. Instead, all they got from them was another lame excuse about having to do some final clearing and tidying up, and neither Tyler nor Terry was prepared to embellish or explain further. Had they got themselves into some sort of bother? Gayle wondered. She had always stayed clear of asking about the contents of the family garages, and she really didn't want to know, but the sooner the garages were reduced to heaps of rubble, the better. In reality, the two men were certainly being economical with the truth, but they weren't telling an out and out lie when they described their intended actions as 'final clearing and tidying up'.

The rain, albeit light, had arrived very much as forecast by the time Tyler's van pulled into the space opposite the garage just after 11.00 pm. Tyler switched off the lights before turning the ignition key and silencing the diesel engine. The two men then sat looking ahead at the wall for somewhat longer than usual as if to put off the unpleasant inevitable and build up their courage for the task that lay ahead of them. 'I think we'll do it in two stages.' Tyler suggested, inclining his body towards Terry. 'We'll go in first and put our chum in the blanket so that all we have to do is take one end each; then we'll both come out and close the door. I'll position the van so that as soon as you've opened the door again I can drive up with the side door open and as close as possible to the garage entrance. I'll leave the engine running and come in to help lift him aboard. Once he's on board, we can put the wet dust-sheet in with him and shut the side door of the van. Then I'll pull forward to allow you to close the garage door. There's no need to lock it. You OK with that?' 'Let's bloody do it!' said Terry through gritted teeth.

And that's exactly what happened. They did it. The rain and the time of night meant that the side-street was deserted, and there had been no need for them to pause or to modify the procedure to avoid curious eyes. The dust-sheet beneath the body was soaked, but they quickly transferred the body to the blanket and gathered it around. It not only offered a convenient way of moving the body from the floor to the van, but it also hid it from view. Within seven minutes the van door was closed and Tyler was in the driver's seat and edging away from the front of the garage to allow Terry to pull down the up-and-over door. Within another thirty seconds, Terry was in his seat, and the van was pulling into the side street, turning left and making its way to the Weston Road at Ashton Gate.

At about the same time, the young man who lived in Yatton was at the wheel of his VW Golf GTi crossing the swing bridge over the River Avon and heading north-west up the same road, which would take him and his three young passengers much of the way home. He was perfectly sober, having drunk nothing more powerful than Coca Cola, and although the same couldn't be said about his passengers, all were in good humour, noisily exchanging views about the girls they'd met in the course of the evening. The driver was careful not to exceed the 30 mph speed limit, which applied until the junction with the Long Ashton Park & Ride, but then accelerated to 60 mph, a speed he held for the full dual carriageway stretch of the road which passed under a pedestrian walkway almost at its top end. Once back in the built up area of Cleeve, he allowed his speed to fall to 50 mph, which, although well above the limit, seemed reasonable. There was hardly any traffic, after all. He was still doing 50 mph on the approach to Backwell, and he could see that a car was holding its position at the exit to The George car park on the right. He rightly judged that the driver had seen him coming and was waiting for him to pass before pulling across and following him up to the traffic lights at the crossroad about half a mile ahead, and he therefore kept his speed up. With his attention on the car on the far side of The George, he completely failed to notice the vehicle that was beginning to enter the road from a lane on the near side of the pub. The lane offered an alternative, if narrow and tortuous, route from Nailsea, and all vehicles were required to stop before entering the main road. The driver of the vehicle entering from the lane had paused, rather than stopped, had seen no traffic approaching from his right and had completely misjudged the speed of the VW Golf approaching from his left. He pulled across the nearside lane and turned right, into the path of the oncoming VW. The young man from Yatton hit the brake pedal. Had his brakes been in tip-top condition, it might have been possible to avoid a collision, but they weren't. As police investigators would discover when they examined the remains of the car in days to come, one of the bleed nipples had not been properly tightened and had been leaking fluid each time the brakes were applied. As a direct result, although the brake fluid in the system was fresh, its level in the reservoir was dangerously low, and there was air in the VW's brake system. The resulting collision killed the passenger in the other car and spun the vehicle round and over onto the south-bound lane, while the VW, its driver and front-seat passenger fatally injured, came to rest across the north-bound lane.

Chapter 20

At the time the collision occurred, Tyler and Terry were joining the Weston Road at the same junction the VW had passed on its way out of Bristol fifteen minutes earlier. Both the brothers were relieved that the first part of their operation that evening had gone so well, and they felt far more confident about what they still had to do than when they had arrived at the garage half an hour earlier. Tyler's attention to his speed as they drove up the hill, by-passing Long Ashton, was immaculate. The last thing he and Terry could afford was to be hauled over for speeding with a body in the van! However, as they passed under the pedestrian walkway, Tyler's heart sank and he felt cold fear in his stomach. There in his mirror, coming up fast behind him, was a police car with its blue lights flashing! 'Cops!' he shouted to Terry, who immediately looked over his right shoulder then glanced at Tyler, the blood draining from his face, before fixing his eyes, too, on the road ahead. They were both sitting bolt upright as the police car pulled out, came abreast and sped past with not even a glance from the driver or his colleague. The first was concentrating on the road ahead, and the second was talking into his radio.

Both Tyler and Terry visibly relaxed from the stiff posture they had adopted, stomach muscles clenched, when the police car had been behind them. They pressed on, intending to continue through Cleeve and Backwell and to take a back route to the road that would eventually lead them to the bridge over the river. It soon became apparent, however, that they would have to think again because, as they passed through the outskirts of Backwell Farleigh, they could see the blue flashing lights of the now stationary police car ahead of them and a policeman in a reflective vest waving lighted batons at the car in front of them. There was only the one car, and as the policeman bent to talk to its driver, presumably to instructed him to find an alternative route to his destination, Tyler took the initiative. Slowing, checking behind him, and then executing a U-turn he turned back the way he and Terry had come, his mind working furiously. Just to be on the safe side, he put his arm out of the window and waved his thanks to the policeman who he could see in his rear view watching while the other car also executed a U-turn.

Had he not been so anxious about the position he and Terry now found themselves in, had the sudden turn of events not brought back that familiar feeling of fear in the pit of his stomach and a bead of sweat to his forehead and had he been able to think clearly he may have realised that there was still a route available to him. About a mile further on, the A370 crossed over the B3130, a minor road which led through the village of Wraxall to Nailsea, but as he approached it, he was distracted by an oncoming ambulance, its lights flashing and its siren wailing, and the realisation only dawned on him as the B3130 flashed beneath them and the car behind them, its nearside indicator flashing, entered the slip road and disappeared from view.

At this stage, all Tyler wanted to do was bring the whole nightmare to an end. Why had Dad got him and Terry into this? he asked himself; why had he and Terry been behaving as if it was they who had committed the crime when they hadn't had a clue about the man in the grey suit in the freezer in Garage No 2 until a couple of weeks ago? They'd dealt with the freezer (that was bad enough), the garage was now empty; and in a little more than 24 hours the Council would own it and all the other garages in the side-street in Bedminster, but they had to get rid of the body because the road would soon be crawling with cops and emergency vehicles. They simply couldn't take it back to the garage. That was unthinkable. They had to find somewhere to dump it right away!

The lay-by that suddenly presented itself was too good to overlook. It was long and deep, and the road was quieter than usual because any traffic originating south of the scene of the accident was being turned back or diverted. Tyler swung the van into the lay-by, braked and switched the engine and lights off. In the sudden silence he turned to Terry and said 'Let's do it!' Terry was only too happy to comply, and he and his older brother leapt from the van simultaneously. Tyler slid open the side door, which was conveniently facing away from the road, and he and Terry took their respective ends of the blanket in which the body was still wrapped, lifted it and carried it urgently across to the bushes at the side of the lay-by. They let it fall to the ground with far less respect than they had treated it when loading it in the garage. Transferring their grips to the same hem of the blanket edge and pulling it upwards, they rolled the body unceremoniously away until the blanket was free. The man in the grey suit lay on his side in the gentle rain. His head was at an abnormal angle and one leg was bent unnaturally beneath the other, but his upper body was hidden in the foliage, and all that protruded was a leg and a stockinged foot. 'Shit!' exclaimed Tyler looking down at the foot. He turned quickly back to the van, threw open the rear door and urgently felt around the floor. 'Got it!' he said and, half turning, tossed the shoe that had been there for some days towards the body. Terry threw the blanket into the side entrance of the van, slid the door closed with a bang and leapt into the passenger seat. The whole operation had taken less than two minutes and during that time not one vehicle had driven past. They'd done it! Their relief was palpable, and Terry wouldn't admit it but he felt close to tears. Tyler grinned and punched the air as they joined the carriageway bound for Bristol and home.

∞∞∞∞∞∞∞∞

Tyler was a different man on the Sunday morning, Gayle noticed. She had still been awake when he crept into bed well after midnight the previous night, but she continued to feign sleep even when he put his hand lightly on her shoulder, and he had not persisted. He was up early for a Saturday, but she snoozed on until, at the usual time, he brought her up her mug of tea. 'Good morning,' he said as he placed the mug on her bedside table, 'I thought we'd give Ma a ring to see if she'd like to go out for lunch today. What do you think?' 'It depends where we go,' Gayle answered cautiously. 'I'm always happy not to have to cook.' 'We could try the pub in Portbury,' Tyler suggested, 'We've had good meals there before; you know what you're getting there and the prices are OK.' 'Fine by me,' said Gayle with the hint of a smile. Whatever he and Terry had been up to the previous night must have gone well, she thought, but she couldn't help adding 'Not spending the day at the garage, then?' 'No,' said Tyler. 'That's all done and dusted.'

After breakfast and after 'phoning Gloria, who jumped at the chance of eating out with them, Terry spent half an hour or so tidying up his van. This was not unusual behaviour, but he seldom used the vacuum cleaner on the inside as he did that morning. The two wet dust-sheets went into the recycling bin for collection the following Tuesday, but the blanket, neatly folded, went back into his tool-shed. By the time he and Gayle climbed aboard to collect Gloria from her home in Pill, the interior of the van was cleaner than it had been for a very long time.

On the way to Pill, they had the radio tuned to BBC Radio Bristol, and they heard a detailed report of the terrible accident that had happened on the Weston road the previous night. For Gayle it was, indeed, news, and she shook her head in disbelief at the thought of three needless deaths. The collision was not, of course, news to Tyler, but much of the detail was, and it was therefore reasonably easy to react as though he was learning of the accident for the first time.

He was much more interested to learn whether a body had been discovered on the Long Ashton by-pass, but the news came to an end without mention of it, and Tyler breathed a sigh of relief. It would, of course, be discovered soon, but the longer the man in the grey suit remained unremarked in his present resting place, the better.

PART TWO

Chapter 21

D I Knight sat at his desk in the CID section of Bridewell Police Station in the centre of Bristol and looked through his open door into the adjacent incident room. It was 9.30 am on the Tuesday after the body had been discovered on the Long Ashton by-pass, and he was expecting to hear from the pathology lab before lunch, if only for a summary of initial findings. Dr Suzanne Howard, who had attended the scene on her motor bike and led the forensic team that gathered there, had promised that she would give the autopsy due priority. She and her assistant had examined the body and its immediate surrounds thoroughly before giving the go-ahead for removal to the mortuary, and the road had been reopened at midday, and the corpse would have reached the mortuary by lunchtime, but it was a Sunday, and although the death was suspicious, it was not yet a murder inquiry and did not justify an immediate autopsy and the over-time bill that would go with it.

Knight had spent Monday dealing with loose ends on two of the other cases he was investigating and putting his core team together, at least on paper. It was a small team because it was by no means clear that a murder had been committed at this stage. Knight was fairly sure it had, but a lot would depend on Dr Howard's judgement of cause of death. He mulled over the observations he had made on arriving in the office on the Sunday morning: white male probably about 40; clean shaven; well dressed for a day in the office of a bank or a legal firm or even an investment firm– something like that; fair haired and of moderate build, and with well-manicured fingernails. Perhaps his job involved dealing with customers face to face; perhaps they were well-heeled, clients rather than customers.

What was a concern was the absence of watch and wallet. Although not every time, by any means, but more commonly than one might think, the watch could be a handy indicator of time of death. When extreme violence had occurred, or there had been no movement for prolonged periods wrist watches often stopped, and those that also displayed the date could be a particularly helpful indicator. But the watch, the man had worn was absent.

The absence of the wallet was also a real disadvantage. With its customary contents of credit and debit cards, business cards and driving licence, a wallet made it relatively simple to make an early identification of the deceased. Without the help of a wallet and all it contained, the investigating team would, initially at least, have to rely on someone reporting the man in the grey suit as missing. The spouse or partner would usually be the first to register a report, but in the event that the deceased was not married or in a co-habiting relationship, it was likely to be the employer who would do so. However, a report by the latter could take time to materialise if the employee was relatively junior or given to taking days off, for example.

The search of the lay-by and the side of the road had yielded the usual well-weathered rubbish, but there had been an empty new Red Bull can on the verge, and, who knows, if nothing else, it might be possible to test it for fingerprints and get a conviction for throwing litter from a vehicle!

Knight looked at his watch. It was 10.05 am and time for his first coffee of the day. He stood up to make the short journey to the kettle that was perched on a filing cabinet in a corner of his office just as the telephone buzzed. 'Knight!' he said. 'It's Dr Suzanne Howard,' said the voice on the other end. 'There are still some tests I need to run, but I thought I would lose no time in 'phoning you. Are you sitting down?' 'No, as it turns out,' said Knight. 'I was just about to get myself a coffee, but that can wait. What have you got for me?' 'Well,' replied Dr Howard, 'the cause of death was relatively easy to confirm. It was severance of the spinal cord in the cervical area. Both vertebrae C2 and C3 had been well and truly broken, and it looks to me as if it was an intentional act by a third party. Had he hanged himself he would normally have died of strangulation and asphyxia, but even if he had known how to fashion and position a hangman's knot, the damage would have been consistent with a linear force being applied. In 'Mr Grey's' case - I hope you don't mind the short hand - it looks as though the force was applied at ninety degrees to neck, first one way and then the other, probably to make absolutely sure. His head was attached simply by soft tissue.'

'So, we have a murder inquiry, then,' said Knight 'are you able to offer an estimate of time of death?' 'Well that's why I asked if you were sitting down,' replied Dr Howard. 'The short answer is 'No', not with any accuracy at the moment. As I said, there are more procedures I can and will try on 'Mr Grey', but at the moment all I can say is that he died between a week and perhaps eight years ago.' 'Run that past me again,' asked DI Knight, momentarily taken aback and unable to grasp what he had just heard.

'I believe our Mr Grey was frozen very soon after death,' was the reply, 'and he may have remained frozen for days, months or even years. He would have been placed in something like a chest freezer within five to six hours of death. Judging by the pooling of the blood on his buttocks, the soles of his feet and his hands and wrist, I imagine he would have been frozen in a seated position with his knees bent to his chin, perhaps, and his head between them. I was first alerted at the side of the road by his core temperature, which was well below ambient, but when I performed the autopsy I found that the contents of his stomach were still partly frozen. On that basis, though I cannot yet offer much help on the time of death, I estimate that had he been left to thaw in an ordinary unheated room, he would have been removed from the freezer about three to four days before he was found.'

Knight was silent. He had to mull this over, and he needed his coffee even more than he had ten minutes before.

Unbeknown to Dr Howard, her chosen nickname for the person whose cadaver she had been working on was most appropriate. 'Mr Grey', in his lifetime, had never desired nor achieved prominence. He had preferred life in the background and, sometimes, in the shadows.

Chapter 22

Right, listen up!' The conversation between the members of the small group standing and sitting in the Incident Room came to a halt, and the faces turned to face the front of the room and the white board on the wall as DI Knight strode in with a memo pad in his hand. He had been bringing up to date his immediate superior, Detective Superintendent Victor (Vic) Nolan who had subsequently politely declined Knight's invitation to sit in on the briefing. The exchange between the two men, who were of similar age, had been constructive, and Knight felt very comfortable with the outcome.

It was 2.00 pm on the Tuesday, just over two days had passed since the body had been discovered, and it was time to get the investigation moving, to set the initial priorities and to develop some momentum. There had been a press enquiry on the Monday, and the discovery of a body of a man on the Long Ashton by-pass in 'suspicious circumstances' had made the evening paper. It may have warranted more than the small column on page three had the press not enough on their hands with the awful collision that had occurred further up the A370 on Saturday night. He wondered if the officers attending that incident had seen anything that might help his investigation. He would get someone to ask.

'In summary, we have, as I suspected, a murder to investigate, but it's one with a difference.' Knight looked around the room at the members of the team he had hand-picked, thus diverting many from other tasks that he (and more importantly, DSI Nolan) agreed were of lesser importance. The more able the individual, the harder it usually was to pry them away from other leaders, and it was helpful to have the added authority when it was needed.

'The victim is male, about forty years of age. He has fair hair and was dressed in a grey suit that might suggest a white-collar occupation. He had no distinguishing marks on his body and no form of immediate identification on him when he was spotted by a dog-walker, although partly hidden by vegetation, at the edge of the city-bound lay-by on the Long Ashton by-pass at around 7.30 am on Sunday. The 999 call came in from the dog-walker at 7.38 am. Cause of death is clearly a broken neck, a very well and, we believe, intentionally broken neck, but although there were already some noticeable signs of decomposition, we do not know, with any degree of accuracy at this stage, when the victim died. We don't know because he wasn't wearing a watch and, more importantly, it appears that the corpse was deep-frozen after death and only recently allowed to thaw. Consequently, pathology can only give us a very wide margin at present. Although they may be able to narrow it down once they've been able to do some additional procedures, the best estimate for time of death is anywhere between a week before he was discovered and ten years before!'

Knight paused, allowing the implications of the bombshell he had just dropped, to register with those who had been listening to what, up until then, had seemed a fairly routine investigation. 'What we can be reasonably sure about was that the deceased would have begun to thaw on the Wednesday or Thursday before he was found, that's assuming he was in an unheated room.'

'Obviously, our first priority will be to achieve a positive ID of the victim. If he did only meet his death a week or so ago, he may not yet have been reported missing, but it shouldn't be long before he is. If he's been dead for years, he ought already to have been reported missing, and so it ought to be relatively easy to create a short list. We'll call him 'Mr Grey' (as in the colour) for the time being. The pathologist has done so already, and we all need to be singing from the same hymn sheet. We don't know if 'Mr Grey' was married because there was no wedding ring, nor was there a mark where it might have been. Pathology will come up with the DNA, which might or might not be helpful, and we'll need to run 'Mr Grey's' fingerprints through the data-base. Again, we may or may not get lucky! Are there any questions at this stage?' Knight paused and looked round the room again. He sensed that interest had been aroused and the challenge of the case he had presented thus far had been accepted with some relish.

The first to speak was Detective Sergeant Jess Bradley. She was a smart and ambitious police officer with a marvellous knack of getting on with people, making them more receptive to her ideas, making them more likely to trust her with information they might not be inclined to give to some of her more clumsy or arrogant colleagues. 'You've not mentioned a mobile phone, so I assume that wasn't anywhere to be found, but I heard they did a search of the side of the road on Sunday. Did anyone come up with anything?' 'Good question,' replied Knight, 'thank you Jess. No, there was no mobile, and yes, there was the usual well-weathered rubbish that people throw out of their cars, but there was also what appeared to be a very recently discarded Red Bull can a hundred yards or so further down the carriageway towards Bristol. We will need fingerprints from that. You never know. Are there any other questions?'

Only one hand went up, that of Sgt Wes Brown. A stocky but fit individual who had proved to be very resourceful in the past; the sort of investigator who wouldn't be put off if he sensed he was onto something. 'Can you say something about the possible means of freezing, boss? I'm assuming we're not talking about liquid nitrogen, particularly if the temperature has been maintained below freezing for years. It would be pretty impossible to keep that sort of process secret for any length of time.' 'I'm sure you're right, Wes,' replied Knight, 'but we can't rule anything out at this stage. What I can say is that the view of pathology is that our 'Mr Grey' may well have been squeezed into a chest freezer for storage within six hours of death. He appears to have been frozen in a sitting position with his knees bent sufficiently to accommodate his height, which was' Knight paused to consult his memo pad,'5ft 8 ins or 173 cms in 'new money', and his head was probably down between his knees.

When the pathologist got to him on Sunday morning at about 8.45 he could have been out of the freezer for about 72 hours or, if the freezer had simply been turned off, perhaps 96 hours. For the moment, as we've got to start somewhere, we will assume that he was removed from the source of refrigeration on the Thursday morning and that he was left at ambient temperature to thaw before being dumped sometime on Saturday night or the early hours of Sunday morning. You'll know about the RTA that occurred late on Saturday night a couple of miles further up the Weston road. It may be that the officers who had the misfortune to be called to that may have seen something while en-route.'

'As I've said, we don't know the time of death, we don't know who our 'Mr Grey' is, we don't know why he was killed and we don't know why he wasn't immediately disposed of. We don't know why his end of life residence in a freezer came to an end when it did, why he was dumped in such a public place and who did the dumping. We also don't know whether, after potentially ten years, whoever did the dumping also killed him. But that's why I've put together such a talented team.' Knight smiled wryly as he offered the compliment to the members assembled in front of him. 'I'll be tasking you individually after we have all had a coffee, but our efforts will now be directed at finding answers to those seven questions as quickly as we can.'

∞∞∞∞∞∞∞∞

The team assembled again in the Incident Room at 4.00 pm.

'Right,' said Knight in his characteristic manner. 'The first question we need the answer to, and we cannot do much without knowing, is who our 'Mr Grey is.' He looked across the room at DS Jess Bradley. 'Jess, I'd like you and Tom to make this the focus of your attention.' He waited for a nod of acknowledgement from Bradley and Tom Fielding. Tom was a Detective Constable. He was two or three years younger than Jess, but despite his lack of experience, he had nevertheless shown himself full of energy and able to think rationally and 'outside the box'. He would complement Jess well, and Knight could see that they were both pleased to be working together. Knight continued, 'We know of Mr Grey what we can see; his height, weight etc, and I'm pretty sure we ought to be able to generate a pretty good computer graphic of his face should we need to make a public appeal. If we do, we should do so nationally because we can't simply assume he was a Bristol man. We have the make of his shoes and the tailor's label in his suit jacket, but until we have a better estimate of how long he's been dead, those will, perhaps, be of less value than they otherwise might. Finally,' Knight concluded, 'we might be lucky with fingerprints, DNA and the missing persons register.' He looked at DS Bradley. 'Is that enough to be going on with?' It was a rhetorical question, and it received a good-natured nod from both her and DC Fielding.

'The other immediate question I want addressing,' continued Knight, 'is who dumped the body. If we can answer that, we will have the answers to many, if not possibly all, the remaining questions'. He paused, 'Max, I would like you and Nicola to focus on this one.' DS Maxwell (Max) Carter and DC Nicola French, like their colleagues Jess and Tom were good team-players but were not slow to show initiative and trust their own judgement. DS Carter was very experienced but might have something to learn from Nicola, who had displayed a natural acumen that was unusual. Knight knew that they shared an interest in Formula 1 racing (as fans rather than competitors, of course) and got on well. Sgt Wes Brown was the only member untasked at this stage, but Knight wanted another pair of legs and eyes on the team as a whole. Wes had considerable 'nous', and you couldn't have too much of that in this business. 'There aren't cameras on the lay-by,' Knight went on, 'but we may be able to pick something up from the cameras on the approach to the Cumberland Basin, and then there's the fingerprints on the Red Bull can that was found on the side of the road. We'll have something from forensics soon, I'm sure, particularly as this is now a murder inquiry. You might also 'put your feelers out' for reports of a chest-freezer being disposed of, and Wes, I'd like you to assist in this search. It's likely that whatever pressures caused someone to take Mr Grey from the relative safety and obscurity of the inside of a freezer and dump him at the side of a public highway might also need to get rid of the freezer in some haste. Freezers are a lot more difficult to shift these days, and anyone who does so legitimately is going to leave a trail we can follow. You need to agree a plan to visit all waste recycling sites, and scrap metal merchants known to us, and you need to get round to them quickly,' Knight concluded.

'We've worked together before, and you all know that I like to be kept 'in the loop' and 'up to speed' at all times. My door will always be open, except when it's closed. We'll all meet again at 5.30 tomorrow evening, but for the moment, keep alert, keep thinking, keep talking to each other and keep talking to me; any questions?'

There was silence.

Chapter 23

Knight returned to his office just as his telephone buzzed. He answered it in his usual brief and business-like way to find Dr Suzanne Howard on the line again. 'Good evening,' she said, 'I have a little more news I'd like to share with you.' 'It's always good to hear from you, Dr Howard,' replied Knight, 'what have you got?' 'Well, first let me say that I'm in touch with some colleagues at Edinburgh University, and they've agreed to have a look at some of Mr Grey's tissue samples with a view to narrowing the unhelpfully wide window I gave you regarding time of death. They've done quite a bit of research into the effect on cell tissue of long-term refrigeration, principally in relation to farm animals, and whereas I don't think for one minute I'm going to be able to talk in terms of days or even months, I'm nevertheless hopeful. In any event, it will be about a week before I can come back to you.' 'I'm very grateful,' replied DI Knight, genuinely, 'and I look forward to hearing from you.' Sensing he was about to put the phone down, Dr Howard quickly went on. 'There's a bit more,' she said. 'OK,' replied Knight expectantly. She continued. 'Our Mr Grey was HIV positive. I'm pretty sure the infection was in its very early stages, and that he may not even have been aware because there is no trace of any antiretroviral drug in his system.' 'Well, well,' said Knight, 'every little helps! Thank you very much. Until next week then, unless, of course you come up with anything more?' 'Actually, I'm hopeful that we will,' replied Dr Howard, 'The search of the area around the body revealed half a footprint in the mud, which we'll be back to you on, and the shoe, which was lying next to the body, had a very clear and very fresh thumbprint on it. Finally, for now, the forensic examination of the grey suit has already yielded some fibres that look as though they might have come from a blanket or travel rug. We'll send a summary through by email tonight.' 'An embarrassment of riches!' said Knight warmly. 'Excellent work, Dr Howard, thank you again very much.' He put the phone down and stuck his head out the office door. 'Jess,' he called, 'I have something for you.' He motioned DS Jess Bradley towards him and continued, 'and bring Max with you.'

∞∞∞∞∞∞∞∞

It was 9.35 on the morning of Wednesday 1st June. After his quick briefing with DS Bradley and DS Carter the evening before, during which he had brought them up to date with the latest information from pathology, Knight had set the daily briefing time on the Wednesday for 4.00 pm. Something new had come in overnight, and he was still looking at the brief report on the screen on his desk when he picked up the telephone and called DSI Nolan's PA. He felt he should update his boss and take the opportunity to outline his views on the way ahead. Experience had taught him that his superiors were far more likely to give him the space to run the investigation as he saw fit if they felt they were 'in the loop' and not being excluded. Not only that, but he didn't underestimate the value of the experience that his boss could bring to bear on his thinking, and it wouldn't be the first time that Nolan's ability to spot the flaws in his reasoning had helped keep him focussed. Ego was all very well, but two heads were definitely better than one in this business! Sandra, DSI Nolan's PA was able to squeeze him in to see his boss at 10.15. There was time for coffee!

It was made immediately clear to him on entering DSI Nolan's office that he would need to get to the point. 'Sit down, Trevor, you've got ten minutes,' Nolan said in a matter of fact way. Knight lowered himself into the seat. 'I just wanted to quickly bring you up to date on where we are with the murder investigation,' he said, 'and to run a few ideas past you if that's OK?' 'That's one minute gone,' replied Nolan with a smile, 'what's new?' 'Well,' said Knight, 'we've discovered that our man in the grey suit was HIV positive, but because it looked like a new infection and because pathology couldn't find any trace of retroviral drugs in his blood we imagine that he may not have been aware he was infected. It is also an indication that he may have been gay. We still don't know who he is or when he was murdered, but I'm hopeful that we will be able to narrow down the focus of the second question in a week. We're looking at missing persons records in our area over the past ten years, but if we draw a blank I'd like to put his face out, not only in our area but nationally. We've not had a lot of media interest, which I'm happy about, but I think we've got an excellent digital likeness and, whether he died five years ago or a week ago, someone will recognise him. I want to keep the fact that he was frozen after death to ourselves for as long as we can, though. The team are already going round all the council tips and waste metal merchants looking for a recently ditched chest freezer, and I'd rather we got round to all of them first so that they're on the lookout, rather than panic our murderer into getting rid of it right away. We believe whoever dumped the body was sure they had thawed it out completely, and so they might just hang on to the freezer long enough for us to find it.' 'They may simply dump it in the country,' interjected Nolan 'might be a good idea to get in touch with local authorities. They're the ones who have to go out and retrieve these things when they're discovered.' 'Agreed!' responded Knight, with a nod. 'So you'll want to set up a press conference?' enquired Nolan. 'Yes,' replied Knight, looking briefly at his watch, 'on Friday if we can.' 'Fine,' said Nolan, standing. 'Sort it out with Sandra on the way out.'

The desks in the incident room were still unoccupied when he walked through on the way to his office. Max, Nicola and Wes were out visiting recycling centres and scrap-metal merchants, while Max and Nicola had gone to see the staff of the Terrence Higgins Trust centre in Old Market. 'THT', as it was commonly called, provided a wide range of support for those infected with the AIDS virus, including confidential testing and counselling. The two police officers had gone armed with the excellent photo-graphic image of the late 'Mr Grey'. If he had suspected he was HIV positive, it was somewhere 'Mr Grey' might well have preferred to go, rather than consult his GP. He checked the case progress file on his desk computer, as he had done before going up to see DSI Nolan, and discovered that the result of the trawl of the national fingerprint database that Jess had initiated before leaving the previous evening had been posted on it. Unfortunately, the thumbprint on the shoe did not match any thumbprint on record, which meant that whoever had thrown or placed the shoe had no police record. 'Damn!' thought Knight. He already knew that the fingerprints found on the Red Bull can were different and had also gone unmatched.

The 4.00 pm briefing didn't take long because there was virtually no progress to report. No-one at the Terrence Higgins centre recognised 'Mr Grey' from the image they'd been shown, and the next step would be to visit the bars and clubs in that and other parts of the city that tended to attract gay men. Max and Nicola would make a start that very night. The other three officers had equally little to report on the outcome of their search for a recently disposed freezer, but at least they were alerting those who worked at these sites to be on the lookout, and that could well pay dividends. The following day they would be contacting the appropriate offices in Bristol, North Somerset and Gloucestershire District Councils on a similar errand, but they would be able to do this from the office, by telephone.

Chapter 24

Knight found that the best time for thinking, for running different scenarios through his mind, for arriving at conclusions that might escape him at his desk, when the expectation of the phone ringing or the 'ping' signifying the arrival of another email message on his desk computer interrupted his train of thought, were the early hours of the morning. It was then that he felt he was at his most creative and most receptive to original ideas. Although he didn't usually have to get out of bed until just before 7.00 am, he would often wake an hour or two earlier, particularly in the summer when it was lighter, and just lie there and run things through in his mind, with the only noise being the deep breathing of his wife beside him. Sometimes he might drift off to sleep again, but unlike dreams (which he forgot within seconds of opening his eyes), he would remember the ideas that had come to him in the early hours, and the conclusions he'd been able to form.

Thursday 2nd June was like that. It started early with the need to get out and visit the en-suite, but although his bladder had been emptied, he didn't go back to sleep immediately on sliding carefully back into his side of the bed. Instead, he lay there savouring the warmth and the comfort and thinking about the case of the man in the grey suit. What story did the fact that the body had been stored, frozen, for perhaps years before being clumsily abandoned at the side of a busy road tell? He wondered. The two actions seemed to contradict each other. Had circumstances changed drastically? Were the advantages gained by long-term storage – the ability to prevent the discovery of the body as well as, perhaps, to hide the fact that a murder had been committed at all – suddenly of no further importance? Why would that be? And if that were, indeed, the case, why not, at least, preserve the mystery by choosing a less public form of disposal; one that would at least offer the chance of the body not being discovered for much longer? Whoever had disposed of the body did not appear to be operating to the same set of parameters or of priorities as the killer. Was it likely, therefore, that they were different parties? Yes, it was certainly likely, and it was a scenario he ought to explore. He recognised this conclusion as one of those early-morning 'Eureka' moments, and he smiled to himself! He wasn't sure how it would influence the course of the investigation, but he had a distinct hunch that he'd hit the nail on the head. And then he fell asleep.

∞∞∞∞∞∞∞

Some 120 miles away, the man who called himself Simon Lee was also awake and thinking. Unlike Knight, he had been awake for some time, and his mind was so active there was little chance of him getting off to sleep before the buzz of his alarm. He was looking back over his life and wondering how different it would have been if the dice had rolled more in his favour, rather than, so often, rolling against him. He was, by three years, the younger of two sons of a painter/decorator and shop assistant in Taunton, Somerset. Although he didn't have many memories of his very early life, he had no reason to believe that it was in any way unusual, but things had changed for the worse when his mother was knocked off her bicycle and killed when he was ten. His dad had done his best, but the first two years after her death were pretty chaotic for the family, and both his and his brother's education had suffered. Then a new and younger woman moved in, his dad's new girl-friend, and she tried to take the place of his mother but failed. Looking back, he realised that neither he nor his elder brother had given her a chance; their resentment had got in the way. She lasted no more than a couple of years before they were on their own again. His brother left school at sixteen and joined their father in the painting and decorating business, which meant that there wouldn't be room for him when he left school, himself. He drifted aimlessly through the remaining three years of secondary education, often in trouble not only at school but also with the local police. Offences such as shoplifting, minor theft, and speeding (in his dad's van) had all been recorded by the time he was seventeen. At eighteen, on impulse and the absence of any better idea, he visited an Army Careers office in Taunton and applied to join The Light Infantry. He was successful, and had his military career been allowed by fate to continue, he certainly wouldn't have ended up in his present predicament. Despite the disdain he had shown for authority in his youth, he had enjoyed the military training and discipline, and he came to pride himself on his physical strength and fitness. Over the next seven years he saw operational action in Northern Ireland and also in Bosnia (as part of the UN Peacekeeping Force), and he achieved promotion to Lance Corporal. And then it was suddenly all over. Some six months after returning with his battalion from training in Kenya, he was diagnosed with AIDS. He'd been infected during a night 'on the town' in Kenya, and he was immediately discharged on medical grounds. What was unknown to his superiors was that the infection arose not from dalliance with the local girls, although it just as easily might, but with a male prostitute he'd met when he'd found himself in a bar by himself. It had been during his initial military training that he had come to terms with the realisation that he was more attracted to men than to women, but he had never allowed his colleagues or superiors to have any grounds for suspecting that he wasn't entirely a testosterone-fuelled heterosexual. He'd played the part with great skill his entire military career, only allowing his true sexuality to surface when on leave and well away from the army.

Returning to civilian life at the age of 25 had been a great shock, and also a great embarrassment. He hadn't dared return to Taunton, finding a life of sorts instead in Bristol, where he had sought the support of Terrence Higgins Trust in Old Market. He'd benefitted from their counselling and, through them, became a local delivery driver for a couple of years before joining a firm of auctioneers as a general assistant. The general assistant role involved conducting house clearances, typically when owners had died, and preparing the saleable contents for auction. The pay wasn't great, but he enjoyed the freedom the role gave him in the early years. Later, when much of the shine had gone, there were other compensations. Provided he acted with care and wasn't too greedy, he was able to do a little private trading of saleable items from house clearances 'on the quiet'. Progressively, however, as time went by, he became more and more dissatisfied with his lot and more and more aware that his mediocre academic qualifications, his lack of a career path and his shortage of any real money offered him very little reason to anticipate any upturn in his fortunes. What he had wanted, what he desperately needed, was a fresh start.

Chapter 25

Friday 3rd June was the last day of the half term holiday, and according to the local forecast it was likely to be mainly dry. Two twelve-year old boys took their mountain bikes up the winding road from Cleeve to do some off-road cycling in the woodland at the top of the hill. The road was sometimes used, mainly by taxi drivers, as a back route to Bristol Airport, but otherwise it was pretty quiet. They climbed the hill in single file, standing on the pedals at the steepest points to exert more pressure and maintain their forward speed. At the top, they pulled into an open area on the left of the road and came to a halt to get their breath back and to take stock of where to go next. One let his bike rest on its side on the ground and, with a brief statement to his friend, disappeared into the trees. 'Just going for a wee,' he said. Three minutes later, he was back in view of his waiting friend and beckoning to him. 'Come and have a look,' he said. 'Bring the bikes.' Curious, his friend followed him, wheeling the mountain bikes along, one with each hand. Just out of sight from the road and in a bit of a dip in the woodland lay a chest freezer. It was on one long side, its underside exposed and the lid lying fully open on the ground. It had certainly not been there when last they had been up there with their bikes, but that had been some months before, and it looked as though it had been plucked from someone's house that very day. It looked completely out of place, as indeed it was, its whiteness and its rectangular shape, contrasting sharply with its leafy surroundings. The two boys stood looking at it, hands on hips. 'Someone's just *dumped* it here,' said one, stating the completely obvious but doing so with such emphasis as to register his disbelief in what his eyes were telling him. Tentatively, for no other reason than it was a strange experience, the two boys circled the freezer together, bending to peer into the interior once they were on the open side. 'There's something inside,' said the other, pointing at a sealed white A5 envelope resting where it had fallen from the side to which it had previously been stuck. He placed his foot gingerly on the inside surface of the open lid, bent forward and picked the envelope up with finger and thumb. It was damp and it bore no marking on front or back, but it definitely contained something. 'Should we open it?' he asked. He didn't know whether they should because although it had clearly been discarded, it was sealed, after all. 'Go on,' said his friend, and so he did. Being damp, the adhesive flap parted with the slightest pressure, and the two boys craned their necks to look inside as the boy who was holding it inserted the first two fingers of his right hand and parted the two sides of the envelope. Inside were some colour photographs, and the boys felt the thrill of illicit adventure as they removed and sifted through them. There were six in all and they all featured the same man. He was either going into or leaving a building, the same building. He was heavy set, looked old enough to be a grandfather, and he was generally wearing a light-coloured open neck shirt, jersey and dark grey trousers. The doorway was the same in all six photographs, which all showed clearly the wall-mounted plaque with the number 147 on it in white on a black background. The only real difference between the photographs was the time and date code printed at the foot of each, but the boys paid little attention to this. Had they looked on the reverse of each photograph, as would the mother of Matthew, the one who'd made the discovery and thereby earned the right to take the envelope and its contents to his home, they would have discovered another similarity: the name 'Harry Davis' written on each in pencil.

Chapter 26

The press conference on Friday morning had gone well, and Knight was pleased. Somehow, the investigation into the murder of a single man found on the side of the road hadn't fired the imagination or the zeal of the local journalists to the same extent as some he had been involved with in the past. First, there was nothing particularly gory about the discovery; second, there was no obvious sexual dimension, and thirdly, there were no grieving relatives, friends or neighbours because no one knew who he was. As a result, Knight had enjoyed a reasonably easy passage, with no difficult questions, and he had deliberately not revealed the fact that his team were scouring the area looking for a recently discarded chest freezer. While there was merit in alerting the general public to the need to report any findings as a matter of urgency, all local authorities and recycling depots had been told, and he felt it was more important, for the moment at least, not to reveal that the effort to disguise the fact that the body had been previously frozen had not succeeded. The other important revelation was the excellent photo-graphic of the face of 'Mr Grey'. It would be on that evening's news and in the papers the following day; it would also be on the Avon & Somerset Police website for some time. It was such a good likeness that he couldn't imagine someone not recognising him, even though 'Mr Grey' may have disappeared from circulation some years before. The investigation was in its infancy, but he acknowledged that his team had few positives to celebrate so far, and the reality was that without a positive identification of the victim or of the person or persons who'd dumped the victim at the side of the Long Ashton by-pass, the inquiry wasn't going anywhere. However, he genuinely felt that the press coverage would generate something for the team to get their teeth into. Finally, he'd also been able to introduce the thought to those attending the press conference that the party who had dumped the body and the killer need not necessarily be one and the same. That acknowledgement might encourage someone involved with the disposal alone to come forward. You never knew!

Knight watched the early evening news bulletin with the investigation team in the incident room. When it was over, he asked DC Tom Fielding to turn the screen off, and he stood with it at his back. 'I know it's been slow going this week,' he said, 'but it's not for want of effort on your part, and you've laid a good foundation; I have a definite feeling we'll be a lot busier next week. We've had good media coverage this evening, and the papers will carry our 'Mr Grey's' picture tomorrow. Unless he's from Mars and floated down from a space ship, someone is going to recognise him, and once we know who he is (or was), we'll be on our way. So, unless you've got a better idea, let's do what the rest of Bristol is doing right now: let's go home and get some rest. We'll meet here again for briefing at 10.00 am on Monday.' Little did he know that some of them would be meeting together a lot earlier.

∞∞∞∞∞∞∞∞

The elderly lady in the flat across the road from the garages in Bedminster watched the same news bulletin with interest, as she did every night. All the garages were empty and had been locked by a man from the Council, and there was nothing of any interest to be seen down there anymore. She had heard that demolition might start as early as the following fortnight, and if so, that would provide an interesting diversion for a while. She felt sorry for the young man whose face appeared on the news bulletin, which she studied; he looked like a nice man, a gentle man, but she had no idea who he was or how close she had come to him on very many occasions as she had made her way past the garages to the entrance to the building in which her flat was situated.

∞∞∞∞∞∞∞

Neither Terry nor Tyler Davis saw the early evening news. Tyler was on his way home from Avonmouth, while Terry was at his local enjoying a drink with his mates, and with Karla. Terry and Karla were still in the pub at 10.00 pm when the news was repeated, but Tyler was at home. He was lying back on the sofa with Gayle curled up beside him, watching television. Gayle felt his body stiffen and the rhythm of his breathing change as the face of the man found on the Long Ashton by-pass filled the twenty-nine inch screen. 'Did you know him?' she asked, her head cocked towards him. Tyler simply shook his head, his attention focussed on the details that were being presented by the detective in charge of the investigation. Tyler had been bracing himself for this all week, but it somehow still caught him out. Fortunately, the police seemed to have no idea who the dead guy was or how he got to the lay-by, and they seemed not to be aware that he had been frozen for years after his murder. He drew a long breath and steadied his nerves. He'd been wise to insist that the body be thawed before being dumped, and wise, too, to ensure that the freezer be dumped separately. As far as he could see, he reassured himself, the police had no link between the body, the freezer, the garage and Harry Davis or any of his sons. He got up as the news ended and the weather forecast began, ostensibly, to make himself a coffee (Gayle never drank coffee or tea at night), but, once in the kitchen, he took his phone out of his pocket with the intention of sending Terry a text. Then he thought better of it and put it back.

∞∞∞∞∞∞∞∞

In London, the man who called himself Simon Lee was bolt upright in his chair. He'd been home since 7.30 pm, he'd made and consumed an evening meal, and he'd settled down to watch television. Even though he had been half anticipating some awful development since his experience on that wet night in Bristol the Friday before, being confronted now by the face of the man he had last seen alive some five years before and whose body he had personally consigned to its resting place in a freezer in Garage No 2 looking out from his television was a shock, a real shock! It meant the beginning of the end of the new start, the new life in London he had engineered and painstakingly developed over the past five years. It was inconceivable, even after that length of time, that the face would go unrecognised, and he now knew he would have to be prepared to move on. However, he recognised there was much to think about and so much more to be done if he was successfully to cover his tracks.

Chapter 27

The boy who had taken the envelope and photographs home with him showed them to his mother, Hilary Russell, and told her where and how he and his friend, Luke, had discovered them. On their own, each of the photographs seemed innocuous to her, but, taken together, she felt there was something ominous and threatening about them. Although there was nothing to suggest why, someone had gone to great lengths to record the regular comings and goings to the house or office which bore the number 147 of the man she assumed to be Harry Davis, having seen the pencilled name on the reverse of each. Closer inspection of the printed time and date on each photograph showed that the time of arrival was consistent – it was always early afternoon – and so was the departure about two hours later. The photographs appeared to have been taken in December 2005, but the envelope, although damp, couldn't possibly have been out in the open since then. When she said as much, her son was quick to reassure her that the freezer in which the envelope had been found had definitely not been there when he and his friend had been up on the hill on their bikes before, but that would have been February or March, and the envelope and its contents had certainly not been exposed to the elements since then. Between the two of them, mother and son concluded that the freezer must only recently have been dumped there. It was a prima facie case of fly-tipping, which really annoyed her, and her first thought was that it should be reported. Although it was too late to telephone the Council that evening, she would do so on the Monday, but she would let Matthew tell his dad all about the find when he got home later that evening, as the boy was clearly itching to do.

The boy's father, Hal Russell, was an actuary at one of the big insurance companies in Bristol and was already edging his way through the Friday night traffic on his way home. It had been a pretty routine sort of day, but then no-one had ever pretended that an actuary's role, although an integral part of the process of insurance risk assessment (and thereby pricing and profit), was exciting. Unusually, some of the sales team had invited him to join them for a drink after work, but he had chosen to drive into Bristol that day so he had politely declined. It just wasn't worth the risk. Once over the Cumberland Basin and past the entrance to the Long Ashton Park and Ride, the traffic on the Weston Road thinned and speeded up. It would slow again on the approach to Backwell Farleigh where the terrible accident had occurred about a week before, and there would, inevitably, be a queue at the traffic lights in Backwell, but he reckoned he'd be home by 6.30 pm, and he was not far off. He pulled into the driveway of his house in Cleeve at 6.32 pm, switched off his lights, reached for his coat and briefcase and crunched across the gravel to the front door. Surprisingly, it was opened from the inside for him by his grinning son, Matthew, whose other hand remained behind his back as though he was concealing something that he was really desperate to show him. 'Hello,' he said with a smile, 'this is an honour. You're usually up to your ears in your tablet. What are you so excited about?' Before he could answer, his mother shouted from the kitchen. 'Let your dad come through the door first, Matthew!' She smiled at her husband as he made his way to her from the hall, his own face registering his curiosity. It then took about three minutes for the story of the boys' find in the woods on the hill on the Wrington Road that morning to come gushing out of the excited Matthew. Hal Russell sat at the kitchen table and listened carefully then sifted through the photographs slowly after putting on his reading glasses. 'Have you reported the freezer?' he asked his wife as she handed him a glass of red wine. 'No, it was too late,' she replied, 'but I will, first thing on Monday. What do you think we ought to do with the photographs?' 'Well,' replied Hal, stroking his chin, 'I have a suggestion.' He paused for effect, looking at his son as he did so. 'I think we ought to take them to the police.' Mathew's eyes widened. 'Not only that, but I think that Luke and Matthew deserve a reward. Why don't you see if Luke can come into Bristol tomorrow? We can all take the envelope to the front desk at Bridewell Police Station and you can tell the sergeant everything you've told me. It's only ten minutes from the office, and we can use my parking space there. Afterwards we can grab a pizza and go to the multi-screen in Cabot Circus; there's bound to be something suitable for family viewing; it's still half term, after all.' 'Good idea,' said Hilary, 'I'll telephone Luke's mum. Let's put the envelope by the telephone so that we don't forget it on the way out.'

For Matthew, it was a great outcome!

Chapter 28

A tall, and once erect, military-looking man, Gregory Carver, now almost 73 years of age, walked with a slight stoop. He walked slowly along the pavement in Clifton Village, a chic and almost anachronistic group of shops and terraced housing in the heart of the predominantly Georgian suburb of Clifton. He paused between two parked cars, giving thanks for the fact that he didn't have to drive to his destination, which was within walking distance of his home, and crossed the road, newspaper under his arm. His destination was the coffee shop he had become a regular customer at since his wife had died some years before. He probably called in for a strong black coffee and a slice of pastry or cake two or three times a week, and the regular staff knew him well. Today, being Saturday, he was served by a girl he had only seen a couple of times before, probably a student at the university, but she took his order and his money with a fresh and ready smile and assured him that she would bring his coffee and cake across to the small table near the gable window. It had just been vacated and promptly cleaned by a young man Carver had got used to seeing on Saturdays, who caught his eye and motioned him over.

Carver loved the smell of fresh coffee and cake and pastry, but he also enjoyed the warmth, informality and companionship the coffee shop offered, with its comfortable mix of furniture and tasteful décor. The young but very able staff brought the place alive, and he always felt younger on leaving. It was too easy to fall into the habit of not going out, and, in the years immediately after his wife had passed away, he had been only too ready to adopt the life of a recluse. He'd cut himself off from mutual friends, and without any family to turn to (they had not been able to have children) he'd concentrated solely on administering his business. The business was simply a portfolio of residential and office property in the Clifton and Hotwells areas, a portfolio he had built-up largely in the sixties and seventies. It had yielded more than enough income for him and his wife to be able to enjoy their old age, particularly as they had no children and grandchildren and weren't concerned about whom, other than charities, to leave their money to. They had travelled extensively in their sixties and had particularly enjoyed the world cruise that had taken them away for three months from January 2006, but within a few weeks of returning from that cruise his wife, who was two years his senior, was diagnosed with cancer of the liver and spleen. Her death a mere four months later brought their hopes and plans to an abrupt and cruel end.

It was his GP who had helped to bring him to his senses, suggesting that although two years had passed since his wife's death, he seek professional bereavement counselling. It started when she had invited him to make an appointment to review his regular medication, but, alerted to his obvious deterioration due to poor eating habits, lack of company and a cessation of regular exercise, had then asked him to make a further appointment with a practice nurse for routine tests.

At the appointment that followed those tests, his GP had not minced her words, and he had appreciated her honesty. He was never fat, but his weight had fallen and his blood pressure and cholesterol were both markedly raised. She had looked at him, her right elbow on the edge of her desk, hands crossed in front of her and head inclined towards him and had bluntly warned, 'Unless you pick yourself up, Mr Carver, unless you take a greater interest in living, you will die long before you should.' It was not the approach she would make to all her patients, by any means, but she felt it would work with him. 'It is largely up to you, but I'm going to refer you to an organisation that can work with you to turn things round, and I very much hope you will accept my recommendation and referral.' Although he didn't know what to expect from counselling, he had accepted his GP's advice and his presence in the coffee shop that morning, enjoying the, albeit passive, company of others, was testimony to the success of the strategy she had recommended. He was a different man; older, perhaps, but much more like the old Gregory Carver.

He settled down and spread his newspaper on the table. Then, having scanned the front page, he turned it over to look at pages 2 and 3. Casual onlookers would have seen him suddenly lean forward to stare intensely at the right-hand page for a few seconds before sitting back, removing his glasses, passing his left hand over his eyes as if to help them see better, and then, having replaced them, lean forward again to read the article that lay before him. It was the report of an investigation into the suspected murder of a young man. Above it was a large picture of the man's face. It was a face he had immediately recognised as a former tenant, but it was a face he had not seen since well before the world cruise he and his wife had enjoyed in 2006. He remembered the young man because he had been a good and reliable tenant of a flat in Hotwells for some years, but shortly after returning from the cruise, Carver discovered that he had vacated the furnished flat with absolutely no notice, and it had surprised him. It had been so unlike the young man, who always paid his rent on time and had been no trouble at all, and although many tenants had passed through his hands over the years, he recalled the incident as if it were the day before. He could certainly remember his face, and it was the face in the paper on the table in front of him. What is more, Carver could even remember his name. And now, it seemed, the young man was dead, and there was a telephone number to ring. He would telephone as soon as he got home and had retrieved the file from the cabinet in his study just to make sure he had the name right. Fortunately, he never threw any of his tenant files away. Well, well, he thought, sipping his coffee.

Chapter 29

A re you doing anything, Jess?' asked Knight when DS Jess Bradley answered her home telephone at 12.15 pm on the Saturday. He hadn't announced himself because there was no need to; she would recognise his voice and would also be looking at the caller ID on her telephone. Although he'd only spoken five words, Jess immediately sensed that there had been a development and that Knight was optimistic about it. 'Good afternoon, sir,' she replied, 'no, not doing much, thanks; been shopping and thinking about going out for a run while the weather holds. Why, has something come up?' It was clearly a rhetorical question. 'Sure has,' replied Knight, 'There have been some calls to the operations room today from people responding to the photo-graphic of 'Mr Grey' on the news last night and in the paper this morning. You and Tom can sift through them on Monday, but one in particular looks very promising, and I'd like to follow it up today. It was from someone who rents out flats in Hotwells and claims our Mr Grey was a tenant of his until early 2006. The guy lives in Clifton, but the parking's pretty awful there on a Saturday so I'm happy to pick you up from Bridewell in 40 minutes if that's OK with you.' 'I'll be there for one o clock, sir,' Jess Bradley replied. 'Thanks,' said Knight, and rang off.

Having travelled from Bridewell in Knight's car, and having parked a block and a half from the address the operations room had given them, the two detectives stood outside a detached three-storey town house in a quiet backstreet. The house looked in good condition, but although the garden was tidy it had seen better days. 'What do you reckon this is worth?' mused Knight, realising that the answer would be a great deal more than he could ever afford. 'Well over a million,' replied Bradley, 'shall I ring the doorbell?' Knight nodded, and they stood patiently waiting to be let in to meet Mr Gregory Carver who had phoned in earlier that day. The door, as it turned out, was opened by Mr Carver himself, who smiled to indicate that he was clearly expecting them. 'Good afternoon,' opened Knight, 'Mr Carver?' he inquired. 'That is correct,' replied Carver, 'I imagine you are police officers?' 'I am Detective Inspector Knight and this is Detective Sergeant Bradley,' Knight confirmed, and before he could say any more or show his warrant card, Carver swung the door open and motioned them both inside. Once in the entrance hall, he ushered them into the front room, which, like the garden, thought Knight, was tidy and respectable, but no more than that. There were only two framed photographs on display. The black and white one on the mantelpiece was a wedding photograph, and although Carver was then some fifty years younger, he was clearly recognisable. He stood slim and erect in a dark suit, towering over his much shorter bride. The other picture was a colour photograph taken of the same couple but in more recent years. Both were formally dressed and stood arm in arm smiling at the camera. Carver followed his gaze to the colour photograph. 'That was the last photo of the two of us,' he explained, 'we took a world cruise in January 2006. It was taken before the last formal dinner before docking at Southampton in mid-March. I'm afraid things aren't as smart as they were when my wife was alive. In fact the whole place is far too big for one person, but we lived here for 30 years, and it would be difficult to leave it all behind. Please sit down. Can I get you both a cup of tea?' Knight shook his head. 'Not for me right now, thank you,' he answered, looking across to Jess Bradley with raised eyebrows.' 'Nor me, but thank you,' she responded, following his lead. They were both impatient to hear what Mr Carver had to say.

'Mr Carver, we're investigating the death of a young man whose body was found a week ago on the side of a road near Long Ashton. He had nothing on him that would enable us to identify him, but I believe you may be able to help us?' Knight opened. 'I certainly can,' replied Carver reaching for a slim brown folder which rested on the table beside his chair. 'I saw his picture in the paper this morning, and although it's a good five years since I saw him last, I had no doubt, whatsoever.' Carver paused, Knight nodded encouragement, and he continued. 'He was a tenant of mine for a number of years. I own a number of flats and offices, and he rented one of each. The flat is in Hotwells, and the office, it's very small, only suitable for a one-man operation, is in St Paul's along the Gloucester Road. While we were away on our cruise, he up and left both properties. I only discovered on our return that the rent for each had not been paid at the end of March, and when he didn't return my calls to his office and to the flat, I went round to both. They were locked, but when I opened them with my master keys I found his keys inside on the floor as though they'd been dropped through the letterbox. The office and the flat were both furnished, and everything was there that should have been there, but he had taken all his personal belongings. I waited a couple of weeks and then I let the properties again. The rent was, and still is, my pension, you see.' Knight nodded. 'What was his name and what can you tell us about his personal circumstances?' he asked. 'His name is (or was) Simon Lee,' replied Mr Carver. 'He was a financial adviser and mortgage broker. He was always very polite, and I never had any complaints from his neighbours in Hotwells or on the Gloucester Road. He kept himself to himself as far as I could see, but he was a perfect tenant.' 'You say it's a good five years since you last saw him,' observed Knight, 'but could you possibly be more specific?' 'Hmm,' mused Carver, that's tricky. It's the troublesome tenants I tend to see; not the good ones, but I certainly spoke to him by telephone at his office a fortnight or so before we went on our cruise. I wanted to explain that I would be away for three months, and I asked that he deal direct with my odd-job man if there were any building or services problems while I was away. It was definitely him.' 'Presumably he was single?' asked Knight. 'He certainly wasn't married, and I wasn't aware of any partner or girl-friend,' replied Carver, 'but, as I say, he seemed to keep himself to himself.' 'And what about his sexuality?' Knight asked, looking intently at Mr Carver. 'Are you asking me if he was a homosexual?' Carver responded, returning his gaze. 'I'm trying to determine whether he might have been,' answered Knight. 'It has a bearing on the investigation.' 'Well, I couldn't say for sure, and I certainly wouldn't swear to it,' replied Carver, 'but if you were to tell me that he was, I wouldn't be all that surprised. That's only an opinion.' 'Thank you very much Mr Carver, that's very helpful' said Knight without explaining why. 'You presumably had a written rental agreement with him, did you?' 'Yes,' replied Carver leaning across and offering Knight the slim brown A4 folder, 'I keep all my tenant agreements. This is Mr Lee's.' Knight took the folder and opened it up on his lap. There were only a few enclosures held together with old-fashioned file tags, the metal ones that tended to rust after years in musty old cabinets. Knight scanned the contents. He saw name, date of birth and National Insurance number on the rental agreement. There was no passport number recorded, but there was a driver's licence number, and there were also details of the bank account from which the rent for each property was paid by Standing Order from June 2000. Knight handed the folder to Jess Bradley, who also could not help but flick through the contents. 'May we take this folder with us, Mr Carver?' Knight asked. 'We will, of course, let you have it back as soon as we can.' 'Of course,' replied Carver, 'I'm pleased to be of help and,' pre-empting Knight's next request, 'should anything else come to mind, I will be pleased to let you know.' With that, Carver stood and extended his hand. Knight and DS Bradley took it in turn, followed him to the front door and left with a final wave. 'I'd like you to put a quick note on the system for the record as soon as we get back, Jess', said Knight as they walked quickly back to the car, 'but don't put the name against the case until you and Tom have cross-checked, and there's no pointin starting that process until Monday because DVLA and the others won't be open 'til then.'

Chapter 30

Knight dropped DS Bradley at Bridewell Police Station and headed home. It was 3.15 and there was still something of the afternoon for him to salvage. He felt quietly satisfied, and he hummed a tune as he made his way home. Mr Carver's information was good quality stuff, and he was optimistic that it wouldn't take Jess and Tom long to corroborate it. Then there were the other two telephone calls for them to follow up. He was sure that, by the end of Monday, they'd be able to confirm the identification and start calling 'Mr Grey' Simon Lee. According to Mr Carver, Simon Lee was alive and well in January 2006 and he hoped the information he was expecting to receive from Dr Howard and her colleagues at Edinburgh University would at least not conflict with that date and, at best, might help to narrow-down further the probable date of death.

As DS Bradley went into the building, the Desk Sergeant called across to her. 'Do you have a moment, DS Bradley?' he asked, and before she could reply he went on, 'I may have something of interest to you.' Jess smiled, recognising that she could hardly refuse, and stepped over to the desk. 'We had a family in a few hours ago,' said the sergeant, 'mother and father and two twelve year old boys. They left this.' He picked up a white A5 envelope from the tray behind the desk. 'It has some photographs in it,' he continued, and, holding the envelope at one corner, he slid the photographs onto the desk. 'I doubt that there'll be any original fingerprints on them because the boys and the parents have been all over them, but there's a time and date on each, as well as a name in pencil on the back.' DS Bradley looked at the photographs and the envelope and looked up at the sergeant. 'So why me?' she asked, eyebrows raised. 'Well,' answered the Desk Sergeant, 'I was on duty last week, and I remember Max Carter and DC French doing the rounds of metal merchants and recycling centres. The two boys found the envelope yesterday. It was in a chest-freezer that had been dumped off the road between Cleeve and the airport.' 'Thank you,' said Jess, not even trying to hide her smile, 'do we know exactly where to look?' 'We have a general description,' answered the Desk Sergeant, but I think the family are still in town, and I have a mobile number.' 'Could you let me have it, please?' asked Jess, 'I need to contact DI Knight right away.'

Before 'phoning her boss, Jess scrolled through the contacts on her mobile phone and rang Max Carter, who answered within a couple of rings. She quickly brought him up to date with all the Desk Sergeant had revealed, and he confirmed that he would be on his way in within minutes. She then telephoned the mobile number entered by the Desk Sergeant on the visit record alongside the name Mr H Russell. The telephone rang and went automatically to voicemail. She identified herself and asked that Mr Russell call the desk at Bridewell Police Station as a matter of urgency. Then she called DI Knight. He had just parked his car in the driveway of his family home when the call came through. He remained in the driver's seat and put his mobile to his ear. He remained motionless as Jess Bradley reported the facts to him, ending with the news that Max Carter was already en-route to Bristol. 'Do we have an address for Mr Russell?' he asked when Jess finished. 'Yes, we do,' replied Jess reaching for the print-out of the logged record that the Desk Sergeant had already produced, 'it's 25 Brockley Avenue, Cleeve,BS49 3PU.' 'It's not too far out of my way,' said Knight, 'I'll call there just in case. In the meantime, get the Desk to ask the family to drop whatever they're doing and get to Bridewell. Tell Max to alert the forensic people that we will need them. As soon as we've got the exact directions, we'll all need to take a look at the freezer. Once you've done all that, you can go home, Jess. You've done well.' 'Thank you, sir,' acknowledged DS Bradley, but before she had ended the call, DI Knight had started the car and was engaging gear.

Hal Russell's mobile was set to voicemail because he, his wife and the two boys were watching a film at the multiplex cinema in the centre of Bristol. It was therefore an hour before he obeyed the urgent summons to contact the police at Bridewell. By then, DI Knight, DS Carter and two members of the forensic pathology team were gathered there, drinking coffee and impatiently clock-watching. The Desk Sergeant reassured himself that he couldn't have recorded the location of the freezer any more accurately than he had because, after all, only the two boys had been there, but he wasn't sure that DI Knight was hugely sympathetic. He would be going off shift at 6.00 pm and was hoping that the call from Mr Russell would come through before that. Fortunately it did, and because the cinema was only a ten minute walk away, the two boys and Mr and Mrs Russell were soon standing at the desk in the lobby. It was agreed that the boys would direct Mr Russell and his wife to the location, with Knight, Carter and the forensic team following immediately behind. At the end of the cavalcade would be a police car with two uniformed officers equipped to cordon-off and guard the freezer until, after initial examination, it was taken away for much closer scrutiny. The boys were particularly excited.

They were even more excited as they led the detectives through the trees and bushes and proudly revealed their find of the previous day to them. Knight gave a cursory glance at the freezer, noting its orientation and its condition. It didn't look as though it had been out in the open all that long at all. 'Where did you find the envelope?' he asked the two boys. 'It was here,' answered Luke bending forward and pointing to the spot where the envelope had been. 'And how did you get it out?' Knight followed up. 'I put my foot here and reached in like this,' answered Luke, going through the motions. 'Did you see anyone when you were both up here, anyone on foot or in a van or truck?' continued Knight. 'No,' the boys said in unison, shaking their heads. 'Well, Luke and Matthew,' Knight went on, 'you have both acted very responsibly, and you may actually have helped to solve a real crime. Well done! We'll take over now. I think you can both go home.' Looking across at one of the uniformed constables, he said, 'please escort these two budding detectives back to the car.'

Ten minutes later, Knight was on his way home, too. He had left the constables controlling access, the forensic team beginning their initial examination and DS Carter in overall control. Already on its way to the site was a recovery vehicle, and Knight imagined that it wouldn't be too long before the freezer was under wraps and safely on its way back to Bristol for a thorough and detailed inspection. The freezer might turn out not to have anything at all to do with the case of Mr Grey, but Knight had a strong hunch that it would, and he knew he wouldn't have to wait very long to find out.

Chapter 31

D I Knight got in good and early on Monday morning, made a coffee and sat down at his desk to review everything that had been recorded to do with the case since the Friday afternoon. He scrolled down the data on the screen on his desk before him. He read quickly through Jess Bradley's report of the conversation with Mr Carver and skipped the record of incoming calls to the operations room to read Max Carter's brief account of the handling of the freezer find. The initial forensic examination had been concluded before dark, and the freezer was safely stored by 7.30 pm. Max reported that fingerprints had been found around the base at each end, different fingerprints, and this tended to indicate that two people (most likely men) had carried the freezer to the glade in the wood where the boys had found it. He was also able to report that they had taken numerous samples from inside it. It was amazing what could be found in corners and cracks. The detailed examination would involve completely dismantling the freezer, and would take a few days, but Knight was confident that there would be something to report from the initial investigation within 24 hours. He returned to the records logged by those in the operations room who'd taken the telephone calls. The first was Mr Carver, but then there were two from others who claimed to recognise the deceased. Only two? What did that say about 'Mr Grey's' public profile, he wondered. He would have expected there to be more. The first was a man called Alan Clarke, who rang from a Bristol address to say that he may have seen the man whose face appeared in the paper in a bar 'some time ago'; the second was also a man, also local, who said the deceased had helped him arrange a mortgage seven years before. His name was Peter Maybury. Max and Nicola would visit both men as soon as appointments could be made with them. Recognising someone seen in a bar was one thing, but Knight expected that the visit to Peter Maybury would be more productive. Mr Carver had said that Simon Lee was a Financial Adviser and Mortgage Broker, and Maybury might be able to provide corroboration. He sent a quick email to DSI Nolan's PA to draw her attention to the logged events of the weekend and to tell her boss that the team briefing would start at 10.00 am.

'Good morning, one and all,' said Knight addressing the five members of his team. 'As you all know if you've read through the logged events on the internal management system that we've had a pretty eventful weekend. We have a top quality ID of the deceased from his landlord, who is sure he was alive at the beginning of 2006 and who has provided us with his tenant file; Jess and Tom will be digging-in to that from today. The landlord may also be able to provide details of neighbours not only at the deceased's home but also at his office, if asked. They'll also be following-up the other two calls that came in. It is highly likely, but I want positive confirmation before we flag the name up, that the deceased's name was Simon Lee and that he was single and, quite possibly, gay. He was self-employed as a Financial Adviser and Mortgage Broker, and we may be able to find out more about him from Financial Services Authority (FSA) because he would have had to have been registered with them in order to work with mortgage companies and insurance firms. There will therefore also be people in local insurance and mortgage companies in the city who had dealings with him. His tenant file also gives us his bank account details, and that will offer rich pickings. He appears to have disappeared in the first quarter of 2006, but I will be very interested to know how long transactions continued after then.' Knight paused and looked across to DS Wes Brown 'Wes, I know I asked you to work with Max and Nicola, but I think Jess and Tom would benefit from your help on this one.' Wes nodded just as DSI Nolan slipped into the room, motioning to Knight with his hand to carry on.

'Max,' Knight continued, 'thanks for your report. Until we have something positive from forensics that links the freezer to the deceased, there's not a great deal we can reasonably do, and I suppose the same goes for the photographs, but I don't think it would be a waste of time to circulate them internally while we're waiting and to do some initial investigation into the name 'Harry Davis' and the possible location of the premises he appears to have been frequenting. Let me know the minute you and Nicola come up with anything, whether it's to do with our investigation or not.' DS Carter half-raised his right hand. 'I'd like to circulate one of the photographs among patrol officers,' he suggested, 'the premises looks more like a shop or maybe a town house than one you'd expect to find in the suburbs; it would be helpful to have lots of eyes looking out for No 147 while we're trying to narrow it down.' 'Good idea,' replied Knight, 'I'm aware you've all got a lot of digging to do now that we have a possible ID on the body and a potential link with the freezer. I want to keep the momentum up, and if we need more officers drafted in, I would be happy to ask for them.' Knight looked across to where DSI Nolan had been, but he had already slipped out.

Chapter 32

D S Wes Brown moved over to join DS Jess Bradley and DC Tom Fielding after Knight returned to his room. 'How can I help?' he said, addressing his question to Jess. 'Well let's look at what we've got to do,' she replied. 'We ought to give priority to the other two callers, but there are also some further questions I'd like to ask the landlord, Mr Carver. Let me deal with him because he's already met me, but perhaps you could follow up the other two callers?' Brown nodded. 'Then there's the data in the client file. We need to do the usual checks with DVLA, HMR&C and, of course, his bank as well as the FSA, and we'll need to get 'out and about' among the local insurance and mortgage people, as well as any of his previous neighbours we might dig up. I would be grateful, Wes, if you would deal with the FSA and handle the initial trawl of insurance and mortgage companies. It may be that the caller who claims to have had a mortgage arranged by our Mr Lee will be able to point us to at least one mortgage company that he introduced business to. Let's get on with it, shall we?' DS Brown nodded again, and DS Bradley reached for a telephone.

Mr Carver wasn't in when Bradley called, but she left a brief message on his answer-phone and, turning to the copy of the rental agreement she had made, she underlined the driving licence number that Mr Carver had recorded as part of the usual identity check. Looking sideways at Tom Fielding, who was speaking to someone at HMR&C, she got through to a number she had often used before at the DVLA. The voice on the other end was familiar, as was hers to the man who answered the telephone, and the formalities were quickly dealt with. 'This is a murder inquiry,' she said. 'We have a name and a driving licence number, and we'd be very grateful for whatever information you might be able to give us.' 'Off you go,' responded the man at the DVLA, and Bradley read the details to him. After a short pause, he came back to her with confirmation that the licence had been issued on 6th March 1989 to Mr Simon Lee, whose date of birth was 13th January 1969. His home address at the time was Flat 2, 88 Oak Tree Road, Locking, Weston-super-Mare. The licence was 'clean' – no endorsements or speeding offences had been recorded- and the only other information the DVLA records showed was a change of address to Flat 1, 27 Rowntree Court, Hotwells, Bristol on 31st March 2006, when the licence had also been upgraded from paper to plastic. Jess Bradley checked the address against that on the rental agreement, and it matched. That was a good start. She thanked the provider of the information and sat back to log the details she had been provided with.

'I've checked with the good people at HMR&C,' said Fielding. He waited until she finished updating the computer record of the investigation before continuing. 'They were able to confirm that Mr Lee was a self-employed Financial Adviser but served notice in March 2006 that he was packing it in and would be moving away from Bristol, possibly to work for someone. The last tax return was sent to them in May that year, and the balance of income tax was paid by cheque.

They've had no dealings with him since. I asked them to send us a copy of any correspondence from him and all the tax returns he submitted, and they will, but it could take five working days.' 'OK,' replied DS Bradley, 'will you deal with the bank, now? I'm hoping for a call from the landlord, Mr Carver. I'll get you a coffee in the meantime.' 'Thanks,' answered Fielding, 'but if you don't mind, I'd prefer to deal with the bank in person. There's a branch in Corn Street, and I could be there in ten minutes.' 'Go ahead,' Bradley answered, 'I look forward to hearing what you come back with.'

Corn Street, a cobbled street in the historic centre of Bristol and the historic buildings along each side of it went largely unscathed during the blitz in 1940 unlike much of the centre, which was destroyed. As he walked up the slight hill towards one of two banks at the top of the street, DC Fielding relished being able to act alone and without what seemed like constant supervision. He entered the bank, which had long been of the modern open plan design, and went across to a young woman at the enquiries and help desk. He identified himself, enjoying the moment he presented his warrant card and asked if there was someone he could talk privately with. The girl looked at her watch, asked him to wait for a minute, and disappeared through an adjacent door. After a short time, she re-emerged and motioned him through, passing him to a middle aged man who identified himself as Mr Royal, the branch manager, before resuming her post at the enquiries and help desk. 'Would you like to come into my office?' the manager enquired, motioning him through. 'Please do sit down. How may we help you?' DC Fielding produced a photo-copy of the tenant agreement and placed it on the desk between them. 'We're trying to trace this man,' he said, pointing with his index finger to the name Simon Lee. 'Judging by this rental agreement, he had an account with your bank, if not this branch, in June 2000. We would very much like to know all you can tell us about the account.' 'The first thing I need to do is to see whether the account is still live,' said Mr Royal, 'and if it is, I can give you all you need right away. If it isn't, it may take a little longer because I don't have immediate access to closed accounts, other than to confirm that they're closed. But, never fear, I do know someone who can.' He smiled and tapped his way into the screen.

After what seemed a lot of tapping, the manager confirmed that the account had, indeed, once existed but was now closed. He picked up the telephone and referred to a branch directory, dialled, checked his watch, and waited. Fielding checked his watch, too (it seemed everyone else was doing it) and he found the time to be 11.45. Too early for lunch, he hoped. The call was answered, and the manager identified himself and explained what he wanted. 'I wondered if you might be able to help,' he said to the person on the other end then, having listened for a few more moments, he turned to Fielding and said, 'The account was held by the Clifton Branch, which is where it was opened. If you want printed statements for the lifetime of the account, we can get them sent to your office, but it's probably best if I let you explain what you need, yourself. The lady on the other end is Pamela.' Fielding felt elated. It was all going so well, and he was sure that he wouldn't have made such good progress had he tried to navigate his way through the bank's call-centres himself. 'Good morning, Pamela,' he started, 'we will certainly need copies of all the statements.' He then gave her the address to which they should be sent and his contact number at the police station. 'But while you have the account on the screen, could you please tell me when it was opened, when it was closed and by whom?' he asked. He jotted some notes on the reverse of the tenant agreement as she answered. 'And what was the new address?' he asked, jotting the answer down, too. Finally, he asked, very politely, that she send the police copies of all the correspondence she had. The exchange complete and proving more fruitful than he could have hoped, he thanked 'Pamela' profusely and ended the call. Fielding handed the telephone back to Mr Royal, thanked him for his help and left. He was quite pleased with himself. So much so that he had to stop himself from running down the hill he had walked up half an hour or so before.

Chapter 33

When he arrived back at his work station in the incident room, DS Bradley was on the telephone to Mr Carver so Fielding made himself a coffee and waited. He watched as she ended the call and made notes on a pad then took a seat at the same desk. 'How did it go?' he was asked. 'Very helpful, actually,' he replied, 'the bank will be sending us copies of all the statements issued to Simon Lee. It seems he opened the account in 2000, but he wrote to them twice in 2006. First, in March to tell them of a change of address to another flat in Hotwells – I've got the address -and then in mid-April to cancel his standing orders and to close the account at the end of June. He asked for a cheque for the balance to be sent to the new Hotwells address. If they still have the original letters, they'll send us photocopies; if all they have are scanned copies, they'll send them by email.' DS Bradley was pleased as Mr Carver had not been able to give her more information because he didn't own the neighbouring offices or flats. 'Let me have a quick word with the boss,' she said, 'then we'll go and have a look at the new address in Hotwells. What is it?' 'It's Flat 3, 14 Amber Way, ' he replied, checking the note he'd made on the reverse of the copy of the tenant agreement he had taken to the bank. 'It's not that far from the first flat he was in.'

Jess Bradley walked across the Incident Room and poked her head round the frame of the door into DI Knight's office. 'Is the door open, sir?' she asked. 'Sure is,' replied DI Knight, looking up from the screen he was studying. He was due in court that afternoon in relation to a case he'd been lead investigator for since early February, and he was rehearsing some of the salient points he would need to remember if he was called to give evidence for the prosecution. 'DC Fielding had a productive morning,' she said, advancing a couple of paces into his office. 'We've learnt that Simon Lee wrote to his bank in Clifton twice in early 2006: first, to tell them of a change in address – he was intending to move to another flat in Hotwells – and second, a couple of months later, to cancel his standing orders, close the account from the end of June and ask for a cheque for the remaining balance to be sent to the new address. I'm told we will either get hard copies of the letters from the bank, along with all the bank statements they sent him since he opened the account in 2000, or we'll get scanned copies by email. Fielding is putting the report of his discussion with the bank on the system as I speak, and we're going out to see if anyone's home at the second address in Hotwells.' Knight was pleased, and he showed it. 'That's good news, Jess. I think we'll ditch the 'Mr Grey' tag now and start calling the deceased 'Simon Lee'. I think it's also time we started putting a time-line together on the system and on the board. We can start with Simon Lee's date of birth and work forward. There seems to be a lot happening in 2006, and I want to see how it all fits together. I'll ask Nicola to put everything we know so far in date order. Let me know what you find in Hotwells.'

Jess and Tom were able to park quite near to 14 Amber Way. The time of day helped. Once everyone was back from work, it would be impossible. They walked up a short path to the front door of the terraced house and studied the names against the four flats the building contained. Flat 3 would probably be one of the two on the top floor, and Jess looked up, but saw no sign of life at either of the two windows. It was lunch time; neither a good nor a bad time to find someone in. The name against Flat 3 was Brigitte Kirby. She pressed the button and waited. She and Tom were in luck because a girl's voice squeezed tinnily out of the speaker above the button, 'hello, who's there, please?' Jess replied, 'hello, I'm Detective Sergeant Bradley and my colleague is Detective Constable Fielding; we're with Avon and Somerset CID. We have ID, but I'm afraid you'll have to let us in before we can show you. May we come in?' 'What do you want to see me for?' The voice replied. 'I'm sorry, but I can't say. If you'll come down, I'd be happy to explain. Don't worry; you're not in trouble. This is just part of a routine investigation.' Jess had deliberately omitted the word 'murder' at this early stage in the proceedings! 'Hold on,' said the voice, 'I'll be right down.' Sensible girl, thought Bradley.

Brigitte Kirby overcame her initial reticence and invited them up to her one-bedroom flat. It turned out she was a student in her final year at Bristol University. There was no need for her to be at the university that day, and she was catching up on some reading in preparation for a lecture the following day. She had been a tenant of Flat 3 since 2008 and knew absolutely nothing about anyone who might have lived there before her. The only piece of potentially useful information she was able to give was the identity of her landlord. She showed them a copy of her rental agreement with a company called Davis Properties Ltd. The directors of the company were Mr H and Mrs G Davis, and the letting was administered by a firm of solicitors in Pill. Tom Fielding made a note of the solicitor's contact details, but neither he nor Jess Bradley made the connection between Mr H Davis and the name that had been pencilled on the back of the six photographs.

Chapter 34

The two detectives lost no time in getting back to the police station. Knight was still attending court, and they therefore found his desk empty. There was still ample time to get to Pill before offices closed for the day, so they decided to take the initiative and visit the solicitor who acted for Davis Properties Ltd right away. They needed to confirm the lettings history of the flat they had just visited. It would only be necessary to go back to 2006 to confirm the letting to Simon Lee, but they might also determine how long he was in residence. They got back in the unmarked police car together and set off for Pill. They could have telephoned ahead to make an appointment, but that wasn't DI Knight's style and so, following suit, they intended to call on the solicitor unannounced. Knight maintained that although there was always the chance of the person he wished to see being out, there was an even chance that they would be in and much more to be gained by observation of their reaction to a surprise visit from the CID. It was nearly always an instructive exercise.

Pill is a relatively small village, and Tom Fielding had the full address of Gordon Long, Solicitors, from the letter the current tenant of Flat 3, 14 Amber Way had shown him; so the office was easy to find. It was on a ground floor at the corner of a block in which there were two charity shops and a stationery shop. They opened the glass-fronted door and found themselves in a small waiting room beyond which was an open door into an office. A bell had sounded on their entry, and a woman in her mid-thirties with her hair tightly drawn up in a bun appeared. 'Good afternoon,' she said, 'I'm Stephanie, Mr Long's secretary. May I help?' 'Is Mr Long in?' asked Jess, returning her gaze. 'He is, but he's busy at the moment,' replied Stephanie, wondering who these two were. They certainly weren't locals. 'I'm DS Bradley and this is DC Fielding,' Jess announced as they both reached for their warrant cards. 'We won't take up much time, but we're conducting a murder inquiry and we believe Mr Long might be able to help. May we go in?' Stephanie was taken aback not only by the surprise visit but also by Jess Bradley's forthright approach. She blinked and half turned to face Gordon Long who'd overheard the exchange and had come through into the outer office. 'I'm Gordon Long,' he said, 'please do come through.' He preceded them into his office, stood behind his desk and motioned to two chairs. 'Please do sit down,' he said, and did so himself. He looked across at the two detectives and said, 'Over to you. How can I help?' He seemed composed, Jess thought. 'As I said to your secretary,' she answered, 'ours is a murder inquiry, but you're not a suspect, I promise. We believe you may be able to help us establish the movements of the deceased some years ago.' Gordon Long smiled politely to acknowledge the reassurance that he wasn't a suspect. 'Go on,' he said. 'We understand that you act for Davis Properties Ltd, and that the company rents flats in Hotwells,' continued Jess. 'That is correct,' replied Long, 'the company has three flats there, and they all currently have tenants.' 'Thank you,' acknowledged Jess, 'we're particularly interested in Flat 3, 14 Amber Way. We have met the current tenant and understand that she has been there almost three years. We need to know who the flat was rented to a little before her tenancy commenced. We're also particularly interested in the year 2006.' Jess paused. Gordon Long had listened carefully and seemed entirely at ease. 'I'm sure I can help,' he responded. Raising his voice slightly, he asked Stephanie to bring in the tenancy file for Flat 3. Stephanie was already at the filing cabinet; she had been listening to the complete exchange and was relieved that it wasn't Terry Davis in trouble again. She answered briefly and almost immediately brought the file through and placed it in Gordon Long's outstretched hand. 'Right,' said Long, opening the file and looking at the most recent enclosures. 'You say you've met Miss Kirby. Her tenancy started in September 2008. Before her, the flat was let to a Mr William Parker. He wasn't a university student. He needed temporary accommodation having recently moved to Bristol. He was selling his previous home and buying somewhere within commuting distance. He thought he'd only need to rent for six to nine months, but he was a tenant for exactly two years. He was there between July 2006 and July 2008. Does that help?' 'Yes it does,' replied Jess, 'but what about the first half of 2006?' 'Again, we had a young man in the flat before Mr Parker,' Long continued, 'he, too, was in for three years, but he wasn't at the university either. He worked for a firm of auctioneers in the city. He left at the end of May 2006.' DS Jess Bradley felt her pulse quicken as Gordon Long mentioned the date, but nothing else seemed to match; for a start, Simon Lee was a Financial Adviser, and he had left his flat in Hotwells in March 2006, judging by the letter he wrote to the bank. However, only a month later, in April 2006, he closed his account and asked for the balance to be sent to him at Flat 3.'And what was his name?' she asked. 'He was a Mr Spencer Maine,' was Gordon's answer. Jess paused; then asked, 'do you have a forwarding address for Mr Maine?' 'Interesting you should ask that,' replied Gordon, 'we do, but the copy of the termination of tenancy we sent to him at his new address was returned undelivered, and it's still here on file.' He pointed to an envelope. 'You have been very helpful, Mr Long,' said Jess, 'and if you could let us have a copy of Mr Maine's tenancy agreement, we will go away and leave you in peace.' 'Certainly,' answered Long. He was just about to summon Stephanie when she appeared, arm outstretched. He smiled at her, knowingly, and handed her the folder.

DC Jess Bradley was deep in thought as the two detectives waited in the outer office for Stephanie to produce the copy of Spencer Maine's tenancy agreement. Assuming the dates and addresses they had gathered so far were correct, she thought, the only way the facts fitted together was for Simon Lee to have moved in with Spencer Maine after he left his own flat. It was only a one bedroom flat, but there was already a suspicion that Simon Lee might have been gay, so it was possible. She stepped back towards the solicitor's office and cleared her throat to attract his attention. 'Would the tenancy agreement have allowed Mr Maine to have shared the flat with someone?' she asked. 'Certainly not,' was the reply. 'We don't allow it.'

Chapter 35

When the two detectives got back to the incident room, Knight was back at his desk, but with him in his office were DS Carter and DC French. DS Wes Brown was at his own desk updating the case file after his visits to the two individuals who had phoned in over the weekend. 'I'll be right with you, Jess,' he said. 'OK,' she replied, 'it would be good if we could both catch up.' She waited as he put the finishing touches to his brief report but, rather than read it off the screen, she asked him how the visits had gone. He explained that he had met with Peter Maybury and with Alan Clarke. Peter Maybury was a self-employed general handyman and white goods repairman. He had no doubt the picture in the media was Simon Lee, who he remembered very well and was fulsome in his praise for his help in getting a mortgage to buy a small house in Bradley Stoke in 2004 when all other avenues seemed closed. He didn't know where Simon lived, but he had visited his office in Gloucester Road two or three times in late 2003/early 2004. He had supplied Wes with details of his mortgage lender, and Wes had called in to the offices before returning to his desk, but hadn't been able to do much more than confirm that the mortgage existed and had been introduced by Simon Lee. The representative who had dealt with Simon Lee was no longer with the mortgage company, but at least DS Brown had her name.

Allan Clarke, on the other hand, was unemployed and, DS Brown suspected, likely to remain so. He was on benefits, and, judging from the state of his flat, was inclined to spend what little money he received on liquid, rather than solid, sustenance. He claimed to have recognised Simon Lee as someone he'd seen in a bar in Bristol sometime in the past twelve months but couldn't say where or who he was with. DS Brown was disinclined to give much credence to what he had to say.

Just as he came to the end of his narrative, Max Carter and Nicola French emerged from Knight's office and called across to the three in the incident room that it was their turn. Jess Bradley led and Tom Fielding brought up the rear with a chair of his own. They had barely sat down when Knight said, 'I'll hear what you've got to say very soon, but let me quickly bring you up to date with developments. First, we've had a positive match between fibres found in the freezer and Simon Lee's suit.' He paused, and then he continued. 'I'm equally delighted to say that we've also had a positive match between the thumb-print we found on the shoe and the prints we found at one end of the base of the freezer. Sadly, they're not ones we know about, they're not on the database, and the prints that were found at the other end of the freezer weren't quite good enough to offer us anything useful. Finally, I've had a further report from pathology. They are prepared to refine their estimate of time of death to a maximum of eight and a minimum of three years before the body was found. That means between 2003 and 2008. We already know he was alive in early January 2006 because Mr Carver, his landlord, spoke to him by telephone, but by April that year he had disappeared; so we're going to focus on 2006, and, as a first priority, I want you to look at all missing person reports recorded in the Avon and Somerset area after April that year.' Jess and Tom exchanged a glance. It was clearly he, rather than she, who would be trawling through the missing persons records!

'Over to you,' said Knight, looking from Wes Brown to Jess Bradley and back again. DS Brown took the initiative and briefly reported the outcome of the two follow-up meetings he had arranged that day. It didn't take long. He then handed the floor to DS Bradley who, following on from the outcome of DC Fielding's trip to the bank in Corn Street, which she had reported earlier, then took him through their visit to Flat 3, 14 Amber Way and, from there, to their visit to Gordon Long's office. She showed Knight the copy of the tenancy agreement that had been prepared for Spencer Maine and explained that her next step (DS Fielding would be occupied with the missing persons search) would be to use the data recorded on the agreement to identify and locate him. She paused as Knight put his hand up, palm forward, and said, with his eyes focussing on the tenancy agreement which lay on the desk in front of him 'I see the directors of Davis Properties Ltd are H and G Davis?' 'Yes,' said Jess, smiling and nodding. 'Any idea what the 'H' stands for?' he asked, looking up at her. 'Not yet,' she replied, realising, too late, the connection, 'but it won't take long'. 'If it turns out to be 'Harry', you will tell me, won't you?' asked Knight, signalling that he hadn't been fooled by her quick reply. The name

'Harry Davis' had been pencilled on the reverse of all six photographs of a man in his early sixties entering and leaving a premises identified only by the number 147. Both Jess and Tom knew that and should have spotted the possible connection. Jess mentally kicked herself.

∞∞∞∞∞∞∞

A quick visit to the Companies House website immediately after they were released from the meeting in Knight's office revealed that one of the directors of Davis Properties Ltd was, indeed, Mr Harry Davis, and Jess reported the outcome immediately. Knight decided that Gordon Long's office was worthy of another visit in the morning and that he and Jess would make the call. They would call on Harry Davis immediately afterwards if the solicitor was able positively to identify him as the subject of the photographs. He instructed DS Bradley to arrange a time with the solicitor (he felt it was more appropriate to do so for the second meeting). They would travel together from the police station, and he'd have the photographs with him. DC Fielding would go out with DS Brown to the address in Locking to where Simon Lee's first driving licence had been sent twenty two years before, and then Fielding would check the missing persons register.

Chapter 36

The meeting with Gordon Long was arranged for 9.15 the next morning (he explained that he generally didn't see clients before 9.30 am, but he was free until mid-morning that day. DI Knight and DS Bradley arrived in Pill at 9.00 am and Knight parked a block away from Gordon Long's office but within sight of it. 'What's he like?' asked Knight, motioning towards the office with his chin. 'He was helpful,' answered Bradley, 'and he came across as very efficient; seemed to have everything at his fingertips.' 'We'll see what he makes of the photographs,' said Knight. 'If it does turn out to be the Harry Davis, we'll go along to see Mr Davis immediately afterwards.' Looking at his watch, he said, 'Time to go.'

The door leading into the office was open, and the two detectives walked into the reception area with a polite tap on it. Both Stephanie and Gordon Long were standing with their backs half turned, and they both turned to acknowledge the arrivals, immediately recognising DS Bradley. 'Good morning, Mr Long,' said Knight holding his warrant card in the palm of his hand, 'you already know DS Bradley; I'm Detective Inspector Knight. Thank you for letting us have another word with you.' 'No problem at all,' replied Long, 'please come through to my office. Could I interest you both in a coffee?' 'Thank you, but no,' replied Knight, answering for both, 'this may not take long at all, and we might have to go on to another visit very soon.' He made his way into the solicitor's office, followed by Bradley. They waited until Gordon Long was with them, and then DS Bradley asked politely if the interconnecting door could be closed. Much to Stephanie's disappointment, Long obliged, and all that could then be heard from the inner office was the murmur of voices.

Long sat down at his desk, motioned for the police officers to follow suit, and raised his eyebrows as if to say 'Off you go'. DI Knight reached into his inner coat pocket and produced one of the six photographs. Watching the face of the man opposite him intently, he laid it down on the desk, face up, and asked, 'We wondered if you might recognise this man?' It was obvious from the change in Gordon Long's expression that he did, and the fact that he made no apparent attempt to mask his surprise was also noted by Knight. His brow furrowed; he nodded and looked up to meet DI Knight's gaze. 'Yes, I do,' he said, 'It's a photograph of Harry Davis.' 'You may pick it up if you want to look at it more closely,' said Knight, 'you'll see that it was taken on the sixth of December 2005. Can you possibly tell me where it was taken?' 'No, I'm afraid I can't,' answered Long, shaking his head, 'that's not one of the company's properties.' Knight allowed a few more seconds. He was sure that the solicitor's reaction was genuine; he had clearly not seen the photograph before and he didn't know where it was taken. 'When you say it's not one of the properties,' he continued, 'precisely what properties does Davis Properties Ltd let?' 'Not as many as it used to,' replied Long, 'there are now just the three flats in Hotwells, but up to the end of last month there were also five garages in Bedminster. Ownership of the garages has now passed to Bristol City Council under Compulsory Purchase. They'll be knocked down to allow a mall to be built.'

'I think that's just about all,' continued Knight, 'we intend to go on from here to visit Mr Davis this morning. No doubt he'll be able to say what and where No 147 is and why anyone should photograph him entering and leaving. Are we likely to find him in do you think?' Gordon Long's head shot up and he looked first at DS Bradley and then back to DI Knight. 'I'm terribly sorry,' he said, 'but Mr Davis is no longer with us. He passed away a month ago. I thought you knew.'

It was the turn of Knight and Bradley to be surprised. 'You didn't mention that when I called the first time,' challenged Bradley. 'That's a little unfair,' responded Long. 'You didn't ask, and your questions were all about the tenant of one of the flats. It just wasn't relevant!' 'We accept that, Mr Long,' said Knight intervening to placate him and regain the initiative, 'but please tell us more. This is news to us. What was the cause of death for example?' 'He had a heart attack,' responded Long, 'about a month ago; he was cremated at Canford Crematorium. His wife, Gloria, is now the sole director of the company, but I continue to administer the arrangements and, to some extent, her sons, mainly the older one, are now more involved. It's early days for us all, and I'm not sure what will happen eventually.' 'Tell us more about the sons, please,' invited Knight. 'Well,' continued Long, 'Tyler is the older of the two. He works in light engineering at Avonmouth; he's married and lives in Bedminster. Terry, the younger one, is self-employed; he does driveways and that sort of thing. He also lives in Bedminster but with his partner.' 'And the widow, Gloria?' prompted Knight. 'She still lives here in Pill,' said Long, 'but she won't know anything about this,' he motioned to the photograph, 'and if you do plan to call on her, I would ask that she has Tyler and me with her when you do. I'd be there not in a legal capacity but as a friend of many years. Harry's death was a great shock to her because she depended on him for everything, and I don't know how she'dcope with a visit from the police.' 'Hmm,' said Knight, 'OK, I understand that, but I do want to see if Tyler or Terry can cast any light on this photograph. How can we best contact them?' 'I have their mobile numbers,' offered Long. Tyler will be the easier to find, but Terry is seldom at the same place of work for more than a couple of days at a time.' 'Thank you,' replied Knight, 'DS Bradley will take the numbers, but I must ask that you do not communicate this conversation to either of the brothers before we talk to them.' Knight looked directly into Gordon Long's eyes as he spoke, and Long nodded. 'I have no plans or reason to be talking to either in the foreseeable future,' Knight continued, 'and I will definitely not say a word about all this to Gloria.' 'We're already half way to Avonmouth,' mused Knight, 'if you'll tell us where Tyler works and what he looks like, we might get to see him this morning. We'll catch up with the younger brother later.'

A few minutes later, Knight and DS Bradley emerged from the inner office and, avoiding Stephanie's inquisitive stare, left the office and made for their car. Once inside, Knight turned to DS Bradley and asked her to telephone Tyler Davis to see how soon he could see them and where. Not everyone wanted CID to call on them at their business premises, innocent of any wrongdoings or not. He asked that she be not specific about the nature of their inquiry. He felt that a woman's voice might be helpful.

She dialled the number Long had given her, and the call was answered with a guarded 'Hullo'. Her mobile number wouldn't have been recognised by Tyler's phone, and so he was naturally cautious. 'Hello,' replied DS Bradley 'is that Mr Davis?' 'Yep,' answered Tyler, still cautious and expecting a sales pitch to follow. 'This is Detective Sergeant Bradley, Avon and Somerset CID. I'm sorry to trouble you at work,' she said, 'but in the course of one of our investigations we've come across something relating to your late father, Harry Davis, and if you could spare us a few minutes, we feel you may be able to help us understand it. My colleague and I are in the Avonmouth area and wondered if you could see us this morning. We understand if you prefer us not to call on you at work, but there must be somewhere we could meet.' The response was not immediate; in fact it took so long for Tyler to answer that Jess was about to reconfirm the connection, but he did. 'I don't understand what it is you want to talk about,' said Tyler grudgingly. 'I'm afraid we can't be more specific over the telephone,' Jess replied, 'but you'll understand, I'm sure. Could we come to your work or would somewhere neutral be better for you?' Again there was a measurable silence. 'Nah, not work,' said Terry 'and not now. I could meet you during my lunch-break. How about the car park at Gordano Services on the M5 at quarter past one? Who did you say you were, again?' 'I'm Detective Sergeant Bradley, and with me is Detective Inspector Knight,' Jess replied, 'we're not in uniform, and we're in an unmarked car. What car are you driving, so that we can look out for you?' 'I'll be in my van,' replied Terry, 'it's a white Ford Transit.' He ended with the van registration number. It was a Bristol registration issued in the second half of 2004.

'Well done,' said Knight, who had been listening, 'let's get back to the station. It would be a good idea to run Messrs Tyler and Terry Davis through the computer and also check that registration plate before we go out to Gordano.

Chapter 37

Knight and Jess Bradley arrived at the Gordano Services car park at 1.00 pm precisely. It was busy, as usual, but it would be far busier in the holiday season, thought Knight as he selected a bay that allowed them to watch the traffic coming in through the main entrance. At 1.10 pm the white Ford Transit with the Bristol registration plate came into view, and they watched as it swung past and found a bay close to the café and toilets. A couple of minutes later, a man in blue overalls climbed out of the van and stood, with his hands in his pockets, looking up and down the ranks of parked cars. He then climbed up into the driver's seat again and sat, with the door open. Knight checked his watch and reached for his door handle. DS Bradley reached for hers, and the two of them got out of the car together and walked across to Tyler's van. Tyler's gaze was fixed on the entrance to the car park, and the first he knew of the presence of the two officers was when Knight came from behind the van to the open driver's door and cleared his throat.

Tyler jumped, momentarily startled, and then stepped out of his van to engage with the two detectives. His discomfort was clear, and both Knight and Bradley sensed his unease immediately, noting the perspiration on his brow and on his upper lip. It could mean something, but, then again, being unsettled by suddenly being called to meet two detectives to discuss your late father could be construed as a perfectly normal reaction! Knight showed him his warrant card and introduced himself and DS Bradley, and he concluded the introduction by thanking Tyler for giving up part of his lunch hour to see them. He had decided not to mention their earlier meeting with the solicitor unless specifically asked. He had also decided not to reveal the source of the photographs. 'As DS Bradley mentioned when she phoned, Mr Davis,' Knight said, 'we came across something that appears to relate to your late father in the course of an investigation, and we are hoping you might be able to help us understand it.' Although Knight paused to allow Tyler to respond, he continued to regard the two officers warily and didn't say anything. Knight reached into his pocket. 'This is one of six photographs that were taken of your father in December 2005. In all cases, he is entering or leaving the same premises.' He handed the photograph to Tyler and watched him closely. He then continued, 'As you can see, the door and the number, 147, are all that are showing. We know it's five years ago, but can you cast any light on where and what No 147 might be?' Knight then stopped talking and waited for Tyler, who was staring at the photograph, shaking his head and looking very puzzled, to say something. 'I've never seen this photograph before,' said Tyler after what seemed like an age, 'and I don't know anything about the place he's going into. Where did you get it?' 'I'm not at liberty to say right now,' answered Knight, 'but I might be able to reveal that later. Do you think your brother, Terry, might be able to help us?' Genuinely puzzled by the photograph and thinking that the cops seemed to know a lot about the Davis family, Tyler gave a noncommittal reply, 'I don't know, but I'd be surprised if he did.' Knight waited for more, which was not forthcoming, and then he acted on a hunch. The check on the van registration plate had been uneventful- the van had a current MOT and was properly owned, licensed and insured- and Tyler Davis had a clean sheet as far as Avon & Somerset Constabulary was concerned. The same couldn't be said of his younger brother, Terry, who had attracted police attention more than once in the past, but his offences had been relatively minor. 'We know Terry is probably working somewhere today, and we haven't got the time to find him and ask him if the photo' means anything to him,' said Knight, 'but if he, and possibly you, were able to come to the station for a few minutes after work this evening, we could ask him, and, by then, we might also be able to tell you both how we came by the photos of your dad.' Again, he waited in silence for Tyler to consider the request and respond. He was relieved to see Tyler nod thoughtfully and then agree to the proposal. Knight gave him a reassuring smile, thanked him and suggested that he and DS Bradley should make no further inroads into Tyler's lunch hour. They acknowledged each other and he and Jess Bradley returned to their car.

'I'm glad he didn't ask if we had Terry's mobile number,' said Knight as he strapped himself in, 'or I might have had to tell a white lie.' 'Why do you want them both to come to the station?' DS Bradley asked. 'Principally to get Tyler's fingerprints,' answered Knight, 'Terry's are already on record and don't match anything we've seen on this investigation,' he continued, 'but I'd like to get Tyler's if only to eliminate him from our investigation.' Bradley knew Knight better than that. She looked across at him as he sat with the engine running. 'Or confirm your suspicion, sir?' she asked. Knight looked across and smiled. 'Just a hunch, Jess,' he said. 'That van of Tyler's is big enough to carry a freezer. I've asked Nicola to spend some time with Traffic. We'll see if the van was out and about on the night of Saturday 28th May or very early the following morning.'

Something had triggered the sudden disposal of a corpse that had been successfully concealed for five years, and Knight had more than a hunch that the 'something' was the death of Harry Davis which had occurred only weeks before the body of Simon Lee was discovered. He wasn't sure why, but for the first time in this inquiry he sensed a glimmer of light. He engaged gear and moved forward to join the queue waiting to exit the services area.

Chapter 38

The traffic was very light when DS Brown and DC Fielding entered the Weston Road and headed south west, and it wasn't long before they were on the other side of the M5 and turning off the A370 for Locking. In its day, at the heart of the village of Locking had been the RAF's Technical Training centre and, later, its premier training centre for radio technicians, but at the turn of the century all RAF activity at Locking ceased when its role was subsumed by RAF Cosford on the eastern border of Shropshire. At first, there had been grand plans to redevelop the ex-military site, but few had materialised, and Locking remained a quiet village with more than its share of unemployment and the social problems associated with it.

As they cruised along Oak Tree Road, the signs were all too clear that they weren't in the most up-market part of the village, and the small block of flats at No 88 didn't challenge that conclusion. The building, erected in the mid 60's, looked tired and dilapidated; some of its windows were impervious to light, their curtains drawn firmly, and lengths of black cable trailed from shared television aerials, disappearing through holes in walls and window sills into the darkened living spaces within. Flat 2 was a ground-floor flat with a light blue door that was overdue a coat of fresh paint. The garden gate had long since gone, leaving the posts from which it had hung standing pointlessly at the start of a short path that led to the door from the pavement. It looked as though someone had once tried to grow shrubs in a small circular bed to the left of the path, but the shrubs had long given way to grass and dandelions that now almost completely hid a chipped ornamental gnome lying on its side.

'This is a long shot,' muttered Brown, after all, over twenty years had passed since Simon Lee's driving licence had dropped through the door and onto the mat. He rang the bell and was immediately rewarded by the sound of a dog barking furiously and a man's voice shouting 'Shut up!' It didn't sound like a small dog, and he and Tom Fielding took a cautious step back from the door. The barking continued but became more muffled as, judging by the sound of an internal door slamming, the owner had shut the dog away. They heard a security chain being unlatched, and the door opened a few inches to reveal a middle-aged man in a t-shirt and old jeans. He was unshaven and his voice was laden with suspicion. 'Yeah? Whaddya want?' he asked.

'We're police officers,' replied Brown, holding the man's gaze, 'I am Detective Sergeant Brown and this is Detective Constable Fielding.' Reaching for his warrant card, and, from the corner of his eye seeing Fielding doing the same, DS Brown continued, 'We're conducting an investigation into someone who once lived at this address, and we wondered if you might be able to help.' He paused to give the man behind the door an opportunity to invite them in, but it was not forthcoming, and the suspicion in the man's gaze had intensified, if anything. 'Help the police?' the man sneered. 'Why would I want to do that?' 'Because knowingly withholding evidence is an offence, and because this is a murder inquiry,' replied Brown. The man's eyes flicked between the two police officers, but the door didn't open any more than it already was. 'I don't have to invite you in,' he said, 'ask what you want to ask out here!' 'Very well,' replied Brown, 'Would you please tell us who you are, if you're the tenant and how long you have lived here?' 'Two years,' replied the man, 'yes, I am the bloody tenant, and my name is Bill, Bill Fisher. Is that all?' 'Not quite,' answered Brown, 'does the name Lee mean anything to you? A Simon Lee once lived here, but long before your time here. It would be helpful to know of anyone round here with that name.' 'Nah. Never heard of anyone with that name,' was the reply, 'and I don't know anyone.' The man's response seemed genuine, unhelpful though it was, and DS Brown saw little point in continuing the conversation with Mr Bill Fisher. He thanked him, and the two officers walked back to the car. The door slammed shut before they had reached the end of the path.

'What now?' asked Fielding. 'The council offices in Weston are our best bet,' replied Brown, 'we probably should have gone there first, but it's only a small village; I know there's a pub because we passed one on the way in, but on the way out let's see if there's a village store that's been here for twenty years.' The two officers got into their car, aware of the hostile stare they were receiving through the lounge window of Flat 2, and they pulled away from the kerb. There was a village store cum post office, but the couple who were running it had only been doing so for four years having moved to the village from the West Midlands, and so without wasting any more time the officers headed for the offices of North Somerset Council in the centre of Weston-super-Mare.

Their visit to the Council housing department was far more fruitful than their morning expedition to the village of Locking. Not only were they each treated to a cup of tea once they had identified themselves but they came away with confirmation from the tenancy records and from the electoral roll that Simon Lee and his mother, Mrs Susan Jane Lee, had lived at Flat 2, 88 Oak Tree Road between April 1986 (when Simon would have been 17) and June 1991. Her marital status was shown as 'divorcee'. In the electoral roll of 1992, however, the records indicated that by then there were three adults in the flat because Mrs Lee had a partner, a Mr Gareth Rees. By 1993 Simon Lee had moved out, and his mother and her partner had done so in April 1994. The couple seemed to have made no application for housing in North Somerset, and the assumption was that they had either gone into private accommodation or had left the county altogether. There was no forwarding address for Simon Lee, but the two officers felt fairly satisfied with their day's work as they drove back to share their information with the investigating team in Bristol. DC Fielding also had other work to do there. It wouldn't take long because the missing persons register was now on line and easily accessible, but he was keen to see if it would yield another piece of the jigsaw picture of Simon Lee which was slowly developing.

∞∞∞∞∞∞∞∞∞

As it turned out, DC Fielding's search of the missing persons register when back at his desk took no more than 25 minutes and revealed absolutely nothing. Simon Lee, the man in the grey suit, who was born in 1969, was issued with his first driving licence in 1989 and had been invisible for the period between 1993 when he left the flat he shared with his mother in Locking and 2000 when he had rented a flat in Hotwells. He had lived there until apparently doing a runner in early 2006, and had not been heard of again until his body had turned up, partly frozen, at the side of the Long Ashton by-pass in 2011.

Chapter 39

It was 6.15 pm when Tyler and Terry set out from Tyler's van, parked on the third floor of a multi-story car park in Rupert Street to walk the few hundred yards to Bridewell Police Station for their meeting with DI Knight. They were curious, suspicious and apprehensive; neither had any inkling of why their dad would have been photographed entering and leaving anywhere, and the number 147 meant absolutely nothing to them. They were hoping to learn more, but their memories of their illegal dumping of the body were still fresh in their minds, and they were wary of a police trap. Not to turn up, however, not to have accepted DI Knight's invitation, would only have created suspicion. They had agreed that, wherever possible, Tyler would do the talking. His mouth was dry as the pair presented themselves at the front desk and he announced who they were and why they were there to the Desk Sergeant. He had been briefed to expect them and asked them to take a seat while someone came to escort them to their meeting. Within a couple of minutes, DS Bradley appeared and, with a smile, thanked them both for coming. She confirmed that DI Knight was free, and she invited them to follow her. As she turned into the corridor in which the interview room was situated, she was surprised to see DC Nicola French emerge from the room and turn to walk down the corridor away from them. Their eyes met briefly as she did so and there was an imperceptible smile on Nicola's face.

She ushered the two men into the interview room, and DI Knight stood up and offered his hand to both. There was a water jug and glasses on the table, and although he offered them tea or coffee as an alternative before they sat down facing him, both declined. 'Thank you both very much for coming in to see me this evening,' said DI Knight looking from one to the other of the two men sitting uncomfortably in front of him. 'Terry, we haven't met, and you won't know DS Bradley.' He motioned with his left hand to Jess, who had taken the seat on his right. 'As I explained to Tyler this morning, we are trying to understand and explain why your late father,' he paused and nodded gently to the brothers in recognition of their recent loss, 'would have been of sufficient interest to someone that they would have photographed his arriving at, and leaving, a house or establishment over a period of weeks. We showed one of a sequence of photographs to Tyler this morning in the hope that he might be able to cast any light on it, but here,' he reached into a folder on the desk and brought out the six photographs and spread them out for the two brothers to see, 'are all the photographs in question.' He waited while Terry and Tyler examined the photographs and then continued. 'If you turn them over, you'll see the name 'Harry Davis' has been pencilled on them, and I'm sure you will both confirm that that's exactly who they show.' Again he waited, and the two Davis boys followed his invitation. They looked puzzled and worried, but that's exactly how he would have felt in their position, he thought.

'Terry,' he said, looking directly at the younger brother, 'Tyler has not been able to say where or what No 147 might be. Can you cast any light on where these photographs were taken? You'll have seen that they were taken on Tuesdays over a period of two weeks from 6th December 2005, and they seem to show your dad arriving at No 147 at about a quarter to two and leaving about two hours later.' He stopped talking, poured a tumbler of water for himself and sipped at it while watching for any reactions. Both shook their heads incredulously, exchanged glances briefly and returned his gaze. 'No,' replied Terry, 'I don't know where it is.' 'Until very recently, nor did we,' said Knight, 'but one of our uniformed officers on patrol around Old Market recognised it today'. The news came as a surprise to DS Bradley, but she didn't let it show on her face. '147 Old Market is the address of a massage parlour,' continued Knight, 'it's called 'Sweet Caramel' and it's run by a couple named Shandy and Carl Stewart.'

If it was possible for the faces of the two men to turn paler than they already were, they did. They looked at each other again, this time in unfeigned astonishment, and Knight felt for them momentarily. Their dad had only been dead a matter of weeks and now they had learned, possibly for the first time, that he had been regularly and routinely 'playing away'. 'Ma mustn't find out!' said Tyler, reaching for a tumbler himself and grimly fixing DI Knight with his stare. 'It'll kill her!' 'There's no immediate reason for us to tell her,' replied Knight. 'Your dad wasn't exactly breaking the law, but what he was doing, and his need to keep it from you all, seems to have given someone a lever over him. It would seem to me that your dad was being blackmailed. What I want to know is why and by whom. I want to know who took these pictures. Think back; ask yourselves whether you saw any tell-tale signs in his behaviour; if he was paying someone to keep quiet, were there signs of any financial problems as a result?' Knight paused as the questions registered with the two brothers. 'I know you want to get home,' he said, 'but let me give you a few minutes to talk among yourselves. DC Bradley and I will be back shortly.' With that, he stood up, and Jess followed him out of the room.

∞∞∞∞∞∞∞

'When did you get the report identifying the massage parlour, sir,' asked Jess as they walked along the corridor. 'About five minutes before you brought them in to the interview room,' answered Knight. 'Nicola got to me just before you did. Good timing, hey?' He smiled, and Jess detected more than a hint of satisfaction in his voice. 'And what now, sir?' she asked. 'We'll give them a few minutes, but when we go back in I'd like you to be prepared to take both their fingerprints. I think we've already got Terry's on record from when he was a bit younger, but we haven't got Tyler's, and I think it would look better if we invited them together. I don't know how you feel, but I thought their reaction to the revelation of their dad's Tuesday afternoon hobby was genuine surprise. I don't think they knew anything about it, and now Harry Davis is dead he's not going to say much. Remind me; when exactly did he die?' 'First week in May,' answered Jess, 'and he was cremated on the 18th.' 'And the body of Simon Lee is discovered less than a fortnight later. I wonder if that's just a coincidence.' Knight mused.

Twelve minutes later, they returned to the interview room. Knight again felt a twinge of sympathy for the two sons of Harry Davis who had been trying to deal with the news Knight had given them earlier. 'Are you sure you wouldn't like coffee or tea?' he enquired as he approached the desk. 'I'd like something a lot stronger,' replied Tyler, 'but, I'm driving and you're not offering!' Knight smiled, and he and Jess sat down and waited. It was Tyler who broke the silence. 'We don't know anything about dad and the massage parlour, and we never had any idea that he was being blackmailed or anything.' He said. 'We never got involved in the money-side of the business; the only person who did was dad's solicitor, and if he suspected anything, he didn't say anything to us.' 'When you say 'business', Tyler, what exactly do you mean?' asked DI Knight without acknowledging that he and DS Bradley had already spoken with Gordon Long. 'Property rental,' answered Tyler. 'What sort of property, exactly?' prompted Knight, wondering if Tyler's terseness was driven by a concern not to reveal very much about the business. 'Rent from three flats in Hotwells,' was the reply. 'So that's all that Davis Properties Ltd has on its books, then; three flats in Hotwells?' Knight continued to probe for the full answer to the question, an answer that tallied with the account given by Gordon Long. 'It is now,' replied Tyler. 'There *were* five garages in Bedminster also, but they've just been sold to the council to knock down. They're redeveloping.' 'Thank you,' said Knight, resolving to ask the solicitor in Pill in the morning to provide details of the tenants of the five garages. It was time to bring the interview to an end.

'Well,' said Knight, leaning back and tidying-up his folder, I think that's almost it. I really am grateful for you coming in this evening, and I will let you know if we find out anything more about all this. I see no reason at this stage to involve your mother, but I would ask that if you suspect she may have any information that might help to cast light on the possible blackmailing of your dad, you let us know.' He paused, seeking confirmation from the two men, who both nodded their agreement. 'But, before you go, there is one thing you could do for us and that is to provide us with a set of each of your fingerprints. You don't have to, but it will help to eliminate you from our inquiries and once we've done so and the inquiry is over, they will be deleted if not needed. DS Bradley has the forms you'll need to sign to record your consent, and she's also got the means to take the prints now. It will only take a few minutes. Is that OK?' Terry looked at Tyler; they had no idea that the discovery of the photographs had anything to do with the freezer or the body they'd dumped, but they'd been led skilfully by DI Knight to this point. They nodded, and Jess went swiftly to work.

Chapter 40

Wednesday 6th June made a promising start. The pink dawn sky in the east soon gave way to blue, and it was almost a pleasure driving in to work. DI Knight was at his desk by 8.30, and his team all made their way in over the course of the next 30 minutes. No sooner had DS Bradley removed her coat than she was summoned into his office by a wave from Knight. They both remained standing while he asked that she get on the telephone to Gordon Long, the solicitor in Pill, to find out who the tenants of the five garages in Bedminster were and where the garages were located. Allowing her to leave, he asked her to tell DS Carter and DC French to pop in. 'Nicola's gone back to Traffic, sir,' she said, 'where she's looking through the camera footage, but I'll tell Max.'

'You wanted me, sir?' asked Max Carter as he entered Knight's office. 'Yes, Max,' he replied. 'How's Nicola doing?' 'She's getting square eyes, sir,' Max answered with a smile, 'because she's been reviewing the traffic camera coverage of the roads leading to and from the Cumberland Basin. She's concentrating on night time traffic and on the two weeks before the date the freezer was discovered. That's a lot of viewing!' 'OK, I'll have a word with her when she's next in,' said Knight, but this morning I'd like you to go take a look at the garages that Harry Davis rented out and the people who rented them. Jess is speaking to the solicitor who administered the Davis properties now. They're no longer owned by the Davis company; they're council property now and they'll soon be knocked down. I don't know when, but, as I say, get along there this morning, please.' Carter was just about to leave the office when Jess Bradley reappeared at the door. 'If he's nothing else, that solicitor's pretty efficient,' she remarked. 'He was able to give me all the detail while I waited. Interestingly, two of the garages were rented by none other than Tyler and Terry Davis, two were rented by people who live in Bedminster, and I have their names and addresses, and the fifth, apparently, was a mystery to Mr Long. He says that the rental was a private arrangement between the late Harry Davis and the tenant. He has no paperwork on the deal, and he never knew the identity of the tenant. He says that the rent was always paid in cash and by post.' 'That will give you something to get your teeth into,' said Knight to DS Carter. He was about to say more when the office telephone buzzed; before the two detectives left the room, Knight had the telephone to his ear and was listening intently.

Later that morning, the elderly lady in the flat across the road from the garages had read her morning paper and poured herself a first coffee and was looking out at the blue skies and wondering whether to go out for a walk when she saw a police car pull into the cul de sac on the other side of the road. It was the first activity she had seen since the man from the council had put padlocks on all the garage doors a week before, and she was pleased with the unexpected distraction. She watched as a man in a suit got out on the passenger side and wandered round the garages, checking the padlocks on each of the doors. He then returned to the police car, opened the passenger door and, with one hand on the vehicle roof and one on the top of the door he paused and took a look around. He looked up at the flat across the road and, despite the net curtain, could make out the shape of a person apparently looking down on him. He seemed to be on the point of shutting the car door and coming across the road, but instead he lowered himself into the seat and the car pulled away. The next stop would be Bristol City Council offices. The man in the suit, DS Carter, needed to find whoever had the keys for the five padlocks.

It was lunchtime when DS Carter returned to Bridewell. He had with him five brand new keys on a single keyring; each key had a large tag attached to it with string, and on each tag was a number from one to five. His intention was to take a quick lunch, check on the availability of DC French, and return to inspect the interior of the five garages. In his pocket he had a piece of paper with the names of the tenants and the garage numbers that correlated with them: No 1 was rented to a Miss Marshall, who, judging by her address, didn't live far from it; No 2 simply had a question mark against it; No 3 was rented to a Mr David Belmann who had a shop nearby; No 4 was rented to Tyler Davis, and No 5 to Terry Davis. It was these two garages which were of prime interest, but the mysterious letting arrangement of Garage No 2 meant that it would also merit attention. He was in the canteen about to place his order when his mobile phone rang. It was DS Bradley. There had been a development. He was to tell DC French to get to the incident room immediately, and he was to do the same.

Chapter 41

The detectives gathered in the incident room adjacent to DI Knight's office and had just been joined by DC French and four uniformed police sergeants when Knight walked in from the corridor opposite. He had been bringing DCI Nolan up to date with the latest development, which he was about to reveal to the team, and the immediate action he was about to put in motion.

'DS Bradley will now tell you what she told me fifteen minutes ago,' said Knight, standing facing the group. He turned to Bradley, who hadn't been expecting that the meeting would start exactly this way but who stood up, cleared her voice and announced that the fingerprints taken from Tyler Davis the previous evening matched the fingerprints found on the abandoned freezer and the thumbprint on the loose shoe found by the partly frozen body of Simon Lee. Glancing at DI Knight, she sat down and watched as the news was digested by the men and women who shared the room with her: faces smiled, heads nodded and glances were triumphantly exchanged. 'Thank you, Jess,' said Knight, looking round the room and waiting as attention became focussed on him. 'Later this afternoon,' he continued, 'we are going to arrest Tyler Davis, and we are also going to arrest his brother Terry. We've nothing hard on Terry, but Tyler couldn't have acted alone. He must have had someone to help him move the freezer, at least, and it's my hunch that the 'someone' is his young brother. I've applied for a warrant to search both their homes, and we shall also set forensics loose on Tyler's Transit. With the agreement of Bristol City Council,' he nodded to DS Carter, 'we'll also take a close look inside the garages they rented from their father's company. We'll meet Tyler as he leaves work in Avonmouth, and we'll be waiting for Terry when he gets home from wherever he's working today. I don't know if either will want to engage the services of their family solicitor, Gordon Long, but we will not permit that on the grounds that he, quite possibly, could be complicit in the crime. In fact, he might be happier not to be called to help because he's not a practising criminal lawyer. We'll offer them the services of one of our usual firms.' Knight paused briefly; then he continued. 'I'm as happy about this as you are, and who knows where the questioning will take us, but I must emphasise that while we appear to be on the brink of establishing who transported Simon Lee's body to the Long Ashton bypass, that doesn't necessarily mean the same person or persons killed him. Remember that his death appears to have occurred around five years ago. Yes, it could have been Tyler or Terry, or both, but it could equally have been their dad, who regrettably is now nothing more than a pile of ashes, and the murder may even have some connection with the attempt by someone to blackmail him. So, let's get on with the job this evening, but let's not lose sight of the main focus of this investigation, the murder of Simon Lee. Are there any questions or points?'

Nicola French caught his eye. 'You have something for us, Nicola?' he asked. 'Yes, sir,' said Nicola as she rose to her feet, 'I would have been in to tell you earlier, but I've just come straight in. I was just about to call it a day when I came across some footage that had been automatically flagged for examination but hadn't warranted further action by the traffic division. It shows Tyler Davis and Terry Davis coming into Bristol at 11.45 on the night of 25th May in Tyler's Transit van. I initially recognised it from the registration you logged after your meeting with him at Gordano Services, but the reason it had been flagged was that one of the registration plates, the front one, was almost entirely obscured by a rag.' 'Great news, Nicola!' said Knight. 'What day of the week was that?' 'It was a Wednesday, sir,' she answered, 'ten days before the two boys discovered the freezer.' 'Is there anything else before we decide who's doing what tonight?' asked Knight looking round the room. His gaze rested on DC Tom Fielding who appeared to be trying to decide whether to prolong the briefing. 'Only to say, sir, that I'm expecting the copies of Simon Lee's bank statements to arrive tomorrow, and I shall also, hopefully, be hearing from the DVLA as well.' 'Excellent' said Knight encouragingly, 'it's good to keep the focus on Simon Lee. Let me know if you find anything.' With that, the meeting ended and DI Knight took the three detective sergeants into his office to plan the action that would take place at the end of the day.

Chapter 42

When Tyler Davis emerged from his work place, he was surprised to see a police car parked alongside his van with two uniformed policemen in it and DI Knight and DS Bradley standing alongside it. He walked towards them carefully, trying to disguise the panic he could feel rising from the very pit of his stomach. His heart was already beating much faster when the two uniformed officers got out and DI Knight took two steps towards him. 'Tyler Davis,' he said, slightly raising his voice to be heard over the sound of a nearby car engine, 'I am arresting you in connection with the murder of Mr Simon Lee. You do not have to say anything, but, it may harm your defence if you do not mention when questioned something which you later rely on in court. Anything you do say may be given in evidence.' Before Tyler knew it, the two uniformed officers had handcuffed his hands behind his back and he was being guided to the rear seat of the police car. 'Two things before you get in,' said Knight, 'your mobile and the keys for your van, please.'

An hour later, Gayle Davis answered a knock on the door to find DC Tom Fielding and a uniformed police officer on her doorstep, with a man and a woman carrying holdalls on the path behind them. Following procedure, he identified himself, explained that her husband had been arrested and was in police custody and that a warrant had been issued to permit the house and any adjoining buildings to be searched. He asked for her full cooperation in order for the search to be concluded in as short a time as possible; Gayle stepped aside in amazement and shock to let the party in and closed the front door behind them.

At about the same time, Terry Davis, parked his van on the side of the road opposite his terraced house in Bedminster, and was arrested by DS Carter as he stepped from it onto the pavement. As he was bundled into the police car and invited to hand over his phone and the keys of his small van, he caught sight of Karla answering the door to DC French, accompanied by one policeman in uniform and two people carrying holdalls. He couldn't wave to reassure her because his hands were cuffed behind him.

By the time Terry was read his rights, relieved of his belt, shoe-laces and the contents of his pockets and taken to his cell, Tyler was already being questioned by DI Knight. He knew beyond doubt that Tyler had been involved in the dumping of the freezer and of the body, and Tyler was therefore guilty, at least of complicity in, albeit five years after, the murder of Simon Lee. What he really wanted to know was who killed Simon Lee. He decided to start with that very question. 'Tyler,' he said, looking directly into Tyler's eyes. 'Who killed Simon Lee?' Tyler looked at him blankly. 'Who's Simon Lee?' he said. 'Simon Lee is, or was, the man whose body was dumped at the side of the Long Ashton by-pass,' replied Knight, 'he was wearing a grey suit, and one of his shoes had fallen off. It wasn't that long ago. It was in the paper and on TV. Surely you remember?' 'No comment!' was Tyler's reply. 'Well, Tyler, I must inform you that your thumb-print was found on the loose shoe. How did that come to be there, do you think?' asked Knight. 'No comment,' was the answer. Knight continued. 'We found your thumb-print on his shoe, Tyler, and we found your fingerprints on the freezer from which Simon Lee was taken before being dumped at the side of the road. As we speak, Tyler, your home is being searched, your van is being forensically examined, and your mobile phone is being analysed. You really would be surprised what a mine of information mobile phones can be,. I expect that by this time tomorrow we will have a lot more proof of your involvement in the death of Simon Lee. Who killed him, Tyler?' 'No comment,' was Tyler's reply, but somehow it lacked conviction. 'You'll have all night to give your answer to that question lots more thought,' said Knight. 'Interview terminated at 7.00 pm on Wednesday 8th June 2011.'

Although Knight realised he had far less evidence of Terry's involvement, he decided to follow a similar line of questioning to that he had embarked on with his older brother. The interview commenced at 7.30 pm. 'Terry,' Knight asked. 'Who killed Simon Lee?' The question was met with the same uncomprehending stare as it had when directed at his brother. Terry shrugged, looked briefly at the lawyer who was sitting on his right, and answered, 'I dunno no-one named Simon Lee'. 'You may not know his name, Terry, but Simon Lee is the name of the dead man whose body recently turned up on the Long Ashton by-pass. You will have seen his picture on TV. We didn't know his name then, but we know it now. I've just been talking to Tyler about him. I know Tyler knows him because we found Tyler's thumb-print on one of Simon Lees' shoes. I want to know who killed him, Terry. Can you tell me? Knight asked. He had been observing Terry closely, and, as with Tyler, he was sure that the name 'Simon Lee' meant nothing to him. He was equally sure, however that Terry was Tyler's accomplice when the freezer, at least, was moved. One man might be able to move a body, but not a chest freezer. 'Did you help Tyler move the body, Terry?' Knight asked innocently. Terry didn't say anything. He was clearly unsure how to answer the question, and his eyes flicked from left to right. Knight waited and then posed the question again. 'Did you help Tyler move the body of Simon Lee, Terry?' he repeated. 'No!' came the short response. 'Do you know who did, Terry?' Knight asked gently. 'No,' said Terry, then, reconsidering the wisdom of his answer, he said, 'I know nothing about the bloody body!' 'And what about the freezer, Terry?' Knight continued, watching for his reaction. It was clear that Terry was scared. 'What about the freezer? Tyler couldn't have moved that on his own. Did you help him dump that, too?' 'Do I have to answer?' Terry asked the lawyer who had been patiently listening. 'You don't *have* to.' was the reply. 'In that case I won't,' blurted Terry defiantly. 'OK, Terry,' said Knight, sitting back in his chair and preparing to leave. 'It's been a long day. We will speak again tomorrow. By then we will have the results of the search of your and your brother's house and car, and we'll have the analysis of your, and his, mobile phones, which will not only tell us who you've been speaking to but will also tell us where you've been. Oh, and

I'll also show you an interesting photograph we've got. Remember, we want to know who killed Simon Lee. You'll be able to give the question lots of thought in your cell tonight. Interview terminated at 8.00 pm on Wednesday 8th June 2011.'

CHAPTER 43

The first thing DS Wes Brown did on the Thursday morning was to follow up the patrol officer's identification of the premises that Harry Davis had been photographed entering and leaving in December 2005. He decided to walk to Old Market from Bridewell. It would only take ten to fifteen minutes. His route took him across Castle Park and then across the dual carriageway that separated the centre of Bristol from St Phillips. He crossed by the pedestrian bridge before entering Market Street. He then crossed Jacob Street and continued on the south side of the road, noting that the odd numbers decreased as he went east. He found No 147 where he had been told it would be, half way along the next block. There was nothing outwardly to suggest what purpose the premises might serve, but he knew what business was conducted there from the report he'd read. The area was well known for the number of similar establishments that had sprung up there to service the sex trade, and he didn't expect that the occupants would be brimming over with cooperation so early in the day, particularly when he revealed his identity. He tried the door; it was locked. He rang the doorbell and waited. There was no immediate response, and so he rang the bell again. He peered through the window looking out on the main street, but there was a blind in place; he was considering exploring the rear approach to the building when he heard the sound of a key being inserted into the lock. The door was partly opened by a large unnaturally blonde woman in a top and skirt that were too small for her. She peered at her caller with a frown. 'We don't open until after lunch,' she said, 'what do you want?' 'I wonder if I might speak to the manager? I'm Detective Sergeant Brown,' Wes replied, producing a warrant card. The frown on the woman's face intensified, and she stared at Brown for a few seconds, wondering what to do. Then, having decided that co-operation was probably the best course of action in the long run; she stood back, swung the door more open and said, 'I'm busy, but come in.'

Wes Brown stepped forward and found himself in what looked like a reception room, and there was a strong smell of cheap air-freshener. A desk stood beside the corridor that led off from the room, and behind it was a single chair. The woman walked past the desk into the corridor, and she motioned Brown to follow her. Four paces later, she turned right into the first of three doorways leading off from the corridor. There was a leather couch down one side of the room she ushered Brown into and a large mirror on the wall opposite. A hand-basin was in the corner at the far end of the room and there was a chair beside it. The smell of air-freshener was, if anything, even stronger. She stood with her back to the far wall, with one hand on the back of the chair and said, 'I'm Shandy. My husband and I own and run 'Sweet Caramel. How can I help you?' 'You could start by telling me what sort of business you have here,' replied DS Brown. 'It's no secret,' she replied 'not from your lot or from anyone who chooses to give us their custom. All you need do is look at our website. We offer two basic services. We have a range of attractive escorts for those who want to go out on the town, and we offer a massage service on the premises for those who prefer to stay in. Here,' she said, smiling sweetly, 'please have one of our business cards. You never know, you might like to become one of our customers, yourself.' Brown glanced at the card. He could see that the proprietors were listed as Shandy and Carl Stewart. He decided on a more formal style of approach. 'Mrs Stewart,' he said, 'we are currently engaged in a murder inquiry.' He paused, waiting to see if the statement had the desired effect. It seemed to because her smile quickly disappeared. He felt in his jacket pocket and pulled out a copy of one of the photographs of Harry Davis outside the front door. 'We believe this man was a regular visitor to these premises about five years ago. Do you recognise him?' He handed the photograph to her and continued to study her as she moved across to better light and peered at it. She, again, seemed to consider her options before answering. 'Normally, we would be very reluctant to reveal the identity of our clients because our discretion is very important to them,' she answered. She paused, appearing to invite some acknowledgement, some acceptance of that basic principle before continuing. Brown nodded. She went on, 'However, we do try to stay within the law.' She looked at the photograph, again and then looked up to meet Wes Brown's gaze. 'I do remember this gentleman,' she said, 'he used to be a regular, but I haven't seen him for years. Has he been murdered?' 'No,' replied Brown, 'he died fairly recently but of natural causes. Could you say exactly when he last came here?' Shandy Stewart looked thoughtful, whether it was for effect or whether she was genuinely reflecting on Brown's question was hard to say. 'It would have been at least three years ago because Robin, his favourite, has been gone for that time, and he stopped coming well before Robin moved on. We only knew him as 'Harry'. I don't know where he lived or what he did because we don't ask for that sort of information, and even if we did, we would only be told lies. I do remember that he was a regular afternoon visitor, but that's about all.' Wes was making brief notes but paused to ask, 'What about records of regular visits?' Shandy smiled and answered, 'I keep old appointments books, but only for six years for tax purposes. Do you want me to tell you exactly when his last visit was?' Wes nodded. 'That would be helpful,' he replied, feeling mildly surprised at the extent of Shandy's cooperation. 'Take a seat,' she said, 'I'll only be five minutes.' She left the room and returned a couple of minutes later with three A4 sized appointments books, one each for the three years 2008, 2007 and 2006. She sat on the couch and, looking across at Brown, reassured him it wouldn't take long. She knew what she was looking for, and it didn't. 'Robin's last appointment with him was Tuesday 14th June 2006,' she said. 'Robin moved on at the end of February 2007.' Looking up from his notepad, Wes asked, 'And do you know where she went?' Shandy looked mildly amused. 'She?' she queried, 'Robin was a masseur, a young man, and a very good looking one.' Closing the appointment book, she stood up and motioned her hand towards the door into the corridor. 'And now DS Brown, I don't think I have any more for you, and I have a business to run.' DS Brown, accepting that he had derived as much from Shandy as he could reasonably have expected, thanked her and made his way through reception and out onto the pavement. Turning left, he reached for his mobile phone, but then replaced it and lengthened his pace. He would be back at Bridewell within fifteen minutes.

∞∞∞∞∞∞∞

At much the same time as DS Brown knocked on the door of 'Sweet Caramel', DS Carter was inserting a key into the padlock of Garage No 4, watched by DC French. Behind them in the cul de sac were two police cars. Two uniformed officers were putting tape across the access to the garages, and two members of the forensics team were waiting behind him to see what would be revealed when, with gloved hand, he lifted the garage door. As expected, the garage was empty, as was No 5, but 'empty' could still mean rich pickings for the forensics team. A small crowd of curious onlookers had gathered in the road, and as Carter glanced at them he caught sight, once more, of a figure looking down from the flat beyond and above the small crowd. 'No time like the present,' he thought. He gave a friendly wave and, leaving DC French with the search party, he walked across the road, through the open glass doorway that led into the stairwell and up the 27 stairs to the door of the flat on the first floor. He knocked, and the door was almost immediately opened by an elderly lady with immaculate grey hair and bright blue eyes behind a pair of NHS spectacles. Having identified himself, he was invited in with a smile and a wave of the lady's hand and asked whether he would prefer tea or coffee. 'I've only got Instant, I'm afraid,' she added.

It didn't take long for DS Carter to discover what a mine of information the lady, Mrs Peabody, represented. Not only had she observed the comings and goings across the road since she had stopped going out as much but had kept records, by date and time, in her own prim hand, in an exercise book. The jottings went back almost three years, but it was the early months of 2011 that looked particularly promising. It became clear very quickly to Carter that as soon as the forensics team had finished with Garages No 4 and 5, they should switch their attention to Garage No 2. After his second coffee, he prised himself away and left. On his way down the stairs to brief the forensics team, he took out his mobile phone and brought DI Knight up to date with the news of Mrs Peabody's revelations.

∞∞∞∞∞∞∞

At the very time that DS Carter and DI Knight were talking by phone, a panel van drew up outside a terraced house in the London borough of Clapham. The building had been modified to provide three apartments, one on each floor. The driver checked the address against a list lying on the passenger seat beside him, switched the van's ignition off and got out. He opened the rear door of the van, removed a metal fence-post spike and a lump-hammer and selected a suitable spot in the small front garden adjacent to the low brick wall that separated it from the pavement. He went down on one knee and, holding the metal spike in place with his left hand, drove it in with the hammer in his right. Satisfied that it was secure, he returned to the van, tossed the hammer back in, extracted an estate agent's 'apartment for sale' sign on a pole and returned to insert the pole into the aperture in the metal spike. He stood back to ensure the sign post was vertical, went back to his van, closed the rear door and drove away.

CHAPTER 44

DI Knight was aware that he had enough evidence to charge Tyler Davis and therefore to hold him in custody until he did. The case against Terry, however, was, at best, circumstantial and, unless something positive was forthcoming from the interviews he would conduct that day, and/or from the forensic searches that had taken place the previous night, he would be under pressure to release Terry as early as Saturday evening. However, he was fairly confident that something would come up, and he therefore decided to have a word with Tyler first, probably just before lunch.

He went out into the incident room to see who was there and found DS Jess Bradley and DC Fielding poring over the contents of an A4 sized manila envelope that lay at the side of the desk. 'What have we got here?' he asked. The two officers looked up. 'We've just had this delivered, sir,' replied Bradley. 'Copies of bank statements issued to Simon Lee and of the correspondence between him and the bank during the life of his account. Tom's going to go over it all this morning. We're expecting to hear from HMR&C tomorrow or Monday, but we've already heard from DVLA,' she said, holding up a smaller brown envelope. 'We're just about to open it.' 'Good,' replied Knight. 'Let's hope we come up with something. Where are the others?' Looking quickly round the room, Jess replied, 'DS Carter and DC French are with the forensic team at the garages in Bedminster, sir, and DS Brown is probably on his way back from the massage parlour in Old Market. Do you want me to come in on any interviews with the Tyler boys this morning?' 'Yes, I think so, Jess,' replied Knight. I've got a meeting with the boss this morning to bring him up to date and decide what we're going to release to the press, but you and I'll see Tyler first just before lunch, and we'll let Terry stew a little longer. I'll want to know whatever comes in from last night's searches or this morning's activities, so either you or Tom text me if I'm not here beforehand.' 'Will do, sir,' was Jess' reply.

An hour and a half later DS Brown phoned in with the news that the object of Harry Davis' visits to Sweet Caramel had been a masseur named Robin, and shortly after that came a report from DS Carter of an eyewitness account of two men identified as Tyler and Terry Davis covertly loading a large, freezer-sized item into Terry's Transit from one of the garages owned by Harry Davis Properties Ltd on the same night as the two had been photographed driving back into Bristol with the front registration plate obscured. Tom Fielding alerted Knight by text, as instructed, and briefed him when he rang back. Knight sounded pleased. Tom then returned to the papers in front of him. He'd found something odd, but he wanted to discuss it with DS Bradley before he raised it with the detective inspector, and she had gone to sort out the arrangements for the interviews with Tyler and Terry Davis. The telephone on his desk buzzed again. It was turning out to be a busy Thursday.

It was a few minutes after midday when DI Knight and DS Bradley walked into the interview room in which Tyler and the solicitor who had attended him the previous evening were seated. Knight nodded to them both and positioned himself in the chair immediately facing Tyler over the desk that separated the two. He got the interview under way immediately, glancing up at the ceiling-mounted CCTV camera to ensure that it was on and running, and declaring the start time of the interview. He then paused, looked across at Tyler and asked him the same question he had asked the previous night. 'Tyler,' he said, 'who killed Simon Lee?' He felt that Tyler had had plenty of time to review the situation he found himself in and, hopefully, to recognise the futility of continuing to be obdurate in the face of the evidence already in the hands of the police. He was right. Tyler's mind had refused to recognise the demands of his body for the rest it needed at the end of the day, and had been going over and over the implications and likely outcomes of his predicament. He was not a murderer, but he sensed that there was considerable risk that he could be painted as one, and he was scared. He had been allowed to phone Gayle, with a uniformed policeman in attendance, and she was distraught. She had watched as the police had searched the house leaving nothing, no matter how personal, untouched and unexamined, and she described to Tyler the sense of foreboding she had felt when the search had extended to his shed, and a travel rug had been bagged and taken away. He had meant to do something with the blanket, wash it or have it dry-cleaned or simply dispose of it, but he had not got round to it. All he had done was to honour his dad's last wish that he get rid of the contents of Garage No 2, presumably to protect his name, but he had made a complete mess of it. Not only that, but he could tell by the line of questioning that he was now 'in the frame' as a possible murder suspect. He had to come clean. The damage had already been done, but he would do his best to protect his younger brother; as far as he could tell, they didn't have anything on him.

'I don't know,' answered Tyler. 'It wasn't me. I didn't know who he was until you used his name last night. I never saw him alive.' Knight cocked his head. He was encouraged. 'Tell me more,' he said. Tyler swallowed and took a nervous glance at the solicitor sitting impassively beside him. 'The first time I laid my eyes on him was in one of the other garages,' he said. 'He was well dead. He was in the freezer you found and was frozen solid. I don't know how long he'd been there; all I know is that I found him after my dad died and I was getting the garages ready for sale to the council. I didn't tell the police 'cos I was worried that my dad might have been blamed, and that would have killed my mum. I got someone I met in a pub to help me; paid him a bloody fortune; dumped the freezer first and the body a couple of nights later. I'm not a murderer. I didn't kill the bloke.' Knight sat back and waited for more, but Tyler remained impassive, staring at the floor. It was as if he'd delivered a statement he had been rehearsing for hours and was relieved to have got it off his chest. It was clear he was protecting Terry. Knight decided to expose this lie and see how he responded. 'The guy you met in the pub,' said Knight, 'which pub was that, when did you meet him and where can we find him?' He waited for the reply, but Tyler was clearly struggling to put together a plausible answer and failing. Knight reached into his folder. 'I am presenting you with street camera print of you and your brother, Terry Davis driving into Bristol at 11.45 pm on 25th May 2011,' he said, placing the photograph on the desk in full view. 'We believe this was the night you got rid of the freezer, Tyler,' he said. 'That's Terry, your brother, with you. You're on the way home. The front registration plate is partly obscured by a rag, but the rear is not. It may come as a surprise to you that we also have an eye witness who saw the pair of you loading your van from the garage, No 2 of the five, earlier in the night. Are you sure you want to persist with your story that you were helped by a man you met in a pub?' Tyler put his head in his hands and slumped forward, his shoulders shaking as he sobbed. 'Interview suspended at 12.34 pm,' declared Knight and, with a glance at DS Bradley he said 'It's time for lunch. We'll speak again later, Tyler,' and he walked out. It would be Terry's turn next.

CHAPTER 45

And it was Terry's turn an hour later. Unlike his brother, Terry was cocky and self-assured. No sooner had the interview got under way than he demanded to know why he had been arrested, why he'd been detained for almost 24 hours before having the chance to challenge anyone in authority and when he would be released. DI Knight took full advantage of the opportunity. 'You have been arrested in connection with the murder of Simon Lee, whose body was found at the side of the Long Ashton by-pass on the morning of Sunday 29th May,' he answered. 'I am sorry that I wasn't able to get round to you until now, but I needed to interview your brother, Tyler, who is also under arrest, and I needed to review the evidence we've been collecting. As you, like him, are suspected of involvement in a serious crime, we are permitted to hold you for 36 hours without charging you, but we can extend that period with the help of the courts. My question to you is a simple one: who killed Simon Lee?'

Terry looked at his attending solicitor, who simply nodded his head. He glared at DI Knight and almost shouted his answer. 'I don't know, but I do know that it wasn't me!' Knight persevered. 'Who do you *think* may have killed him then, Terry? Could it have been Tyler or could it have been your dad? You see, we know where Simon Lee's body was stored before he was taken to the lay-by. He was stored in one of the garages that your dad rented out. Not your garage; we've checked that, and not Tyler's garage; we've checked that, too, but it was stored in garage No 2, and we believe he had been stored there for a very long time. We found traces of his DNA on the garage floor this afternoon, and we found fibres from the blanket that he had been covered in or carried in. We also found those fibres in your brother's van, and we found the blanket in your brother's shed.' Knight paused and sat back, watching as the colour drained from Terry's face and his rate of breathing increased. All of a sudden, he was a lot less cocky, but he found it in him to come back at his questioner. 'My dad did not kill the bloke; nor did my brother; nor did I, and I do not know who did!' Knight remained impassive and returned to the cross-examination. 'Did you help your brother dispose of a freezer on the night of Wednesday 25th May?' he asked. 'No,' Terry responded shortly. 'You don't seem surprised at the question,' Knight observed. Terry just shrugged, but silently he realised he'd been caught out by not reacting with surprise. 'You see, Terry, we have an eye witness who will testify that you and your brother loaded his van from No 2 garage on the night of Wednesday 25th May.' Terry glanced at the attending solicitor, who remained impassive. 'Then they're lying,' he replied. 'I know nothing about a freezer.' Knight responded immediately. 'We think you do, 'he said. 'You see, your and Tyler's mobile' phones and our traffic cameras don't lie. We've compared them and we've found that you were together on the night of 25th May and that you travelled together to the area where we later found the freezer. You returned to Bristol just before midnight that night. I am showing you a copy of a photograph taken by one of our traffic cameras.' Knight paused long enough for Terry to study the photograph, and then continued, 'Your phones also revealed to us that, on the night of Saturday 28th May, you were both in the vicinity of the spot where the body of Simon Lee was found.'

Knight paused again; there was no response from Terry and so he continued. 'You asked me at the beginning of this interview why you had been arrested, Terry, and I hope you now know the position you're in. You are under suspicion that you murdered or were complicit in the murder of Simon Lee, whose body was kept in a freezer in a garage owned by your father, until you and your brother disposed of that freezer on the night of 25th May, leaving the body on the garage floor. We believe you disposed of the body three nights later. I'm not charging you at this stage. Instead I'm going to give you time to think about all that you've heard this afternoon, and then we'll speak again.' Terry remained silent, his gaze fixed on the desk in front of him. 'Interview suspended at 2.30 pm,' declared Knight, who stood up and left the room without a backward glance.

When back in his office, Knight called the three detective sergeants, Jess Bradley, Max Carter and Wes Brown into his office. He gave them a quick résumé of the interviews with the two Davis brothers and acknowledged that although he was now confident that it was they who had disposed of the freezer and the body, he was now far from sure they had anything to do with the murder of Simon Lee. He wondered whether Harry Davis might have had more to do with it. After all, Simon Lee was HIV positive, and the evidence thus far had shown that Harry Davis might have had homosexual inclinations; so there might have been a link there. The photographs found in the freezer suggested that Harry Davis was being blackmailed; could the blackmailer have been Simon Lee? And who was the mystery tenant of Garage No 2? Could it be that there was no tenant? Could it be that Harry Davis had invented the mystery tenant simply to allow him to use the garage to store the body of Simon Lee who had been blackmailing him? Would the body of Simon Lee still have been in the freezer in Garage No 2 were it not for the sale of the garages to the city council or was it the death of Harry Davis that had precipitated the need to clear the garage?

CHAPTER 46

Immediately after their discussion with DI Knight, DS Bradley and DS Brown left in an unmarked car to travel to Pill to see the solicitor, Gordon Long. Knight's instructions to them were to thoroughly re-examine the question of the identity of the tenant of Garage No 2, leaving the solicitor in no doubt about the seriousness of the possible charges against the Davis brothers. Knight remained behind to interview Tyler and Terry again.

Jess Bradley opted to take the passenger seat and, as they left Bristol westbound for Pill, she dialled Gordon Long's office, offered apologies for the short notice, and alerted Stephanie to their impending arrival. Fortunately, Gordon Long was in and would be free to speak with them. Stephanie asked what the subject might be, but Jess simply answered that the solicitor would know.

'Good afternoon Mr Long,' she said as the two detectives were ushered in by the ever-inquisitive Stephanie. 'You know who I am, but,' indicating her colleague with her hand, 'you will not have met Detective Sergeant Brown before.' Long switched his gaze briefly to DS Brown. 'Thank you,' he said, 'I'm pleased to meet another member of the force; I hope the Detective Inspector is well.' He raised his eyebrows and the tone of his voice as he finished the sentence. 'Yes, thank you,' replied Jess with a reassuring smile. 'He's just a little busy at the moment.' The pair sat down at the chairs that had been arranged for them, while Long closed the door. 'So, how can I help you on this occasion?' he asked as he took his seat opposite them. Jess had the lead. 'When I telephoned a few days ago,' she said, 'you kindly gave me what details you held on the identity of the tenants of the five garages in Bedminster. Our investigation has since thrown up an important lead that we need urgently to follow up in relation to one of them. I know you indicated that your records were sketchy, but we really do need *anything* and *everything* you have about the tenant of Garage No 2.'

Long sat back in his seat with a bemused frown on his face. 'I can only give you what I have,' he said, 'and that' he pointed to his head, 'is all in here. As I've already told you, it was a private arrangement between Harry Davis and the tenant; there was no paperwork that I was party to. I didn't even know the tenant's name.' Jess cocked her head to one side. 'How did you feel about that?' she asked. 'Frankly, I was never happy about it,' Long replied, 'but Harry wouldn't budge. As long as the rent was paid, Harry said he was happy to look after the administration, and, to the best of my knowledge, the rent never failed.' Keeping eye contact with Long, Jess replied, 'So you'll have the tenant's bank details somewhere, then?' Long shook his head. 'No,' he answered, 'the rent was always paid in cash and by post. Only the first envelope came through this office, and I got the impression that was a mistake. All the subsequent ones went to Harry, presumably at home.' Jess raised her eyebrows. 'So you have absolutely no idea who the tenant is, where the tenant is and how to contact the tenant?' she asked, incredulously. 'Surely, as the property administrator you had an obligation to advise the tenant about the impending sale to the council, for example?' 'I certainly did,' confirmed Long, 'and I did all I possibly could, but eventually I had to refer the problem to the sole surviving director, Harry's widow, Gloria. I made her aware of the problem with just under a fortnight to go, and in the absence of any contact with the tenant we gained access to the garage with Tyler's help. He had to cut the padlock away, and when he opened the garage it was empty.' Jess and Wes Brown exchanged a quick glance, which Long picked up. 'You seem surprised,' he said. 'We are *very* surprised, Mr Long,' confirmed Jess. 'Were you present when Tyler Davis opened the garage?' 'No, I wasn't,' replied Long. 'Tyler reported the fact to me by telephone, and it was a great relief'. 'Would you tell us when this telephone conversation took place?' replied Jess. 'Certainly,' answered Long. 'The transfer of ownership took place at the end of May, Tuesday the 31st, and Tyler phoned me the previous week. On behalf of his mother, I had asked him to help on the Wednesday, and he reported to me on the morning of the following day. He and Terry had been tidying their own garages the previous night, in any case.'

It had become clear from the conversation that the solicitor was unaware that Tyler and Terry were in custody, but that wasn't all that surprising. The two men had been arrested less than 24 hours before, and neither had asked that the family solicitor attend them. Whether he would have been able or willing to do so, had he been asked, was another matter, but nothing in his demeanour or conversation at this stage intimated that he knew what had happened in the past 24 hours. Jess decided to break the news then and there. She felt it might help to encourage Mr Long to dig out of his memory whatever small fact he might not, consciously or unconsciously, have revealed.

'It may not have been such a relief had you inspected the garage yourself Mr Long,' said Jess, speaking deliberately more slowly. 'You see, we have forensic evidence that the body of the man whose murder we're investigating was stored in that garage until the Saturday before ownership was transferred. We also have forensic and other evidence that identifies Tyler Davis as party to the removal of the body on the Saturday night, the night it was dumped at the side of the Long Ashton by-pass. We strongly suspect that it was Terry Davis who helped him. Both Tyler and Terry are currently in custody, and we expect that at least one of them will be charged very soon. If there is anything else you know, or even suspect, about the arrangement between Harry Davis and the tenant of that garage, you need to share it with us.' Both detectives studied the solicitor closely. They were sure from his reaction that the news of the arrests and the suspected contents of the garage had come as a shock. They waited. Long looked at them both. 'I had no idea,' he said, 'no idea at all. I've been entirely honest with you. I was always uncomfortable with the lack of anything official in regard to that garage. I had no way of knowing if Harry had told the tenant about the compulsory purchase; after all, it was only finalised a week or so before he dropped dead. The last thing I did before putting it in Gloria's (and Tyler's) hands was the only thing I could do. It was a long shot, but I sent a text out to a mobile number I found on Harry's mobile phone. There was no name in his contacts list, only the words 'Garage Two', but, as I say, there was a mobile phone number. The text message didn't 'bounce' back, and so I imagined it had been delivered. I waited a few days, but when I still had no reply, I tried 'phoning instead. When I did, I found that the line had been disconnected.' Long paused and reached into his desk drawer. 'Here's Harry's phone,' he said. 'It's on a pay-as-you-go contract, and there's still some credit on the account, but, as I say, if you try ringing the number I texted, it sounds as though the phone on the other end has been disconnected.'

DS Brown picked the phone up, looked at it briefly, fished a plastic evidence bag from his jacket pocket, slid it in and handed it to Jess Bradley. The two detectives thanked Derek Long and made their way back to their car. 'What did you think, Wes?' asked Jess. 'He's kosher,' was the reply. 'It looks like there definitely was a tenant, so that eliminates one of the DI's possible scenarios. It's a pity we can't talk to old Harry Davis.'

CHAPTER 47

It was 3.00 pm on Thursday 9th June when DI Knight faced Tyler Davis across the desk in the interview room for the third time. On this occasion he did so with DS Carter to his left. Tyler looked dejected. He sighed audibly as Knight addressed him. 'I have asked you before, Tyler,' he said, 'but we need to know who killed Simon Lee, and unless you can convince me that it wasn't you, it is likely that you will be charged before the evening is out. This is your chance. Do you have anything to say?' Knight sat back and rested his forearms in his lap. He waited, resisting the urge to break the silence that followed and focussed on the clock high on the wall behind Tyler. Almost a minute and a half elapsed before Tyler responded, his voice breaking as he did so. 'My dad asked me to do it,' he said. 'It was the last thing he said. I had to. We were in the ambulance. He was dying.' 'What did he ask you to do, Tyler,' said Knight. 'To clear the bloody garage; to get rid of whatever was in it without my mum, without anyone, knowing about it,' he replied. 'I asked Terry to help me. He was family. But he didn't know what the hell was in there, and I didn't know until we opened the bloody door. I swear! We just did what dad asked.' Tyler's voice broke again, and Knight waited until he regained his composure. 'Tell me what you found, Tyler,' he said.

'There was a special padlock on the door,' replied Tyler after taking another deep breath. 'We didn't have the key. I had to cut it off. When we opened the door, all that was in there was a chest-freezer up against the far wall. We could see that it was plugged in, and when we got up to it we could see that it was on. We lifted the lid. We didn't know what was inside at first, but then we could see it was a body – frozen solid. We were just gobsmacked. Terry had to go out to be sick.' DI Knight broke in with a question. 'Are you sure there was nothing else in the garage, Tyler, nothing on the floor at all, nothing on any shelves, nothing hanging on the walls?' he asked. 'Absolutely not!' was Tyler's reply. 'It was dusty inside, but it was empty apart from the freezer. There was nothing else.' Knight studied him. 'Thank you,' he said. 'I'm sorry to have interrupted. Please continue.'

'We didn't do anything when we found it,' Tyler went on, 'but I had to put a padlock of our own on the door, and we had to decide how we were going to get rid of the freezer and the body. Terry helped me, but I was the one who decided what to do. We dumped the freezer first, and we left the body on the garage floor for a few days to thaw. It would have ended up in the river near Yatton had it not been for the bad accident on the Weston road. We had to turn back and we dumped it in the lay-by. It was my plan; dad asked me, not Terry; Terry can't tell you anything more. It was my fault it has all ended like this.'

'Thank you, Tyler,' said Knight. 'Everything you've said has been recorded and, personally, I have little doubt that you're telling me the truth, but I must ask you one final question. Now that you've had plenty of time to look back at what your dad asked you to do and what you found in the garage that your dad asked you to clear, do you think that your dad might have killed Simon Lee?' Tyler buried his head in his hands. 'I can't think that,' he sobbed, 'I can't'.

'Interview terminated.' said Knight. It had taken 45 minutes. The interview with Terry wouldn't take as long.

∞∞∞∞∞∞∞

Faced with the weight of evidence that had been accumulated against the two brothers and with Tyler's confession, Terry accepted that there was little to be gained from protesting both his ignorance and his innocence, and the interview with him that followed was over in half an hour. It was long enough for Terry to give an account of his involvement and for DI Knight to be reassured that his account corroborated with that given earlier that afternoon by his older brother. It was plain to Knight that the first time the brothers had come into contact with Simon Lee was many years after his death and confinement in the freezer in the garage in Bedminster. The two would still be charged; they had, after all, attempted to conceal the crime that had taken place years before, but there would be no opposition from the police to their being released on bail pending their appearance in court as both had confessed and neither was considered to be a danger to the public.

The afternoon's interviews left DI Knight with mixed emotions because, whereas the confession of the two men had resolved the questions posed at the beginning of the inquiry – who disposed of the body, how and why – he didn't feel that much progress had been made in the search for Simon Lee's killer. Certainly, Harry Davis remained a prime suspect, but there was nothing so far to take it beyond a suspicion. Judging by Tyler's testimony, his father knew what the garage contained, but the words he had uttered to Tyler as he lay dying in the ambulance did not amount to a confession by any means. The murder of Simon Lee could possibly have been the reason for his being blackmailed, but why threaten to expose someone for visiting a massage parlour when there was a body in a garage? Could it be that the blackmailing, if that is what was happening, was being conducted by none other than the killer of Simon Lee and was intended to ensure that Harry keep his mouth shut about what was in Garage No 2? There had been a time when Knight had entertained doubts about there being a tenant of Garage No 2 at all, but the report from the two detective sergeants who had been to talk to the solicitor in Pill seemed to verify the existence of the tenant, the shadowy figure whose name did not even appear on Harry Davis' mobile phone against the number that was listed there. The mobile would be looked at by the technical team, but Knight did not hold out much hope that it would reveal any secrets about the identity of the tenant. Knight resolved to get the team together on the Friday morning to bring them up to date with the afternoon's developments and determine the next steps in the investigation.

PART THREE

Chapter 48

At an estate agents in Clapham, the door was unlocked a couple of minutes before 9.00 am on Friday to admit a man known to his fellow office-workers as Simon Lee. Those who had already arrived and those who had yet to come were aware that he had handed in his notice earlier in the week and had been surprised because he seemed to have settled in well over the years, and, although he tended to keep himself to himself he had proved to be an effective salesman and a dependable source of revenue to the business. As he had reassured the partners that he was not switching to a competitor (as so often happened when head-hunters tempted agents with juicier packages elsewhere) but, instead, was planning a year-out during which he would go travelling abroad, he had been permitted to work his notice. He took off his coat, hung it on the stand out of sight of visiting customers, and looked through the diary that had been prepared for him by the secretary he shared with two other agents in the office. He saw that he had two viewings that day, both in the morning. With the consent of the partners, who had also been surprised that he was selling, rather than renting-out his apartment while he was away, he had placed his own apartment with the agency, negotiating a reduced commission, and although the 'For Sale' sign had only gone up that week, the website was already attracting considerable interest. Neither of the viewings that morning was for his apartment, but he wasn't overly concerned. He had maintained the property to a good standard, and he was very confident that, in Clapham South, it would not be on the market long, particularly as, in the interest of a quick sale, he hadn't been greedy and had asked a fair price. He would have preferred to leave the estate agents immediately, rather than work his notice period, but he had to be realistic and to accept that no matter how quickly he found a buyer, conveyancing would take a minimum of six weeks. By July he was hoping to be well away and starting a new life in his own name. Simon Lee had served him well, but the longer he continued to use the name and persona he had so cunningly and brutally stolen five years before, the more danger he would now be in.

∞∞∞∞∞∞∞

In Bristol that morning, DI Knight was parking his car. There was always something good about Friday, he thought as he switched the ignition off and reached across to the passenger seat for the battered briefcase that he'd tossed there before leaving home. Even when he was in the middle of a case or on standby, when weekends tended to merge with all the other days of the week, there was something good about Fridays. He looked forward to getting the team together after coffee – his second of the day, having enjoyed his first with egg on toast for breakfast at home. As he walked through the door of his office, he glanced across into the incident room and saw that DS Bradley and DC Fielding were already in and seemed to be looking closely at various papers spread on the surface of Fielding's desk. He put his briefcase in its usual place, behind his chair, took his jacket off, hung it on the hook behind his door, and, mug in hand, walked across the corridor to where the main kettle was plugged in. It was already hot, so he wasn't the first to use it that morning. Having filled his mug and added a spoon and a half of instant coffee (always that way round), he strolled across to Bradley and Fielding with it steaming in his hand. Anticipating his arrival, the two detectives bade him good morning. 'Good morning,' he responded, 'something interesting?'

'Quite possibly, sir,' replied DS Bradley. 'Tom's been looking through the copies of statements and letters between Simon Lee and his bank. Lee opened his current account with them in 2000, and he closed it in April 2006. The income and outgoings are all pretty unremarkable, although we fail to see how he managed to cope because he was earning barely enough to cover his overheads. What is interesting is that the signatures on the two letters he wrote to the bank are pretty much the same, but they're quite different from the only other signature we have. He wrote to the bank in March 2006 to tell them he was moving to the other flat in Hotwells and he wrote again on 14th April asking them to cancel all his standing orders, close the account from the end of June and send him a cheque for what little balance remained. We've compared the signatures on those two letters with the one on the tenancy agreement six years earlier provided by Mr Carver.' Jess paused and arranged the two one-page printed letters on one side of the desk and the tenancy agreement on the other. 'It may well be that his signature changed in that time,' she continued, 'but I'm pretty sure that by the time I was in my early thirties my signature was pretty consistent.' 'Do we not have anything else to compare them with?' asked Knight rhetorically. 'Not at the moment, sir,' Jess replied, but we're hoping to hear from the DVLA today and from the tax office on Monday. I don't want to 'start any hares running'. I think we should wait to see what comes from them.' Knight listened and nodded. 'OK,' he said. 'Good work, Tom. Don't wait until Monday, though, Jess, let's look at this again once you hear from DVLA.' 'Will do, sir,' said Jess. Knight then walked across to the white board on the wall between the incident room and his office and wrote in capitals with a black erasable marker pen MEETING HERE AT 10.30 TODAY before returning to his office with his coffee.

At shortly after 10.00 am a manila envelope was delivered to DC Tom Fielding in the incident room at Bridewell police station. It was from the DVLA and inside it was a copy of the application Simon Lee had made for a new photo-card driver's licence at the end of March 2006 to replace the paper one he had been granted in 1989. His home address on the application was shown as Flat 3, 14 Amber Way, Hotwells, Bristol, and this was the address on the photocopy of the new licence also in the DVLA envelope. DC Fielding recognised the address as being the same address as that which appeared on Spencer Maine's tenancy agreement with Harry Davis Properties Ltd. It looked as though the two were cohabiting, after all, unbeknown to Gordon Long, the solicitor who administered the letting on behalf of Harry and Gloria Davis. He turned to the signature on the application (and reproduced on the face of the new plastic driver's licence). It was the same as the ones on the letters to the bank. All were different to the one on the tenancy agreement signed in 2000 for Flat 1, 27 Rowntree Court. Fielding laid the papers out side by side on the desk and looked at each, trying to decide what to make of the difference in signatures. Suddenly he bent forward, peering intently at the copy of the new driving licence. It was only a photocopy, but it was the photograph, rather than the signature, that had caught his attention. It was definitely not that of Simon Lee. He walked across to DS Bradley, who was talking to DS Carter and hovered until he caught her attention. 'You must come and look at this before the meeting,' he said urgently.

Chapter 49

The two detectives walked back to the desk on which Fielding had arranged the papers he had received from the bank and the DVLA. The bank statements were piled neatly at one corner of the desk, but in the centre were the copies of Simon Lee's letters to the bank, the copy of the rental agreement he'd signed some five years earlier, and the photocopy of the new driving licence issued to Simon Lee that had arrived that morning. Bradley had already been shown the letters and had noted the difference in the signatures between them and the rental agreement that Fielding had pointed out, but she hadn't seen the driving licence before. She placed both hands on the desk, bent forward to study it and focussed on the signature, which appeared in the centre of the new plastic licence to the right of the photograph. 'Hmm, same signature as the ones on the letters,' she said and looked up at Fielding as if to say 'is that all?' 'Look at the photograph,' he said. It took about a second and a half for the 'penny to drop'. 'That's not the Simon Lee we know,' she said, almost to herself. 'Could it be a mistake?' It was a silly question, but it allowed her more time to consider the implications of the evidence in front of her. 'Everything else tallies,' said Fielding. 'The name, date of birth and the new address all match, but even though there's five years difference, that's definitely not him.' Jess Bradley looked at her watch. It was 10.15. 'The DI needs to know what we've got here,' she said, 'because it could change everything. Well done Tom. Get all these up on the white board.' With that she walked over to DI Knight's office door, knocked briefly and went in without waiting.

By the time the formal briefing got under way, there was a palpable sense of excitement and expectation in the air. All the members of the team had got wind of the latest development and they were keen to explore the implications. DI Knight set the scene. 'Listen up everybody!' he said. 'This is important. You know we've bailed the two Davis brothers and that we know that it was they who transported Simon Lee's body to the Long Ashton by-pass, but we're also sure that they had nothing to do with Simon Lee's death. We think he was killed either by their father, Harry Davis, whose company owned the garage his body was stored in or by whoever it was who rented the garage. We don't know who that was, and we don't know who was putting pressure on Harry Davis by photographing him visiting 'Sweet Caramel' in broad daylight for appointments with a masseur called Robin, but it's my belief that there's a link in there somewhere. So far, one of the other things we don't know is what the motive for the murder of Simon Lee was, but I wouldn't be surprised if we're a lot closer to knowing as a result of what we've discovered today from Tom Fielding's groundwork. With the help of forensic pathology and what we've learned from Simon Lee's landlord, we've been able to come up with an approximate date of death. We know Mr Carver spoke to him in January 2006 but that Lee gave no indication of an intention to move. However, we know that he wrote to tell his bank of a change of address in mid-March and that he wrote again, this time from the new address, on the 14th of April, to stop payment of all standing orders and to close the account from the end of June.' Knight pointed to the copies of the two letters projected onto the whiteboard. 'In between, Simon Lee applied for a new-style driving licence.' Knight pointed again to the board. 'The name and date of birth all tally with what we know about Simon Lee, and the address on the driving licence is the new address Lee told his bank he was moving to. It's a flat owned by Harry Davis Properties Limited, and was already occupied by a single man named Spencer Maine, who continued in residence until the end of May. However, it was against the rules to share the flat, and the company's solicitor was adamant about that. So Simon Lee appears to have vanished into thin air.' Knight took a drink from his mug of coffee before continuing. 'One of the things that has puzzled us,' he said, 'is that Simon Lee was never reported missing, and now I think we know why. He was single, he was self-employed, and he didn't have any close relatives that we've been able to find. But most importantly, his identity didn't disappear; it went on. The signatures on the correspondence don't match the signature on his tenancy agreement five years earlier because it wasn't Simon Lee who signed them. My conclusion is that, by April 2006, Simon Lee was already dead, and that the person who killed him, and may still be posing as him, is very likely the Spencer Maine who lived, on his own, at 14 Amber Way, Hotwells. I believe we're looking at his face right here.' Knight pointed to the photograph on the driving licence on the screen and looked round the room.

Chapter 50

Spencer Maine was deep in thought in London. He had broken with his usual custom of eating a sandwich at his desk in the estate agent's office and was sitting on a park bench at one corner of Clapham Common. His mind was back in Bristol. He remembered the first time he had met Simon Lee in late 2004. It was around lunch time. He was carrying out a minor clearance of a flat in a side street off the Gloucester Road where it passed through St Paul's. The normal complement of two had removed the heavier and more bulky items that morning, and Spencer had returned alone to collect the smaller and more manageable items. It was a custom he had encouraged and developed, and his mate was more than happy to cooperate because it gave him time off for a quick visit to his favourite betting shop. Spencer Maine was happy because it offered him the opportunity to divert the occasional item to the garage he rented in Bedminster. Simon Lee had come down from what turned out to be his office to buy a sandwich at the delicatessen across the road. He'd nodded and smiled as Spencer had prepared to manhandle a mahogany coffee table into the rear of the van, and he had looked up at the name of the auctioneer on the van's side. 'I could be looking for a table like that,' he had said, pleasantly, 'when's the auction?' 'The auction won't be for a couple of weeks,' Spencer Maine had replied, 'but I could let you have it right now if you really wanted it. It would save me off-loading at the other end.' 'Really?' Simon Lee had responded with surprise. 'What sort of price would you be looking for?' Maine shrugged. 'You never know with this sort of furniture,' he answered. 'It could go for as little as ten quid, but if someone really wanted it, the price would be a lot higher. How much did you have in mind to spend?' Simon Lee had bent to examine the table, running his slender fingers over its polished and unscratched surface, before replying. 'It's in very good condition, and it's just the size and colour I've been looking for,' he said. 'I'd be very happy to pick it up for ten pounds, but I suppose I'd be prepared to go up to about forty.' There was something about him, something that Maine found appealing. 'Well, if you really want it,' he said with a smile, holding out his hand, 'just between the two of us, shall we say thirty quid?' He could still remember the smoothness of Simon Lee's skin as they shook hands and the look of delight on Simon's face as he reached for his wallet in his hip pocket. Spencer had then followed Simon across to his office, carrying the table and making a mental note of the office address. It was the start of a beautiful friendship; the sort of friendship that exists between lovers but also between predator and prey and was already scripted to end in tragedy.

The relationship between the two men developed discreetly and steadily, orchestrated subtly but purposefully by Spencer Maine, who grew progressively more interested the more he discovered about the slightly older man, who lived alone not far from Maine's flat; worked alone, had no social partner and seemed to have no contact with relatives. By unstated agreement, they were never seen together in public but would meet, instead, in their flats at night. In the very early days it was Spencer Maine who played host to their evenings together but progressively their trysts shifted to Simon Lee's flat. It was unarguably more tastefully furnished and more comfortable than Spencer Maine's rather austere and functional accommodation, but that was of secondary importance to Maine, who simply wanted to find out more about his new conquest. During their evenings and nights together, they would talk about themselves, their past and their hopes for the future, Spencer Maine usually taking the initiative and skilfully leading Lee to reveal even his most intimate secrets. For his part, however, Spencer Maine was intentionally selective and disingenuous when talking about his army career. He did not reveal the real reason for his discharge from the army, claiming that he was simply a victim of defence cuts, and he never revealed to Lee that he was HIV positive. However, as both men took sensible precautions when they were intimate with each other, it was relatively easy for Spencer Maine to rationalise the morality of his less than honest approach.

The first inkling of the idea that would ultimately determine Simon Lee's fate came as a result of him unwisely taking Spencer Maine into his confidence one night in mid-2005 and revealing more than turned out to be wise about his business interests. He acknowledged that, as a self-employed mortgage broker and financial adviser, a profession that was becoming more and more tightly regulated, he was never going to earn the sort of money he desired unless he was prepared to take risks. Spencer Maine had listened intently and encouragingly. After all, their relationship had only got off the ground because he himself had been prepared to bend the rules for personal profit. As he sat thinking on the park bench, he visualised Simon Lee's face as he recalled the moment when Simon revealed that his business had become much more profitable since he had decided to open his doors to those who preferred to deal in cash. Since then, money laundering and the fraudulent introduction of mortgages had become a second, but more valuable, source of revenue. Simon had looked up at him trustingly as he revealed that he hid the proceeds of his illegal activities from the authorities by simply holding it in cash in a safe in his flat.

Sitting on the bench in London, Spencer Maine smiled to himself. From that point on, unbeknown to Simon Lee, his fate was sealed. It was like a light going on in his head when he realised that there could be no better opportunity for the fresh start that he desired so much. The plan that came together over the remainder of that year was carefully thought through, preparations were discreet and, in early 2006, while Simon Lee's landlord was away on a cruise, ruthlessly executed.

Chapter 51

Unbeknown to Simon Lee, however, he wasn't Spencer Maine's only sexual partner during their relatively short association. There was another man, a far older man, who had visited Maine's flat from time to time before their first meeting but whose visits became less frequent and finally stopped towards the end of 2005, when he found someone else who would satisfy his needs. Theirs was a more one-sided and purely physical affair always conducted in the privacy of Maine's flat. It was a relationship, Maine reassured himself, that he would never have allowed to be cultivated had he not instinctively felt that there could be something to be gained from acquiescing to the older man's desires. The man was a regular but not frequent visitor. He was a local man, a married man and was very cautious lest he be recognised and his double life be uncovered. Their relationship had started by accident after an impromptu visit to Maine's flat by the man, in his capacity as landlord in 2004. The older man's name was Harry Davis.

It was as a result of Davis' clandestine visits to the small flat, and finding it cluttered with small items of stolen furniture waiting for buyers, that, some months into their relationship, he offered Maine the use of one of the garages he owned in Bedminster and was about to become vacant. The fact that the agreement was made with none of the usual paperwork and without the involvement of the solicitor who administered the rented properties, owed much to the secret nature of the relationship between the two men and the desire by Davis to keep it that way. There was already a tenancy agreement in the files for the flat, and that, Davis had reasoned, contained all the necessary data on Spencer Maine. He felt that there was little to be gained by duplication of paperwork, and a 'no frills, cash in hand' agreement was agreed by handshake. But there was one condition which Spencer Maine insisted and to which Harry Davis, mindful of the illicit nature of the likely contents of the garage, agreed: Maine would control access; he would fit his own padlock. In a way, Maine reasoned, the precaution not only offered him the privacy he wanted, but also afforded Davis, as landlord, some security. Should 'the law' ever become involved, he argued, Davis could simply deny that he had ever given the tenant authority to fit a padlock, and he could genuinely say that he was unaware of the garage's contents.

At that stage, Maine's relationship with Lee was in its infancy, and the thought that Maine might take advantage of the opportunity to make a fresh start with a new identity had simply not occurred to him. He shivered as he re-lived the moment many months later when he took Simon Lee's life in the garage and bundled him into the freezer which would become his resting case for the next five years. It was never intended to be as long as that. The freezer was supposed simply to buy time, to allow Lee's disappearance – if at all noticed – to fade from memories and to allow time for Maine to dream up a more permanent solution. One of the problems when stealing someone's identity in such a brutal and final way was the need to ensure that Simon Lee's body was never found because once it was discovered, once it became known that Lee had died, the new identity, which was key to Maine's reinvention, would be worthless.

It was mid-February 2006 when he had enticed Simon Lee to the garage to have a look at an antique chair he had 'borrowed' during a recent house clearance. The freezer, purchased new and delivered to Garage No 2 by the retailer only weeks before, was already in place, operating and empty. To add some mystery, it was covered by an old sheet, and it drew Simon Lee towards it like a moth to a flame. 'What have you got here?' he had asked as he had stepped towards it, and he had watched with a look of puzzlement on his face as, with a flourish, Maine had tugged the sheet off and revealed what it had been covering. 'A freezer?' Lee had asked incredulously. 'What on earth have you got a freezer for?' 'Open it and see' had been Maine's reply.

It was a critical moment, and although it only took a few seconds for Simon Lee to step up to the gently purring freezer and to raise its lid and peer in, it seemed like an age to Maine, whose heart was racing as the plan he had been working on for almost a year was about to come to fruition. Lee felt Maine's chest press against his back and was aware of an arm across his chest and a hand beneath his chin. For a moment, he pressed back into what he thought was a caress, but it was the last thought he had as, with surgical precision, Maine used the heel of his palm to push his chin sharply across to where his left ear had been, breaking his neck. To make sure, he then jerked the head sharply across in the reverse direction, but it wasn't really necessary because Lee was already dead.

Pressing the body against the wall behind the freezer while supporting its weight with his left arm, Maine had then used his right hand to remove Lee's wallet from its usual place in his hip pocket and the contents of his trouser pockets, dropping the wallet, a key-ring, comb, handkerchief and some loose change onto the garage floor. He had then turned Lee's lifeless body round to face away from the narrow end of the freezer and lowered it slowly, seat first, into its emptiness. The body had ended in a sitting position with the knees up either side of Lee's head and needed only a little adjustment to ensure that the lid could be shut properly. Picking up Lee's left wrist, Maine removed his wristwatch, paused and then brought the lid down. He then slumped to the floor as the shock of what he had just done overwhelmed him.

Ten minutes later, having retrieved the contents of Lee's trouser pockets from the floor, he had replaced the sheet over the freezer and, having pushed the garage door up only enough to allow him to leave, had emerged into the fresh air. He had straightened up, pushed the garage door shut, clicked the padlock into place, and was walking swiftly away without looking back. He had done it! There was still a lot to do if his plan was to succeed but there was ample time to do it in. Lee's landlord would not return to Bristol until mid-April by which time all traces of Lee's presence in the flat and office would have been removed, and, to all intents and purposes, he would have disappeared with all his possessions. His bank account would continue to pay the advance rents by he would not owe his landlord anything, and there would be little reason to report Lee's sudden departure to the police.

∞∞∞∞∞∞∞∞

Spencer had spent the first evening and night in Simon Lee's office, having let himself in with one of the keys on the keyring. Having arrived with some flat-pack cardboard boxes from the auction house, he had made them up and then transferred the contents of all drawers and two filing cabinets into the boxes. He knew from his experience at the auctioneer's that it was better to have more boxes partly-filled than fewer packed tight and too heavy for one person to lift. He had disconnected the telephone and having closed the boxes, had left them on the floor and let himself out, planning to return with his employer's van when the opportunity arose later in the week. Then he would transfer the boxes to his garage having taken the precaution of parking well away from the office.

The following night it was the turn of Simon Lee's flat, but he was far more familiar with it and its contents, having paid very close attention each and every time he and Simon had met there in the past year. He would need to remove all the personal papers, files and correspondence in the Edwardian writing desk and the document box at its side, along with all ornaments and personal possessions. As with the office, these would all go into cardboard boxes, as would the contents of Lee's wardrobe and chest of drawers that couldn't be fitted into the two large suitcases and holdall that had been stored under his bed. Small items of furniture that Lee had collected, such as the writing desk and the small antique table that had been his first purchase from Maine would go straight into the van, along with the cardboard boxes, when Maine was able to call with the van and would be transferred to Garage No 2.

In addition to the key for the office door and the key to the flat, there were three other keys on the keyring that Lee had been carrying in his pocket. Two were for filing cabinets in his office, but a third was a very distinctive key with a long shank and a number stamped around the bow. It was the key to the safe that stood on the carpet at the side of the writing desk; the safe in which Lee had disclosed he stored the cash proceeds of the illegal part of his business. He had intimated that there was a considerable sum in the safe, but he had never been more specific and had never opened it in Maine's presence. Maine recalled the mixture of emotions he had felt as he had approached the safe, key in hand, that night, the night after Lee's death. He was excited at the prospect of finding enough cash to help him move and get a new job and make the fresh start in the new identity, but he was also fearful lest Lee had simply been bragging, exaggerating, and that he would be disappointed by what would be revealed. He remembered, too, the relief he had felt to find a lot more cash than he had anticipated. He'd convinced himself that he would be content with something in the order of, say,£20,000 – a year's wages. What he found was over three times that amount: £63,000 in high denomination notes!

The clearing out of the flat and the office had been completed within the first week, but it wasn't until the end of the second that all Lee's belongings had been transferred to the garage and Maine could decide what would be kept and what would be disposed of. Working in the evenings, he unpacked the boxes and separated the contents into piles. Lee's clothing, bed linen, towels and ornaments would find their way to a variety of charity shops, and a charity would also collect the items of furniture by appointment. It was a shame to give it all away, but it would soon be dispersed with hardly any paper trail to follow. The business files and much of the paperwork that had been removed from the office would simply be recycled; while all Lee's personal correspondence and records extracted from his flat would go to Maine's flat, where they could be examined more conveniently.

Once all the boxes had been removed from the office and the flat, Maine had restored the premises to the condition he imagined they would have been in when first rented. All traces of Lee's tenancy were removed, with one exception. The safe in Lee's flat, made by Whitfield's Lock and Safe Company, stood two feet high and must have weighed at least 150 lbs. It had been too heavy for Spencer Maine to handle alone and had therefore been left in the flat with the key in the lock. Finally, Maine had locked the flat and office doors and had slipped the respective keys through the letter boxes and walked away.

∞∞∞∞∞∞∞

Much later, examination of his personal papers revealed that Simon Lee did not appear to have a passport, but there was a birth certificate, and an old-style driving licence that still bore his Locking address. There were pay slips and bank statements and some early correspondence with the local branch of his bank, and there was a letter from a local dentist confirming an appointment. In addition, there were copies of previous income tax returns and letters from HMR&C; from these, it was possible for Maine to extract Lee's National Insurance number. Using his own photograph, he applied for a new driving licence from DVLA in March 2006, giving his own address, and, posing as Lee, he also wrote to advise the bank of a change of address. It would be a temporary measure, which would at least ensure that bank statements would not be pushed through the door of the vacant flat to create any suspicion that Lee's sudden departure was not premeditated. Later in the year, he would close the account entirely and would open a new one with a different bank after arriving in London and as Simon Lee. HMR&C was more problematic, and he felt he needed more time to think about the tactic he would adopt with the Inland Revenue. On one hand, there was little chance of any correspondence coming through the door in the near future, but on the other, the end of the tax year wasn't that far away. He didn't want any loose ends, and he didn't want the tax man pursuing him for unpaid income tax; so he decided to notify HMR&C that Simon had wound-up his business and would pay any outstanding income tax. It wouldn't be much, but it would mean that he would have to submit a final tax return on Simon Lee's behalf. That could be tricky, but he did have the previous year's tax return on which he could base a fake one, and provided he accepted the figure the tax people came up with and paid promptly, that should be that. It was certainly a risk because he planned to continue to use Simon Lee's NI number, but he felt it was a minor one because he would be moving to London (and a different tax office) and he would get a job, rather than being self-employed. This was just one of a number of loose ends still to be tied up, but provided he kept his wits about him and provided the body remained hidden and there was no reason to suspect foul play, he couldn't see why he wouldn't be starting a new life very soon.

Chapter 52

On Monday, 13th June, the anticipated envelope from HMR&C arrived at Bridewell Police Station marked for the personal attention of Detective Constable Fielding. Tom was waiting for it and it didn't take long to compare the signatures on Simon Lee's tax returns with those that had sparked his interest at the end of the previous week and to come to the same conclusion. The signatures on all the tax returns except for one matched the signature on his tenancy agreement and were not the same as those on the letters to his bank in 2006 and on the new driving licence which had been applied for in that year. Interestingly, however, the signature on the final tax return was a closer match to the signatures on the letters to his bank and the one on his driving licence. It was submitted to HMR&C in May 2006, and there was a note to say that all outstanding income tax had been settled in June. Unless his signature had simply changed, it seemed that the Simon Lee who had written to the bank, applied for a new driving licence and settled with HMR&C wasn't the Simon Lee who had signed the tenancy agreement and submitted tax returns before 2006. As DS Bradley wasn't in the incident room, Tom went and told DI Knight himself. Knight smiled and thanked him. It seemed that the conclusion he had come to at the end of the previous week was still sound. He had given the case a lot of thought over the weekend, and he was fairly sure what his next step would be. He put a call through to Sandra, DSI

Nolan's PA and booked 15 minutes with his superior later that morning.

It was 10.30 am when he was ushered in to DSI Nolan's office. Initial pleasantries having quickly been dispensed with, it took only a few minutes to bring Nolan up to date with the progress of the case. He then presented the idea that had been developing in his mind since the previous Friday. 'So far, we've managed to keep the lid on the fact that Simon Lee's body had been frozen for years. The only ones who already know, other than the person who put him in the freezer, are the two Davis brothers, but it's a condition of their bail that they keep their mouths shut. The press have certainly not got any whiff of the fact, and I believe that now plays to our advantage.' Knight paused. 'Go on,' said his boss. 'I would like to call a press conference, sir, and reveal the facts now. I think the fact that Simon Lee's body had been frozen for five years before it was dumped on the Long Ashton bypass means it would be sufficiently newsworthy for the national media to be interested, and we can use that interest to get the face of our suspect, Spencer Maine, on every newspaper and news channel. If he's still in this country, and I have no reason to believe he isn't, he's been presenting himself as Simon Lee for five years, and I cannot believe we're not going to get at least as good a result as we did when we put Lee's face out there.' 'I agree,' said DSI Nolan. 'I'm committed elsewhere this afternoon,' he continued, 'set it up for tomorrow morning. I look forward to it.' Knight nodded, thanked his boss, and left the office. He trotted quickly down the stairs and walked into the incident room below. 'Heads up!' he said to all who were there. 'We're setting up a press conference for tomorrow morning. I want everyone here at midday for an update.' He smiled and went into his office.

∞∞∞∞∞∞∞∞

There was a sense of keen anticipation in the incident room when Knight addressed the team of detectives and support staff at noon, and after he disclosed the tactic that had been agreed with DSI Nolan earlier that day, there was a distinct feeling among the members of the group that the investigation had entered its closing phase. The media would lap it up! The release of the information that the body of Simon Lee had been stored in a freezer for five years before being dumped at the side of a busy road couldn't fail to hit the front pages and prime time television news slots, but the 'icing on the cake' would be the release to the media of Spencer Maine's photograph, the picture of the man who the team believed had stolen Simon Lee's identity and was most likely still to be using it as his own. The photograph was at least five years old; it was the one submitted to DVLA with the request for a new driving licence, but it was the best they had, and anyone who knew the man who called himself Simon Lee would hopefully see the likeness. Spencer Maine's cover would soon be blown, and, at worst, he would be on the run. If he was living and working in Britain, there were therefore certain precautions to be taken ahead of the press conference to ensure that he didn't flee abroad; his photograph and alias would be distributed to all points of departure from the country, and, in case he was already abroad, European police forces would also be alerted. There was much to be done that afternoon.

Chapter 53

Spencer Maine was at his desk in the estate agent's office at 4.15 that Tuesday afternoon when his company iphone, trilled an alert that a new news item had been added to the BBC News Application. He reached across and tapped on the screen to view it, and he sat very still as it opened in front of him. Although he'd been steeling himself for some sudden development in the Bristol murder inquiry and had decided what his course of action would be were his false identity to be exposed, it was still a shock to see his own face staring back at him. He recognised the photograph as the one that also appeared on the driving licence in his wallet, and he quickly read the account of the press briefing that had taken place in Bristol earlier that day. He looked cautiously around the room. Two of the other agents were out of the office, and their desks were bare, but another was on the telephone to a potential client. He switched the iphone off and slipped it into the desk drawer. It was, after all, his employer's property, but the more important reason was that he didn't want it on his person if he needed to lie low to avoid detection. Smart phones could be used to trace their owners, and that was a risk he didn't need to take. He stood up, cleared his desk and walked to the back of the office to collect his coat. Shrugging it on, he paused only to pick up his brief case and then, looking neither left nor right, he walked to the office door, let himself out, and strode quickly in the direction of the nearest tube station, adjusting his scarf so that it obscured the lower half of his face. He reached into his coat pocket and pulled out his personal mobile phone. It was the one on which he had received the call from Harry Davis' lawyer, but it now had a new sim card and a new pay-as-you-go contract. Only one or two people knew his number, and he made a quick call to one of these before entering the tube station and descending the stairs.

∞∞∞∞∞∞∞∞

The face of Spencer Maine, together with the account of Simon Lee's murder, which had already been circulated to holders of millions of smart-phones and tablets late that afternoon, appeared on the TV news at 6.00 pm and was the main story again at 10.00 pm. By then, half a dozen calls had already been received in the specially established call centre in the police headquarters in Bristol. Among them were a call from a man who remembered Maine from his time in the army and one from one of his former employers at the auctioneer in Bristol. Neither had seen him for years, but the most important call came from a partner at the estate agents in Clapham, London who recognised Spencer Maine as the man who still worked for him but who called himself Simon Lee. He was working late, and he was only too pleased to be able to access the employee data and provide them with the address at which Maine now lived.

∞∞∞∞∞∞∞∞

At 3.00 am on the Wednesday, a small convoy of police cars and a van parked silently a block away from Maine's flat in

Clapham South. The flat was unlit but identification was helped by the 'For Sale' sign outside. The first four officers to emerge came from within the van. They were members of the Territorial Support Group (TSG) and were distinctive in what little light spilled from the street lamp on the corner in their blue helmets and black body armour. They filed silently to the front door and waited there as two other uniformed officers found their way silently to cover the rear entrance. The officers at the front didn't bother to ring the doorbell. Instead, maximising the shock and surprise of their arrival, they splintered the front door frame with one swing of a battering ram, its momentum concentrated on a spot equidistant from the door latch and the Yale lock, and they ran in shouting, 'Police, Police, spilling into rooms as doorways presented themselves and heading for the room in which their quarry was most likely to be, the bedroom. But the bedroom, like all the other rooms in the flat, was empty, and the bed had not been slept in. There was none of the usual toiletries in the bathroom, no razor, toothbrush or shaving cream and, while there were some clothes still in the wardrobe, there were many more empty wire and plastic hangers. It looked as if Maine had returned to his flat, but he'd wasted no time. The news was quickly passed back to the operations room in the Metropolitan Police headquarters and from there it was relayed to Bristol. It was the last thing DI Knight wanted to hear.

Chapter 54

Earlier the previous evening, a taxi had pulled up at the corner of a road in Earls Court, and Spencer Maine emerged from it wearing a coat and hat and carrying a small suitcase and a briefcase. He paid the driver without a word, a scarf still covering part of his face despite the relative mildness of the evening, and he watched the taxi drive away before he walked to the corner of the next block, looking briefly over his shoulder before turning into the road that opened up in front of him. Seven minutes later, he lifted the latch on a small iron gate and entered the short path that took him to the front door of a Victorian terraced house that had long been converted to flats. In the fading light, he studied the names on the pad on the side of the entrance and pressed the button beside the one he recognised as the person he had phoned on his way home that afternoon. A voice responded with a guarded 'Hello'. 'Robin?' he replied, bending his head toward the microphone under the pad. 'It's me, Spencer.' The electric lock on the front door opened with a buzzing sound. Maine pushed the door open and entered.

He had known Robin for about seven years. They had met in Bristol. Robin was then newly arrived from Liverpool and was looking for a job. He needed somewhere to sleep until he had got himself sorted out, and Spencer had offered him the couch in his flat. It had taken Robin almost three months to get a permanent position in a massage parlour in Old Market and a shared flat there. Curiously, although there had been some sexual activity between the two of them in the early days, theirs had been a largely platonic relationship and had continued, on and off, even after Maine had moved to London. It had been Robin who had tipped him off that Harry Davis, Maine's landlord and sometime nightly visitor, had become a regular client of Robin's at Sweet Caramel, and that information had been very helpful. The existence of the photographs that Maine had subsequently taken had been enough to help persuade Harry Davis to preserve the special terms for rental of Garage No 2 after his move to London. Then, less than a year after he had arrived in the capital, Robin had turned up on his doorstep once more, looking for a temporary roof over his head, and he'd been able to help. It was now Robin's turn. Judging by his tone of voice over the intercom at the door, Robin hadn't seen the evening news and was unaware that Maine was being hunted as a suspect in a murder case. Maine wasn't sure how he would react once he knew. It would require careful handling. He reached the door of the flat just as it was opened from inside by Robin. 'Well, well,' Robin said with a smile. 'Look who's here! Long time, no see! Do come in.'

Spencer Maine wheeled his suitcase through the open doorway and followed the direction of Robin's outstretched arm into a small sitting room with a couch, one matching easy-chair, a small table and a television set on a stand in the far corner. 'I don't have a spare room, I'm afraid,' said Robin, smiling, 'so it'll have to be the couch for you, but you won't see very much of me at night because I don't usually get back in until gone three in the morning, and I'll be heading straight for bed. You won't see much of me in the morning either because I normally sleep until midday, but we'll have plenty of time to talk in the afternoons. The bathroom and toilet is opposite the kitchen.' He pointed to the short hall at the other end of the room from which two doorways opened, with another door, presumably his bedroom, closed at its end. 'I'm going to have to leave you on your own in an hour or so,' he continued, 'but the TV's in working order, although I don't use it a lot. Unfortunately, I don't have a lot of spare storage space, but I'll move the towels and sheets from the boiler cupboard so that you have somewhere to put your clothes. You'll find a blanket there, too. You were very brief on the phone. I hope everything's OK. How long do you think you'll be with me for?'

Maine had been happy to let Robin do all the talking. It had given him the opportunity to watch his face and gauge his mood, which was very welcoming and upbeat. It confirmed his initial judgement that Robin was completely unaware of the situation Maine now found himself in. He clearly hadn't seen the early evening TV news. He would inevitably find out what had caused Maine to give up his job and flat so suddenly, but it was better that he heard Maine's version of events first. 'I know you've got to get to work, mate,' said Maine placing his suitcase against the near wall and taking off his hat and coat, 'but I need to explain why I'm here.' He smiled wryly. 'Once I have, you may not want me to stay. Can we sit and talk? It won't take long.' 'Sure,' answered Robin, a look of puzzlement replacing his smile of welcome, 'I'm all ears!'

Maine took a deep breath and looked Robin in the eye. 'To put it in a nutshell,' he said, 'I'm a suspect in a murder inquiry.' He paused for effect, watching Robin carefully. 'When I was in Bristol, before we met, I had a relationship with a guy a little older than me. His name was Simon, Simon Lee, and he had a flat not that far from mine. We were very close in all sorts of ways. He liked to experiment, but we had an accident one night, and he died.' He paused again. 'Go on,' said Robin. 'I was scared. I was sure I would get the blame,' continued Maine, 'and even if I didn't, once the news got out I knew I'd lose my job. So I hid his body. He didn't have any other close friends, he was self-employed, and he didn't have any close relatives; so it wasn't that difficult to keep it all quiet. 'But that would have been ages ago,' interjected Robin, 'and you haven't been in Bristol for five years. What's suddenly happened to stir things up now?' 'They found his body' replied Spencer. 'I'd put it in a freezer in a garage I rented in Bedminster. It was only meant to be a temporary measure; I'd hoped to be able to dispose of it properly, but, on my own, that turned out to be much more difficult than I thought it would be. It all worked well until the guy I rented the garage from, my landlord Harry Davis, the guy who used to visit you, had a heart attack and died. Added to that, the garages were sold to Bristol council at about the same time for redevelopment, and someone, probably his sons, discovered Simon's body. For some reason, they didn't report it to the police; they just dumped it at the side of the Long Ashton by-pass. It was on the news last month. And now they're looking for me, and I'm here because I had nowhere else to go. But if you'll have me, I promise I won't be here any longer than absolutely necessary. My picture was on this evening's TV news, and is likely to be in the papers tomorrow, but that won't last forever. I'm going to grow a moustache and dye my hair, and provided I'm careful, I ought to be able to move out in a couple of weeks. I may need your help in getting a new passport. I have some money; perhaps enough to make a new start abroad, but nowhere near what I would have had if the sale of my flat had gone through. I'd got a buyer, and contracts were due to be exchanged in a couple of weeks, but now I won't be able to sign anything, and that's all gone down the drain. It's all gone completely to shit. I'm sorry.'

Maine had said nothing about his theft of Simon Lee's identity. Robin hadn't ever met Simon Lee and had always known Maine as who he really was, and as such, he was one of very few. For example, Maine had also retained his true identity for all his dealings with the hospital at Kings Cross from where he obtained his supply of retro-viral drugs because it was simply far too difficult to do otherwise, and he had also retained his first passport, which was issued when he was in the army, although he had not renewed it before it lapsed in 2004. He knew he would have to deal with the questions that his theft of Simon Lee's identity would raise in Robin's mind, not least because it might challenge his claim that Simon Lee's death was accidental rather than premeditated, but for the moment, he hoped that his sanitised version of events would be enough. Finished, he sat and stared at the floor. The silence seemed to last forever, but was broken by Robin muttering 'Wow! You are in a mess.' He paused briefly before continuing. 'But look, get settled in; give me time to digest all this; let's talk again tomorrow afternoon. If you need something to eat this evening, you'll find bacon and eggs in the fridge and bread and tins of beans in the cupboard. There's coffee and tea there, too. I'll get a couple of pizzas from the 24 hour shop on my way home, and perhaps we can have them for lunch tomorrow?' Maine nodded. Robin stood, paused, acknowledged with a brief nod of his own and went into his room to change. He was clearly overwhelmed by the enormity of all he had heard and, as he had said, he needed time to work it all through. 'At least he hasn't thrown me out,' thought Maine as he slumped back in the seat. He looked forward to being on his own that night; he'd have time to think things through himself.

Chapter 55

Robin returned somewhat later than he had indicated. It was 4.15 am when he gently inserted his key into the door lock and, having let himself in, took the pressure on the Yale lock so that it didn't click shut when he closed the door behind him. He walked carefully and noiselessly past the shape on the couch and on into the kitchen, placing the two frozen pizzas in the fridge and leaving the early morning edition of the newspaper on the work-surface before stepping across to the bathroom, closing the door and switching the light on. Five minutes later, he turned the bathroom light off, opened the door and turned right into his bedroom, gently closing the door behind him. Maine gave no indication of being awake, but he was a light sleeper and had been aware of all that was going on. The last sound he heard as he lay wrapped in a blanket on the couch was the soft click of Robin locking his bedroom door, and he sighed at what that action signified. He would have to tread carefully to restore at least some of the trust that had once existed between the two.

Come the morning, it was Maine's turn to tiptoe around the flat lest he disturbed Robin's sleep. The need to avoid making undue noise made washing and the preparation of breakfast tricky in such a small flat, but it was after all the usual morning activities were over that was particularly difficult. Other than read the early edition of the paper that Robin had brought home, and recoiled at his picture and the account that accompanied it on page 3, there was nothing to do. He couldn't go out because it was too dangerous, and even if there was something worthwhile to watch at that time of the day, he couldn't watch TV lest it woke Robin. If this was going to be the routine, he'd be out of his mind and surrendering to the police within a couple of days. 'Not so fast!' he thought. 'This is exactly what it must be like in prison!' He looked around for a book or magazine, but there was none to be seen and so, with a sigh, he slumped on the couch and attempted to doze.

He had long given up trying to sleep and was standing at the window watching the comings and goings of the people and vehicles on the pavements and roads below him, when he heard the sound of the lock being turned in the bedroom door. He looked at his watch. It was only ten thirty. He turned to face Robin, who emerged in pyjamas and dressing gown, waved a good morning, and went into the bathroom. Ten minutes later he was out again. 'Would you put the kettle on, mate? 'Robin asked before he went into his bedroom, 'I'll be out in a minute, and we can have a coffee and a chat.'

'Did you read the paper?' Robin asked as they sat in the lounge together with their mugs of coffee. 'Yes,' replied Maine, 'there wasn't anything more than I'd already seen on my iphone yesterday afternoon. Did you?' 'Yes, I did,' answered Robin, 'and I'm glad you'd already prepared me for it because it would have been a bit of a shock otherwise, but do I understand that you've been calling yourself Simon Lee for the past five years? What was that all about?' Maine had

had all the previous evening and most of the morning to prepare the answer to the inevitable question Robin had posed. 'I needed a new start, Robin,' he said. 'I'd screwed up my career in the army by not keeping my dick in my trousers; I was dishonourably discharged, and my reputation was shot; I didn't have much money, and I couldn't see a way out of it all. The accident happened in Simon's flat, and my first thought was to hide the body, which I did. I then decided to clean up the flat as best I could to remove all traces of my being there, and while I was doing that I came across all Simon's personal stuff, his birth certificate etc, and I also discovered a locked metal box under his bed. The key was on his key-ring, and when I opened it I found a lot of cash inside. I don't know what he'd been up to, but it had been profitable. He was single; there were no relatives. Simon was dead, and I was as much responsible as he was, but it suddenly seemed to me that all my Christmases had come at once, and the rest is history. I wouldn't have been able to get the mortgage on the flat in Clapham South without that money, and I wouldn't have been able to make the fresh start I needed without losing the baggage I'd accumulated as Spencer Maine.'

Robin nodded his head as if to show that he understood, but Maine couldn't be totally sure until he spoke. 'Well, keeping you off the streets makes me an accomplice, and it jeopardizes all that I've built up here, but you were good to me when I needed a roof over my head, and I ain't going to throw you out now. With my working hours, it's not going to be easy, as you've already seen, and the sooner you're able to go on your way safely, the better. We certainly can't do this for months; it can only be weeks, but I'll do whatever I can to help. What do you need?' 'Something to read, some hair dye and a new passport, in that order,' answered Maine, his relief showing on his face and in his voice. 'The first two are easy,' responded Robin, 'and we'll sort them out today. I'll see what I can do about the third, but I make no promises.' The ground rules had been set and agreed. Maine wasn't sure Robin had completely swallowed his modified version of the events that had led to the situation he'd been presented with, but it was the best he could do.

Chapter 56

Having stayed up until the early hours of the Wednesday morning to hear the result of the raid on Maine's London flat, DI Knight didn't get in to work until midday. He found the members of the team following up telephone calls that had come through to the operations room throughout the previous evening. Among them, DS Bradley was following up with the MoD(Army) an allegation made by one of Maine's ex-army colleagues that he had been discharged on medical grounds, but DS Brown was in London interviewing the people with whom Maine had worked in an effort to paint a clearer picture of the man and, possibly, to determine where he might be hiding.

There had been numerous calls from the local press seeking more information now that their, and the public's interest had been aroused by the revelation that Simon Lee's body had been stored, frozen, for five years. Some had already branched out in investigations of their own, and there had been a complaint to the police from the mother of one of the two schoolboys who had discovered the freezer that a journalist and cameraman had been pestering her for information at home. She was adamant that she had asked them to leave and had not cooperated in the least, but where children were concerned, nothing remained secret for long, and not all parents were as reluctant to share rumours with the press. Neither were all of Tyler Davis' work colleagues, some of whom had witnessed his arrest, while others were simply titillated by what they had learned and more than happy to repeat it. Tyler had not shown up for work since his arrest, and the word was that he would not be coming back at all. The evening edition of the city's newspaper claimed that explicit photographs involving his father, the late Harry Davis, had been found in the freezer that had been abandoned near Bristol airport.

∞∞∞∞∞∞∞

Alone in her home in Pill that evening, the shock Gloria Davis had felt after seeing the television reports and reading the accounts in the Bristol press since the weekend had turned to anger. She reached for her telephone and started dialling. Over the course of the next half hour, she had summoned and cajoled her remaining family as well as her solicitor, Gordon Long, to meet with her at home at 10.30 the following morning. Tyler was doing nothing, anyway (a date for his trial had yet to be set, and he remained on bail), and Gayle agreed to call in sick and accompany him. It was she who had been by Gloria's side more than any other since Tyler and Terry's arrest. Terry was on bail as well, but was trying to continue as normally as possible and had a driveway to work on, but, hearing the tone of his mother's voice, he was happy to postpone it to another day. Karla would not be coming with him; she had packed her bags and gone to live with her sister, but Gloria would not miss her. Gordon Long complied immediately, instructing Stephanie to rearrange his Thursday morning appointments.

∞∞∞∞∞∞∞

Thursday, the day that Gloria had demanded the presence of her family and solicitor, saw the two men in Robin's flat in Earls Court trying, for the second day, to make the best of the situation they found themselves in, but it was already becoming clear that until Maine was able to go out in the morning, at least, the potential for disharmony would remain. It wasn't simply that the apartment wasn't big enough, but it was also the hours that Robin had to keep and the consequent pressure on Maine to avoid disturbing him during the first part of the day. At least he had a book to read and time to ponder his next steps once the hunt for him had dropped off the front pages.

∞∞∞∞∞∞∞

Gordon Long was the first to arrive at Gloria's house, but only by a few seconds. As he walked from his car to the front door, Tyler and Gayle arrived in her small car, and he waited for them to join him, stepping aside to allow Tyler to ring the doorbell. Other than a nod and a brief greeting, nothing was said as they waited for Gloria to come to the door, but come to the door she did. There was a rattle as the privacy chain was removed and it was followed closely by the sound of the key being turned in the lock; then the door swung open to reveal her. Both Tyler and Gordon were surprised because she seemed to have grown an inch or two in stature, and there was an air of confidence about her that they couldn't remember her having for years. 'Hello,' she said, standing back and waving them in, 'Terry not with you?' Tyler bent to kiss her on her cheek, 'No, Ma,' he said, 'he's using a borrowed van until the police are finished with his.' It wasn't a wholly satisfactory answer, but it was the best Tyler could come up with. He went ahead into the lounge followed by Gayle and Gordon Long, but that wasn't where Gloria wanted them. 'We'll use the dining room,' she said. 'Gayle, will you help me with the coffees while we wait for Terry, please? If he's much later, he can look after himself.' Gordon Long and Tyler exchanged the briefest of glances, each with the suggestion of raised eyebrows, before moving into the dining room on the opposite side of the corridor, where they found the dining room table cleared of all table decorations and bearing only mats for the coffee mugs which would shortly appear. There were five chairs: a carver at the head and two armless chairs on each of the longer sides. There was no doubt who the carver was for; so Tyler took one side of the table for himself and Gayle, leaving the side nearest the door for Gordon Long and, eventually, Terry. They had barely sat down when the front door bell rang again. 'Shall I get it, Ma?' asked Tyler. 'Please,' was the brief answer from the kitchen, and Tyler rose and went through to the door, opening it to reveal Terry. 'Come in, watch what you say. She's in a funny mood,' whispered Tyler and motioned Terry to follow him into the dining room. 'Hi, Ma'' shouted Terry from the corridor, puzzlement and uncertainty showing in his voice. 'Nice of you to join us,' was the reply, which was a bit unfair thought Terry; he was only a few minutes late.

'Well,' announced Gloria once coffees had been dispensed and all had taken their place round the table. 'The reason I've asked you all here today is to give you the chance to tell me what the hell's been going on, and I don't just mean these last few weeks. By all accounts, there's been a bloody body in a freezer for five whole years in one of our garages that you, Gordon, manage, and my two magnificent specimens of sons are likely to end up in jail for tipping it at the side of one of the busiest roads into Bristol. To make it worse, I learned from yesterday's paper that there were also some 'photographs' of your late father *inside* that bloody freezer. What in heaven's name has been going on? I know I left the rental business to Harry and to you, Gordon, but I *am* a director of the company - now the *sole* director - and I want to know how much you all knew, and I want the truth. Our name is suddenly worth absolutely nothing here, and I'm a laughing stock and may have to sell-up and move. So who's going to have the guts to go first?' Gloria sat back in her chair and looked defiantly at the three men at which her final question was directed.

Gordon Long was the first to respond. 'The garage in question, Gloria, was Garage no 2. The rental arrangement was conducted privately by Harry. There was no paperwork that I ever saw, and the rent was always paid to him in cash. Although I asked more than once, I was never told who the tenant was.' 'Did Harry know about the body?' challenged Gloria, looking intently at Gordon. 'In truth, I really don't know,' he replied, 'but it now seems that he might have.' Gloria switched her gaze to Tyler and to Terry. 'And what about you two?' she asked. 'Did either of you know who rented the garage? You both used garages virtually next door. You must have seen some comings and goings over the course of five years, surely?' She waited. It was Tyler who elected to reply. He described how he had been alerted by his dying father in the back of an ambulance that there was something in the garage that needed urgently to be disposed of before ownership was transferred to Bristol City Council. He confessed to keeping the disclosure from Gordon Long and sharing it only with Terry, whose help he needed to comply with his father's dying wish, and he described his and Terry's shock at the discovery that they had made when they had first gained entry to the garage. His voice broke as he accounted to his mother and, obliquely, to Gayle, but Gloria's gaze remained steady and uncompromising. 'We had so little time to do it,' he said. 'It was my idea to put the body in a river on the other side of Yatton, but on the night we chose there was a car smash and the road was closed and there were police everywhere. I panicked, but we'd let the body thaw out, and there was nothing on it to identify it; I didn't think they'd trace it to us. I'm sorry.' He sobbed; his head in his hands, his elbows on the table top. 'Do you think your Dad knew what was in the garage? Do you think your Dad had anything to do with putting it there? Do you think he had anything to do with the murder? Tell me!' Gloria demanded, almost shouting. These were questions that Tyler had asked himself many times as he had reflected on the events that had taken their course since his father's fatal heart attack, events that had changed his life so dramatically and cruelly, but all he could do was to shrug his shoulders. He didn't know, but it was becoming difficult to believe that his father was not somehow involved in the attempt, at least, to conceal the murder of the man called Simon Lee.

∞∞∞∞∞∞∞

A nd what about the photographs?' Gloria switched her gaze to the other side of the table. 'Terry, you're not saying much,' she said, her forearms resting on the table in front of her, hands lightly clasped. She was angry, but she was now in total control of her emotions. Terry replied softly. All his usual cockiness and bravado had quickly evaporated. 'We've both seen photographs. The police showed them to us. They don't show anything bad. They just show Dad outside some place in Old Market. There's no-one else in them.' 'What do you mean *some place in Old Market*?' asked Gloria, her eyes slightly narrowed. 'We couldn't tell,' answered Terry, 'but the police said it was a ....massage parlour.' He looked briefly at Tyler, glanced across at his mother and then focussed on the coffee mug in front of him. There was a pause in the proceedings while everyone reflected on what had been said, and then Gloria turned to Gayle and asked her politely but firmly if she would put the kettle on for fresh coffee. When she was out of the room, Gloria turned her gaze back on her two sons. 'Did you really not know that your father had some interest in men?' she said. 'Did you really not know?' The two sons looked at each other, neither sure what was coming next. Gordon Long looked down uncomfortably at his hands. 'I knew he was going somewhere else to satisfy his sexual needs years ago,'

Gloria continued. 'He hadn't always been like that or we would never have married. He was always civil to me and thoughtful and caring, but I saw a change in him six or seven years ago and I sensed that he had become uncomfortable with marital intimacy. At first I thought it was simply a symptom of him growing old, of losing his libido, but then I wondered if he was seeing another woman. Initially, he would invent excuses for being out in the evening. He would tell me he had been somewhere with pals, but when I made enquiries I found he hadn't. Anyway, I could tell by the way he smelt and by the way he behaved when he came home that he'd already been with someone. I didn't confront him. I wanted to be sure of my facts, and I paid someone from my own money to follow him around. I discovered that it wasn't another woman but that he was regularly visiting a man in a flat in Hotwells – one of our bloody flats! I was shocked and revolted at first, and my first reaction was to kick him out! But I didn't. I realised he'd been a good husband and father for almost 40 years, and I felt that counted for something. I began to feel that what was happening to him wasn't his fault. It was something inside him over which he had no control, and I felt sorry for him. I intended never to let on that I knew because I still wanted his company, and I wanted to enjoy our eventual retirement together. It's no fun being on your own at my age, as I've now learned. But something happened. We'd been out to someone's birthday party, and we had both had too much to drink. We got a taxi back here, and something he said in the bedroom, followed by something I said led to a dreadful row. I told him I knew what he was doing. I told him how close I'd come to chucking him out. It shocked him. He went to the spare room, and in the morning he promised me that he would never touch another man again. We never slept in the same bed again, but I believed he kept his promise. When were the photographs taken? Does anyone know?'

It was Gordon Long who answered. 'The photograph I was shown was taken in December 2005,' he said carefully, 'it was taken in daylight; in the afternoon.' Gloria clenched her jaw. 'So, he didn't keep his promise, then,' she said to no-one in particular. It was again Tyler who broke the long silence that followed. He managed to say he was sorry and had 'never realized' before putting his hands to his face and sobbing. Gayle tried to comfort him and Terry said nothing, his face drained of all colour. Gordon Long drew a deep breath and sat back in his chair. Half turning to Gayle, he asked whether she still wanted him there. 'I certainly do!' she replied, 'I want to know what you know about this Spencer Maine that the police are searching for.' It was Gordon Long's turn to feel the strength of her gaze. 'He was a tenant of one of the flats in Hotwells,' he replied. 'He was there for just over two years or so; he left in the Spring of 2006. The police suspect him of the murder of the man whose body was in the freezer because he stole his identity.' Gloria's brow furrowed slightly. 'Which flat?' she asked. She dreaded but expected the answer that came. 'It was Flat 3, 14 Amber Way,' Long replied, staring fixedly at his notebook. All eyes turned to Gloria. She sighed deeply. 'That was the flat he visited in the evenings,' she said. 'So, it looks like Maine was the one who rented the garage from Harry, then?' She looked at Gordon Long. 'It now seems so,' he responded.

'Well, well. This man Mr Maine seems to have been a clever fellow. Not only was he shagging his landlord, but he's been the invisible tenant of one of our garages for over five years, and he somehow managed to store a body in it, perhaps with Harry's help. As a result our lives have been bloody well ruined!' She paused and looked at each of the three men again. 'I'd like to find him before the police do. Can we do that?' she asked, perfectly seriously. 'I don't think we stand a chance,' replied Gordon Long, 'and I wouldn't want to be involved, in any case. I believe the best thing we can do is to help the police. They may already have come to the same conclusions we've just come to, but I wouldn't want to volunteer any information about Harry unless you were all happy that I did so.' 'You won't need to,' said Gloria. 'Ask the detective to come and see me, and, in the meantime, do what you can, please Gordon, to ensure Tyler and Terry have good lawyers before they come to trial.' With that, Gloria stood up. The meeting was over.

Chapter 57

DI Knight put his head into the incident room, caught the eye of DS Bradley, and motioned her into his office. 'You wanted to see me?' he asked. She responded to the wave of his hand and sat down across the desk from him. 'Yes sir,' she said, 'I've now heard from MoD (Army). They've confirmed that Spencer Maine was discharged on medical grounds, alright. He had Aids. He was diagnosed HIV positive after a routine medical test some months after returning from a deployment in Kenya.' 'That's interesting,' mused Knight, 'Simon Lee had early signs, too. Is there any way we can use that information to track him down?' 'I'm not sure, sir; I doubt it because it's no longer as rare as you might think, but he will be relying on retro-viral drugs, and someone will have to be providing the prescriptions.' At that moment, Knight's telephone buzzed. Motioning Jess to stay where she was for the moment, he picked the handset up and answered in his usual way. 'Knight,' he said. He listened to the caller for about twenty five seconds, scrawling 'Gordon Long' on his pad and rotating it so that Jess could read it. Then he said, 'Thank you, Mr Long, I'll call her.' He put the phone down and said, 'Mrs Davis, the late Harry Davis' widow and mother of Tyler and Terry wants to talk to us. You call her, Jess, and set it up for you and me. We can meet here or at her home. Try to find out what it is she wants to say.'

The last place Gloria wanted to meet was her home, and she made that very clear to DS Bradley. She was already the talk of Pill, and any thought of giving the inhabitants even more to gossip about left her cold. She would come to the police station and could do so on Friday morning. When asked what it was she wanted to see DI Knight about, she reacted quite angrily. 'Because you've not had the courtesy to talk to me since this whole thing began,' she said icily, 'and I'm as interested as you are in finding the person responsible for completely ruining my life. Not only is my husband dead, but his reputation is being trashed by the press, and my two sons, who were only trying to clear up the mess, could end up in prison.' There was a pause, and DS Bradley was about to find a way of asking whether she had any information that might be helpful to the police when Gloria continued. 'I simply want to know what's going on. I can be with you as early as ten o'clock tomorrow.' DS Bradley having checked with Knight, they settled on 10.30.

∞∞∞∞∞∞∞

By Friday morning, Spencer Maine was heartily sick of his self-inflicted captivity. He looked at himself in the mirror as he washed and carefully shaved. His appearance had changed considerably. His brown hair (and even his eyebrows) had been dyed blonde, and he was trying to cultivate a neat moustache and a shaped beard that followed his jawline to his chin. He intended to keep it at the length of four or five-day stubble to mask the fact that it was darker than his hair. With a hat and a coat with lapels that could be worn up and around his neck, he was certain that he could not possibly be linked to the picture that had appeared in the paper and on TV a week before. He desperately wanted to get out of the flat and get some exercise and a breath of fresh air, and he was going to do it that morning. He'd heard Robin get home shortly after 3.00 am, and he would be asleep until midday, as was his custom, but just to be on the safe side, Maine left a brief note on the kitchen table to explain his absence. Adjusting his hat and coat, and taking one more look at his reflection in the mirror for reassurance, he quietly eased the lock on the front door and eased himself out. He walked carefully down the stairs to the ground floor, opened the front door and, having closed it behind him, stood still for a few seconds before walking purposefully down the path, and onto the pavement. He turned right and kept walking, relishing the outside air and the feel of a light breeze on his face. He took no notice of other pedestrians, avoiding eye contact and only looking up from time to time. He kept up a brisk pace for a quarter of an hour, turning this way and that so as not to stray too far from the flat, and then he stopped to buy a newspaper from a corner newsagent. A quick scan of the front pages of the various papers on display suggested that sex and politics were now more newsworthy than the hunt for a suspected murderer from Bristol, but he bought a broadsheet and a tabloid from the disinterested man behind the counter and headed back to the flat to read them through after making himself a coffee. It was 10.30 when he let himself in, took off his hat and coat, boiled some water, switched the kettle on and sat on the sofa that had been his bed to read. He paused only to make himself a mug of coffee but found no mention of the hunt for him in the tabloid and only a small item half way through the broadsheet: police had conducted a search of a house in Taunton following a tip-off, but it had turned out to be a misidentification. He sat back in the sofa and gently nodded his head. It was time to go. He had cash, but what he desperately needed was a new identity. He was sure Robin could help, and he'd mentioned it more than once. He would do so again when Robin woke.

Chapter 58

At 10.30 in Bristol, Gloria Davis was sitting quietly in the waiting room in Bridewell police station, when DS Bradley emerged from the corridor and, with a smile, identified himself, and invited her to follow her into an interview room. There were three chairs in the room, arranged around the table. DS Bradley motioned Gloria to one of the chairs, explaining that DI Knight would be along very shortly. She accepted the invitation to a cup of coffee, and DS Bradley disappeared, only to return a couple of minutes later with three. 'I hope you don't mind your coffee in a mug, Mrs Davis,' she said as she placed the three mugs on the table. 'What would it matter if I did,' thought Gloria, but she smiled and briefly shook her head. At that moment, DI Knight strode in with a thin folder in his hand. He introduced himself, apologised for being late and took the seat directly opposite Gloria. 'How may we help, Mrs Davis?' he enquired. He was younger than she expected, Gloria thought, but weren't they all these days?

'I have been the sole director of our rental business since my husband, Harry, died,' she said, looking DI Knight in the eye, 'but despite the fact that the body you found on the by-pass seems to have been stored in a freezer in one of our garages and the man you're looking for, the suspected murderer, once rented a flat from us, you haven't spoken to me once. You've arrested both my sons, and you haven't spoken to me. There are, according to the newspapers and according to my sons and our solicitor, photographs of my late husband, but you haven't once consulted me. I may not be able to add one shred of information that you don't already know, but until you bother to ask, you won't have a clue! I am very cross. My whole life has been turned upside down at the very point that I had been hoping things were going to get a lot better. First, Harry dies of a heart attack and then my sons are arrested. Then I have to learn about the photographs from the papers, and this man, this Spencer Maine, a weird name if I ever heard one, is still on the run. He could be anywhere. It is he who has wrecked our lives. I have no doubt that his involvement with my late husband and the blackmailing that must have been going on contributed to Harry's early death, and now my two sons' lives have been ruined simply because they tried to clear up the mess he and Harry created. Harry is dead, and I can't bring him back, but I want this man found and brought to justice. I want it even more than you do, but why is this the first time we've met?'

'What do you mean when you refer to the suspect's involvement with your late husband, and the blackmailing that must have been going on, Mrs Davis?' asked Knight softly, deflecting the question that Gloria had challenged him with. Gloria allowed a few seconds to pass before replying. She went over the circumstances of her discovery that Harry had been visiting a man in one of their flats, and the promise he had made to her the morning after the row they'd had. She spoke of her disappointment that the photographs seemed to suggest that he had not kept his promise. She again expressed her anger that she had had to call her sons and her solicitor to her home the day before to get all the facts. Knight was more than content to allow her to do all the talking. He had some sympathy for her because none of all that had happened was her fault, but neither was it the fault of the police in general, and his team in particular. He felt that she would probably feel a lot better once she'd made her point and had got her grievance off her chest, but he wasn't going to stay and participate much longer. He now felt sure that Mrs Davis had no information that would help them find Spencer Maine any quicker, and he was about to excuse himself and leave her to DS Bradley when she reached into her handbag and brought out an envelope. She tossed it into the table. 'This arrived in the post a week after Harry died,' she said. 'I had to sign for it. One used to come every six months. If I was in, I'd sign for it, but if Harry was in, he'd sign for it, and he'd never open it in front of me. I assumed he passed it on to Gordon. I should have asked Gordon yesterday, but I only remembered it after he left. I had enough on my mind the week after Harry died, and I just threw it in the tray. That's where it's been ever since. I once asked what it was, and I think he said it was rent for one of the garages, but it was a long time ago, and I can't be sure. It was just one of those regular things that happened.' Knight and Bradley looked down at the envelope then at one another. It was a brown A5 size envelope with a London postmark. Knight used the tip of his pen to turn it over. On the other side was the standard Post Office label valuing the contents for insurance purposes. According to the label, the contents were simply documents, and were of no monetary value. 'Do you mind if we keep this until we've checked it, Mrs Davis?' asked DI Knight. 'Don't bother to mention it to Mr Long just yet, please. That's something we can do, but do let us know if anything similar arrives in future.' Gloria nodded. 'Of course,' she said.

Standing up, Knight thanked Gloria for coming in to see them, reassured her that they would let her know of any significant developments and left DS Bradley to shepherd her out of the building. He took the envelope, placed between two pages of his file, into his office and put in a call to forensics. Although the address was handwritten, the envelope had been handled by too many people for the outside surfaces to be of any value, but the inside surface, the inside of the flap, handled only by the person who had placed the contents in the envelope and sealed it as recently as a month before, could be a potential source of fingerprints. If, as Knight expected, there was money inside the envelope – six months' rent for Garage No 2 - any fingerprint could be that of the man they were hunting: Spencer Maine.

Chapter 59

The atmosphere in the small kitchen in Robin's flat was strained. It was breakfast time for Robin and lunchtime for Maine, but both sat down together to the same meal of bacon, fried eggs, beans and toast that Maine had cooked for them both. He felt it was the least he could do, but he was becoming only too aware that, in the circumstances, the signs were that he had outstayed his welcome. Since returning from his Friday morning expedition, he'd drunk two mugs of coffee and had pored over both the newspapers with great care, but he hadn't discovered anything more about the police investigation than he had spotted with a first cursory glance. He wasn't quite sure what Robin had thought of his decision to take a walk because he hadn't said much. In fact, Robin hadn't said much at all since waking and coming through to the sitting room, seemingly attracted from his bedroom by the smell of bacon frying. What he didn't know was that Robin had heard him leave and had read his short note before returning to his room and trying to get back to sleep. It took him a while because he couldn't stop turning Maine's version of events over and over in his head. The more he had thought about Maine's account of the 'accident' and later discovery that had caused him to be on the run, the more he found himself questioning it. At first, he couldn't put his finger on it, but something about Maine's story or the way he had told it instantly rang alarm bells in his mind. Two days earlier he had gone out to buy some groceries in the afternoon and had made a telephone call to someone he knew in Bristol. After initial pleasantries, he'd asked the surprised recipient of his call what the 'word on the street' was on the cause of Simon Lee's death. The lady on the other end didn't ask him why he wanted to know, in her business her motto was not to ask questions when the answers were likely to be untrue. She had said as much to DS Wes Brown, when he had asked her about the visits of Harry Davis to the business she and her husband ran in Old Market. 'The short answer, my dear, is a broken neck,' she said, 'but there's been no official confirmation. By the way, I had a detective here a couple of weeks ago. He was one of the team investigating the murder, and he was asking about your old client, Harry Davis. You won't know, but he stopped coming here at about the time you left, but it appears that someone took photographs of him entering and leaving the premises on more than one occasion while he was still visiting us.' Robin frowned. Harry Davis was Spencer Maine's landlord, and he remembered chuckling with Maine over a drink about the coincidence that had taken him to Sweet Caramel at the time. 'Thanks, Shandy,' he said, 'that's very interesting. You're a star!' 'Only too pleased to help,' was Shandy's reply. 'You keep safe, baby.' She made a note of Robin's telephone number on a pad and wondered why he had felt the need to seek an answer to the question he'd asked.

Since making that call, Robin had done his best not to let his discomfort show, but he continued to lock his bedroom door when he was out because all his own private papers were now in a briefcase under his bed. He also continued to do so when he was sleeping. It was difficult to imagine how an accident between Maine and Simon Lee could have resulted in a broken neck; a drug overdose perhaps; asphyxiation possibly, but not a broken neck. But if it wasn't an accident, it was murder, and his early suspicion had been well founded. He could be sharing his apartment with someone who had committed premeditated murder, and had then posed as the victim for over five years. That required nerve and planning, and Robin needed to take precautions not least because he didn't want to die in his bed just yet.

It was Robin who broke the silence as they sat at the kitchen table. 'I've made some progress,' he said, sitting back and making eye contact for the first time that morning. 'I think I've found someone who might be able to help you with new papers.' Spencer Maine sat back, visibly taken aback but pleased that it hadn't been left to him to raise the issue. 'Tell me more,' he said. 'I can't tell you a lot,' Robin went on. I'm dealing through a third party I know and trust, and so I won't meet the person who'll do the work for you. Likewise, you won't meet the third party. I think what will happen is that I'll be given a place and date for you to meet your guy, and you'll be on your own. It's bound to involve more than one meeting, but it's the safest way for all of us. I do know you won't have to travel outside London, and after this morning's experiment, you probably feel happy to 'get the ball rolling? Maine was happy, but there were other emotions, too. Yes, he was keen to proceed, but he was also nervous. He could handle himself, and he was sufficiently streetwise to be alert to signs of danger, but it was money that really bothered him. He had money, but until he made contact with the provider of the new papers he so badly needed, he didn't know whether he had enough. He couldn't use it all, in any case, because he would need to reserve enough to live on until he'd found some way of earning again. Judging by Robin's enthusiasm to proceed, he knew he couldn't rely on him to provide a roof over his head for very much longer. 'That sounds good,' he said, smiling and returning Robin's gaze. 'The sooner the better!'

Chapter 60

The weekend passed slowly but without a cross word in the flat in Earls Court. His spirits had lifted since the conversation with Robin on the previous Friday, and Maine sensed that Robin had relaxed somewhat, too. He had slept more, largely because there was only so much day-time TV a sane man could tolerate, and he had read another paperback. Monday was wet and miserable, and by Tuesday he desperately needed to get out into the open again. This time he was more adventurous, buying a paper to avoid making eye contact with other passengers, he ventured onto the tube, taking the Piccadilly line to Hyde Park Corner. There he spent an hour walking in Hyde Park and along the Serpentine, trying to come up with a plan of action. Somehow, he found it easier to think when he was out in the open, but he continually came up against the same buffer: not knowing how much of his cash was going to have to be spent on forged papers. He caught sight of himself in a mirror as he entered the tube station on his way back, and he smiled secretly. Even his own mother wouldn't have recognised him!

Back in the flat, Robin's muted mobile phone flashed once to signify the arrival of a text message, but he didn't discover it until he'd risen, washed and shaved. Then, before moving out into the sitting room and acknowledging Maine who had only recently returned, he picked his phone up from his bedside table and read the short message. It was from Shandy. 'Hope you're OK.' It read. 'Can we speak?' He sat down on the edge of the bed and looked again at the message, thought for a few seconds and then sent a reply. 'Not good now. I'll call later.' He slipped the phone in his pocket and went out to see what was available for breakfast. He would have to go out for provisions later, and he could call then.

∞∞∞∞∞∞∞∞

The only development in Bristol that morning was the receipt by DI Knight of confirmation that a faint, but useable, thumbprint had been lifted from the inside of the flap of the envelope handed in by Gloria Davis. It didn't match any print already in the digital databank, but the working assumption was that it belonged to Spencer Maine because Gloria had reported her husband referring to envelopes such as this as 'rent', and the envelope contained about twice the going rate for a garage in Bristol city. DS Bradbury was still trying to find a way to track down Maine through medical records, but wasn't having very much success. The people she spoke to in the NHS seemed to attach greater importance to patient confidentiality than to the possibility of tracking a murder suspect, particularly one who had moved away over five years before, and in any case, there was no central nationwide data-base. She had discovered that patients undergoing treatment for HIV tended to be looked after by specialist clinics in hospitals rather than by local GPs, and among the hospitals in the Bristol area, the one that handled HIV cases was Southmead hospital, one of the biggest in the

South West. In London, Kings Cross hospital was well known as a point of treatment for HIV, but, as with Bristol, she would need to speak to someone at a higher level if she were to gain access to records, and it was proving difficult. What she had discovered, however, was that established patients were often prescribed a couple of months' worth of retroviral drugs at any one time and would need to report for routine blood tests three or four times a year. She was fairly sure that Maine would still be registered in Bristol in his own name; there were some things it was just too difficult to change.

∞∞∞∞∞∞∞

As had become the norm in Robin's flat, the one shared meal a day, breakfast for Robin and lunch for Maine, was conducted in silence broken by occasional polite conversation. Maine never asked Robin about what he did 'at work', and Robin never asked about what had happened in Bristol, and neither touched on Maine's future plans. The atmosphere was easier than it had been before Robin had already revealed he had identified a possible source of new identity papers, but that, too, was a subject Maine was loath to raise. He knew that Robin would tell him as soon as something had been agreed, and he didn't want to press him unnecessarily. 'I'll need to go out for some groceries this afternoon,' said Robin, 'how are you off for reading matter?' Maine looked up from his plate. There was something odd about the way Robin had asked the question, but Maine couldn't put his finger on what it was that had alerted him.

'I'm OK,' he said, 'I think it's about time I did a bit of my own shopping. I'll be careful, and I'll do it well away from here.' Robin nodded. 'Thanks,' he replied. The last thing he wanted was for Maine to be linked to his address. It would attract attention and media interest, which he did not want, let alone the risk of being charged as an accessory after the act. 'Shall I go out first, or would you prefer to?' he asked. 'Let me go,' was Maine's reply. 'I can go straight away, and I'll only be half an hour.' 'Fine,' said Robin. He was secretly pleased that he would be able to return Shandy's call. He was curious to find out why she had phoned.

Chapter 61

Robin busied himself with domestic chores until Maine, having donned hat and coat in the usual way, announced he was on his way out. He waited by the window until Maine crossed the road and disappeared round the corner, and then he took his mobile phone from his pocket and perched on the arm of a chair so that he could still see across the road below. He was perfectly entitled to make personal calls from his own flat, but he didn't want Maine to suspect that he had intentionally waited until he was alone, and he certainly didn't want him to have the chance to guess who was on the other end.

Shandy answered after three rings. 'Hi, Robin,' she said. 'Hi,' he answered, 'I'm sorry I didn't get back to you earlier. I was asleep. I picked your message up an hour or so ago, but this is the first chance I've had. What's up?' There was a short pause, as though Shandy was trying to decide how best to start. 'I've been a little worried about you, hon,' she said. 'You never said why you rang me to ask the question you did. I wouldn't want you getting yourself into trouble.' She paused and listened, waiting to see how Robin would respond. He wasn't very good at telling lies, particularly unplanned and unrehearsed, and the length of silence that followed only served to confirm her suspicion. His words, therefore, came as no immediate surprise to her. He hadn't been able to talk about the situation to anyone, and, as he struggled to find a plausible reason for telephoning her with the question about the cause of Simon Lee's death after all these years he realised how much he needed someone to confide in. 'I need to know you won't repeat this to anyone,' he said. 'I think I've already guessed, hon,' she replied, 'of course I won't say anything. I didn't text you out of idle curiosity. I'm really worried about what might be going on down there.'

Robin confirmed Shandy's suspicion. He told her how Maine had contacted him, having left his flat in Clapham as soon as he found out that the search for him had switched to London; how he owed Maine for the favours that he had been granted when he was temporarily homeless in Bristol and again in London himself, and how Maine had claimed that Simon Lee's death had been accidental but that he had covered it up as he was sure he would be wrongfully accused. He assured Shandy that it was only a temporary arrangement and that Maine would be on his way once he had new papers, but he acknowledged that he would be much happier when that day came. 'Do you trust him?' Shandy asked. 'Not entirely,' Robin answered, 'but all my personal stuff is under lock and key, and I always lock my bedroom door when I'm sleeping.' He laughed when he made the final point, but his laugh did nothing to reassure Shandy, who had always had a 'soft spot' for Robin and had treated him like the younger brother she'd never had. 'Where is he now?' she asked. 'He's just gone out for a walk and to buy something to read.' 'Is that wise?' she asked, incredulously. 'He always covers up well, and you'd never recognise him from his photograph in the paper' was the answer, 'he's dyed his hair blonde, and he's grown some stubble. He's very careful not to be seen coming and going, and doesn't use any of the local shops. There are a lot of people in Earls Court. It's easier to hide in a crowd.' 'Well,' said Shandy, 'Thank you for being straight with me, Robin, but I want you to promise to come back to me the minute you sense things aren't working out the way you think they should. I've been doing some asking around since we last spoke, and I'm absolutely sure he killed that guy on purpose. He'd been in the army; he's trained to kill people. He stole the guy's identity and he's lived under his name for years, for goodness sake! It was no accident; it had to be planned. The man's dangerous.' Shandy paused but continued before Robin said anything. 'I can help if you want me to. It would only take one phone call, and he'd be picked up when he's out on one of his walks.'

Robin declined Shandy's offer of help but promised to speak again if he felt he needed her help, and he brought the conversation to an end just as Maine appeared, rounding the corner and heading towards the door below. He felt better to have had the chance to speak to someone else and reassured by Shandy's concern. Things would have to get a lot worse before he'd even think of taking her up on her final offer, but the thought didn't entirely go away.

'You're back earlier than I thought you'd be,' said Robin with a smile as Maine came through the door. 'I got a couple of books at a charity shop,' Maine answered, 'and I knew you needed to get out to get some stuff before going to work.'

Robin seemed a lot more cheerful, thought Maine, and wondered what had happened in his absence.

In Bristol, Shandy sat still for a while, staring at her phone and thinking about the conversation she had just had. It had confirmed her worst fears. Robin was not only in touch with Spencer Maine but was sheltering him in his flat. Neighbours were more aware of comings and goings than they might think and noticed new faces and changes in established patterns of behaviour. Even though Maine had changed the colour of his hair, it was only a matter of time before someone 'put two and two together', no matter how careful the two men were. She didn't care what happened to Maine; in fact she wanted him out of the way altogether, but it was the impact on Robin of his being discovered that troubled her. She still didn't know Robin's address, but she now knew he lived in Earls Court, and she knew what changes Maine had made to his appearance. It would be so easy to pass that information through to DS Brown, whose card she held in her hand. Perhaps she might be able to come to some arrangement with Brown, which protected Robin. She was tempted, but she had promised to keep secret all that Robin had disclosed. She decided she would honour that promise, for the time being, at least.

Chapter 62

I don't want to raise false expectations,' Robin had said before leaving for work that evening, 'but I'm hoping that I'll be back with news for you, 'If so, I'll leave you a note.' Maine acknowledged with raised eyebrows and a smile. 'Fingers crossed!' he said.

He waited until Robin had left the building and disappeared round the corner at the end of the road before he retrieved from his suitcase the plastic bag he'd brought his items of personal shopping home in that morning. Inside was a tube of toothpaste, a packet of disposable nail files, two plastic loyalty cards issued by a coffee chain and a tube of glue. He placed these on the kitchen table before returning to his suitcase and, feeling carefully in the external zipped compartment, brought out a square of blue tack he had bought and placed there some days previously. Ever alert for an opportunity, he had managed to take an impression of the bedroom door key while Robin was in the shower. It had only taken a matter of seconds. He sat at the table and glued the two plastic cards firmly together, placing them under a pile of books to set, while he studied the shape in the blue tack. He reached into his pocket for a pen knife whose blade he had always kept sharp. It would have been better to have a Stanley knife, but he was hopeful that the point of the pen knife blade would be sharp enough.

The aim of gluing the two cards together was to give the key he was about to fashion sufficient strength along its length to overcome the inertia of the door lock, rather than simply bending, when it was rotated in the lock. It wasn't a technique that would work on an external door, but he was confident it would be more than a match for the light lock on the internal door. It had worked before. Once he was sure the cards were well glued together, he set to work with knife blade and files, referring repeatedly to the template on the blue tack, and trying the makeshift key out from time to time, feeling where any obstacle or friction might be. It took about forty five minutes and three cautious attempts before the plastic key had the desired effect, and he depressed the door handle and pushed the bedroom door open gently. He entered the bedroom carefully, noting where everything was, before getting down on his knees at the side of the bed. He peered underneath, using the reflected light from the rest of the house rather than switching the bedroom light on, and he reached with both hands for the Samsonite attaché case that lay there. He slid it out into view, being careful not to change its orientation, and he gently lifted it an inch or so above the carpet to gauge its weight. It was far from empty. He put it down again and, craning his head, inspected the lock. It was fairly typical and wasn't something he could fashion a key for, but although he hadn't really expected otherwise, he would really have liked to see what was inside. He was sure that Robin, like Simon Lee, would keep some cash in it, and it was cash he was interested in. If his fears about the cost of getting a new passport and/or driving licence proved to be well founded, he would need more cash. Yes, it would have been nice to be able to see what amount Robin kept for emergencies, but he now knew where the briefcase was, and although he might not be able to unlock it, he knew he could smash his way in if he needed to. But not tonight; this was simply a reconnaissance mission. He replaced the case, retraced his steps, closed and locked the bedroom door and then made sure all signs of his cutting and filing in the kitchen were removed and secreted in his own suitcase. He made a mental note to acquire a hammer and chisel from a hardware store on his next outing. Then he turned on the TV and settled down for the night.

Chapter 63

True to his word, Robin left a note on the breakfast table because Maine, despite his best intention to be awake to receive any news at first hand, was asleep when Robin let himself in at 3.30 that Wednesday morning. As he tiptoed once more past the couch that had served as Maine's bed since that first night two weeks before, Robin held his breath. He simply wanted to get to bed and wasn't in the mood to talk, so he was relieved to reach his bedroom door without hearing a murmur. In fairness, he didn't have anything to add to the instructions he'd been invited to pass on. His role was simply that of messenger, and that's the way he wanted to keep it. Once in his bedroom, he closed the door gently, turned the light on and wrote the instructions on a page in a memo pad he kept on his bedside table. He tore the page out and slipped into the kitchen, where he placed the page under the salt cellar. He paused before returning to the bedroom, looking across the lounge and hearing Maine's regular breathing. Very soon, he told himself, Maine would be gone, and he'd have his flat to himself again.

Maine found the note immediately after waking at 6.30 am. It read: *'The man you are to meet is called 'Henry'. He will be waiting for you at the mock Tudor building in Soho Gardens, a few minutes away from Tottenham Court Road tube station. He has your description and will make contact with you by asking if you can tell him the time. You simply need to answer that your watch has stopped. He will be there between 12.00 and 12.15 this afternoon, which means I probably won't see you before you leave. 'Henry' won't start work without a deposit in advance (don't know how much), and he will need a set of current passport photo's. Good luck. PS. He doesn't know where we live, and I'd prefer to leave it that way.'*

Maine took the note back into the sitting room, found his pocket diary in his suitcase, opened it to the tube map on the inside front page and sat down to plan the journey. He concluded that it would take no longer than half an hour, but he would leave at 10.45 am to allow time to get the photographs done (he'd seen a post office in Earls Court Road, opposite the tube station on a previous outing). He had almost four hours to kill before leaving, but he already felt tense, and he knew he would need all his wits about him. He made himself a coffee and stared out of the window as the street below began to come to life. The coffee mug in both hands, he stood there for some minutes, deep in thought. How much money should he take with him?

The hours passed very slowly for Maine that morning, but eventually it was time to leave. As he let himself out into the corridor and closed the door behind him, he glanced back across the lounge to Robin's bedroom door, which had remained shut all morning, and he smiled to himself. Little did Robin know that he, too, now had a key - of sorts. Depending on the outcome of the meeting with the man called "Henry", he thought, he might be using the key sooner, rather than later, but he didn't want to dwell on that.

He walked down the single flight of stairs, opened the main door and emerged onto the path leading to the pavement. It was a short walk to the post office, and Earls Court tube station was directly opposite. From there he would follow the same route initially as he had done a week before when he'd ventured as far as Hyde Park. This time, however, he would remain on the Piccadilly line for a few more stops, changing to the Northern line at Leicester Square, one stop away from Tottenham Court Road.

The post office was busy, and there was a short queue for the photo booth. Two 'twenty-something' girls were immediately ahead of him, and he was glad he'd allowed extra time because they took far longer than he felt was strictly necessary. However, ten minutes later he entered the forecourt of Earls Court station with four passport photographs in his inside jacket pocket and felt for the travel-card he had purchased at the start of his first outing. He went through the gates and stepped onto the escalator to the platform below. Twenty five minutes later, he emerged from Tottenham Court Road station and turned into Oxford Street, looking as ordinary as all the other people who were going about their business that morning in central London. He turned south into Soho Street, checked his watch, and then continued into the small rectangular park that was Soho Square. He was twenty minutes early.

Chapter 64

A t the centre of the park was a mock Tudor gazebo, which was one of the main attractions of this quaint little park in the centre of London, and it had formed a background to countless photographs taken by tourists and visitors over the years. It was a good choice of meeting point because the building was both prominent and unique. Furthermore, although the park was small, on this early summer morning there were enough sightseers and tourists in the relatively small area to make it easy to blend in. 'Yes,' thought Maine, 'the meeting point had been well chosen.' He decided to mingle with the tourists and wander along the paths, pausing at the statue of King Charles II, over three hundred years old, while keeping a watchful eye on the gazebo. Unlike 'Henry', he had no idea what the person he was here to meet looked like, but virtually everyone in the park was either one of a couple or part of a group, and it shouldn't be too difficult to spot a single man when he appeared. At ten minutes to twelve, he sat down on an unoccupied bench with a view of the gazebo, unfolded his newspaper and skimmed the headlines, checking his watch every couple of minutes; then, with about thirty seconds to go, he stood up, folded the paper and headed for the gazebo, where he stopped and waited. He was scanning the park when a man's voice behind him said, 'Excuse me.' He turned to see a short, rather rotund figure in a lightweight full length overcoat peering at him through wire-framed spectacles. 'I wonder if I might bother you for the time?' The man smiled politely as he spoke. He had a subtle accent that Maine couldn't place. He also had very uneven teeth. 'I'm very sorry,' Maine replied, 'but my watch has stopped.'

The expression on the man's face didn't change, but he kept his eyes on Maine's as he removed his right hand from his coat pocket and offered it. 'I'm 'Henry',' he said. 'I'm Spencer,' replied Maine, shaking his hand. 'Henry' put his hand back in his coat pocket and glanced round the park. 'Let's find a free bench,' he said and moved off.

Once they were both seated, it was 'Henry' who started proceedings. 'So, Spencer,' he said, 'what exactly do you need?' Maine inclined his body towards him and replied, 'In short, I need a new identity. I need to make a completely new start either here or even abroad; I haven't decided yet. What I haven't got is unlimited funds, and before we agree anything, I need to know how much this is likely to cost me.' 'Henry' nodded gently. 'Of course,' he answered, 'but you have to understand that some things are easier than others. With the advance of digital coding and computerised records, it is now virtually impossible to produce a fake passport, for example. It's relatively easy to produce one that will pass a purely visual inspection but it won't get you out of the country because the minute it's electronically scanned, it will fail. It's much the same with modern driving licences: you could have one in your wallet for years, and you could get away with using it as visual ID, but the moment the police take a serious look at it, the game will be up. For people who need to get away urgently, I can, of course, provide passports, but they won't be forgeries, they'll be genuine but lost or stolen and will have a correspondingly short shelf life. It depends what you want. Birth certificates are a little easier if you're over a certain age, and if you're also looking for the sort of evidence that's acceptable as evidence of home address, that, too, is fairly straightforward. Most banks and other agencies merely tick boxes; none actually checks the data they're provided with. As I say, it depends what you want.' 'Henry' sat back and waited for Maine to think about what he had just heard.

'I think, as a minimum, I need a new driving licence and current evidence of home address,' said Maine thoughtfully, 'and a birth certificate wouldn't go amiss. It would be good to have a passport as well, but I think I've come to realise that any thought of starting a new life abroad is unrealistic. If I did have a passport, it would simply be as additional proof of identity, rather than a means of going abroad.' He paused. 'I'd have the lot if I could afford it, but until I know what you would charge, I can't decide,' he continued. 'Henry' shifted in his seat, placed his hands across his lap and smiled again. 'For a passport that would get you out of the country,' he said, 'you have to be looking at ten grand; for one that will suffice internally: five grand. A UK driving licence will also cost you the same; a birth certificate, £2,500, and I can probably let you have a selection of forged utility bills for £1,500. Whatever you ask for, I do nothing without a down-payment of at least 30 percent; the balance to be paid on receipt: cash only, of course.' Maine nodded. It was as bad as he'd expected. He wondered if there was any margin, any room for negotiation, but his first attempt to lead the conversation in that direction was quickly rebuffed. 'That sort of money could be difficult for me,' he said. 'Those are my prices,' was 'Henry's reply. Maine sat back. 'How do I know that I'll ever see you again?' he challenged, 'you could simply take my deposit and disappear, and I'd have absolutely no way of finding you.' 'Henry' shrugged. 'I'm afraid that's the way it has to be,' he said softly but firmly, 'I wouldn't last five minutes in this business if I handed out business cards. You've been referred to me because of my reputation. It's a reputation that's been hard earned over twenty years.'

The meeting terminated with a brief handshake three minutes later. By then, Maine had decided that he would forego the offer of a passport and would settle for a UK driving licence, a birth certificate and false papers intended to provide proof of residence. He'd handed over a deposit of £3,000 in fifty pound notes to a man he had only briefly met, and he'd done so on the basis of a referral and a verbal assurance. He'd also handed over the photographs of himself as proof of what he now looked like. All in all, he had taken a huge risk. Finally, he had confirmed 'Henry's estimate of his age, and with four parting words, 'I'll be in touch,' the man called 'Henry' had departed. Maine continued sitting on the bench until long after 'Henry' had left the park. He had no idea if 'Henry' knew, or had guessed, who he really was, but 'Henry' certainly knew his correct Christian name, and if he had watched television or read the papers in the past few weeks, he would be able to make an educated guess, despite the efforts Maine had made to change his appearance. Maine was unsure just how he felt about what had just happened. He wondered if he had been the world's biggest sucker, or if it wouldn't be long before he was able to start afresh. One thing was sure: he was £3,000 poorer and would soon have to hand over twice that amount.

Chapter 65

Maine stood up, checked his watch, and, with folded newspaper in hand, set out from the park, retracing his steps along Soho Street and right into Oxford Street towards Tottenham Court Road tube station. He was still dwelling on all that had happened over the previous 15 minutes, and he was not paying much attention to his surroundings; so it was not surprising that he failed to notice the young man in track suit and trainers who emerged from the park behind him and followed him at a distance. The young man kept him in sight on the way back to Tottenham Court road and followed him down to the south-bound platform for the Northern Line. He hung back in the corridor leading directly onto the platform, emerging as the train came to a stop and boarding one carriage behind the one Maine was about to step into. He followed through the changes to the Piccadilly line, always leaving his carriage only after Maine had disembarked, and finally he followed him up the escalator at Earls Court. One after the other, they emerged into the afternoon sunlight and, seven minutes later, when Maine turned the corner into the road in which Robin's apartment was located, the young man was still following but from the opposite side of the road. He slowed his pace, pretending to search his pockets, as he looked down the road and watched Maine let himself in. Then, allowing a few minutes, he walked briskly down the same road, mentally noting the number on the door as he passed it.

Robin was up and dressed and relaxing in the lounge as Maine let himself in. 'How did it go?' he enquired as Maine took off his jacket and draped it over the back of a chair. 'As well as it could have, I suppose,' Maine replied, 'let me get myself a coffee, and I'll tell you. Would you like one?' Robin shook his head. 'No thanks,' he answered, 'I'm OK.'

A few minutes later, coffee mug in hand, Maine settled into a chair. 'How much do you want to know?' he asked. 'Whatever you're comfortable with,' answered Robin, 'but I suppose the bottom line is whether this guy "Henry" can help you?' Maine nodded. 'He can, and he says he will, but I don't know how long he'll take, and he doesn't come cheap. I've already paid over thirty percent deposit.' Robin sensed from the way Maine spoke that he didn't really want to say much more, and he didn't press him. He'd heard enough to reassure himself that the process was, at least under way. He hoped it wouldn't take long. He stood up. 'I need to go out and get some bread and milk and stuff,' he said to Maine, 'I'll be back in half an hour.'

Chapter 66

Shandy took one look at her phone when it rang and answered it immediately. 'Hi, Robin,' she answered brightly, 'everything alright?' Robin leaned back against the outside wall of the convenience store a short walk away from his flat. 'Hi, Shandy,' he said, 'sure, everything's OK, but I thought I'd fill you in on the latest development. Is anyone with you?' Shandy relaxed against the back of her chair. She was relieved to hear that all was well, pleased that he had chosen to keep in touch and interested to hear what the latest development was. 'I'm all yours and all ears, Robin,' she answered, 'go ahead, please.' She listened as Robin described how he'd managed to arrange Maine's introduction to someone who might be able to provide the new identity he needed, and he repeated the short and pointed report he'd heard from Maine earlier that afternoon. 'Has he asked you for money?' was Shandy's immediate question. 'No,' Robin replied. 'I don't know how much he's got with him, but I'm sure he's not penniless.' There was a slight pause before Shandy spoke. 'It's just that, don't ask me how, but I have an idea what these things can cost. He'll be looking at something like ten grand if he wants the full suite, and even if he's carrying a wad with him, it'll make a dent in it that will hurt. Please be careful, Robin.' Robin picked up his shopping bag and turned to enter the store. 'I will,' he said. 'I will. I'll be in touch.'

Shandy sat looking at her phone. What she had heard had troubled her even more, and she decided to do something that she never thought she ever would. She reached into the drawer of the desk she was sitting at and pulled out the card DS Wes Brown had left with her. She dialled the number on the card and waited. It was answered after three rings by Wes Brown himself. 'Hello,' she said after he had identified himself, 'it's Shandy from Sweet Caramel in Old Market. You came to see me some weeks ago. I may have some information for you, but I need to talk face to face. Can you come now?' She couldn't see but could sense the interest her invitation had immediately aroused. 'I'll be with you in twenty minutes,' was his reply.

She was ready for him when he arrived and opened the door immediately after his discreet knock had sounded. 'Come through to the office,' she said, 'can I offer you a drink?' Wes smiled politely and shook his head. 'No, thank you,' he said, 'I was finishing one off when you called.' He followed her through to the sparsely furnished room he had seen before and accepted her waved invitation to sit down. He looked at Shandy expectantly and waited for her to speak. 'I need to come to an arrangement with you,' she said cagily. 'I may have some information for you about the whereabouts of the guy you're looking for in connection with the freezer murder, but I want to protect my source. I believe he's got involved against his wishes, and I fear for his safety. I'm worried about what this man Maine might do to him, which is why I'm talking to you now, but I'm also worried about what you might do to him.' She paused and studied Wes Brown's face but got little information from it. 'Just how is your source involved?' asked Wes. 'I believe he's sheltering Maine,' she replied, 'but not because he wants to. He owed Maine a favour and couldn't turn him away when he turned up on his door claiming that the death of the guy in the freezer was an accident.' DS Brown couldn't believe his luck, but it didn't show. 'Does your source know that you're talking to me?' he asked. 'Not exactly,' Shandy replied, 'but he's talking to me, and I think he's asking for help.' That wasn't completely true, Shandy knew, but she felt that the police would be much more likely to treat Robin leniently if they believed he was volunteering the information that would lead to Maine's arrest. 'Tell me more,' said Brown gently.

An hour later, DS Brown knocked and entered his boss' office. He'd set up the meeting by telephone after he'd left Sweet Caramel, and he'd guaranteed DI Knight's interest with the briefest of outlines of what had been revealed to him earlier. DS Bradbury and DS Carter were also there as Brown sat down and explained that he had confirmation that Maine was sheltering in a flat in London, a flat occupied by Robin, the masseur at Sweet Caramel who had looked after Harry Davis and was, as it turned out, an old friend of Spencer Maine. At this stage, he explained that he didn't have the precise address of the flat and neither did his source, Shandy, but he knew it was in Earls Court; he knew what changes Maine had made to his appearance and that he left the flat from time to time; and he knew Maine was already negotiating the purchase of new identity documents.

Brown explained that Shandy was concerned for Robin's safety, and in order to secure her cooperation, he'd promised her that Robin would be treated sympathetically if the flow of information continued and led to Maine's arrest. 'Does this 'Robin' know that Shandy is talking to us?' asked DI Knight. 'No,' replied Brown. 'We have to be careful we don't spook him. Shandy will do all she can to find out where the flat is, but we don't know what Robin will do if he suspects that she wants the information for us.' DI Knight nodded. 'The first thing we need to do is tell the Met what we know,' he said, 'I'll put a call through on the secure line. Wes, you keep things sweet with Shandy. Her priority is to obtain the address, but I agree, we don't want to lose the link by being too impatient.' The meeting was over; the team dispersed and DS Brown moved back to his desk and picked up the telephone.

Chapter 67

When Robin let himself in, his bag of shopping in his hand, Maine was still sitting where he had been when they'd had their brief conversation earlier. He looked up briefly, but it was clear that he was brooding about something, and Robin chose simply to busy himself in the kitchen. 'I've bought a couple of meat pies,' he said, loud enough for Maine to hear, 'I thought we'd have them with mashed potato and peas. You any good at peeling spuds?' The reply sounded forced. 'Not really, but I'll give it a try.'

Conversation over lunch at the small wooden kitchen table was virtually non-existent. Robin tried, but Maine's responses were brief and discouraging; so he gave up. 'I'll do the washing up,' Maine said as he stood up at the end of the meal, and Robin replied with 'great, thank you,' and left him to it. He returned to his bedroom and lay on his back on the bed with his hands under his head, staring at the ceiling and thinking. This couldn't go on for much longer without there being a serious row. He hoped against hope that there would be word from "Henry" soon. He was about to drop off into a light sleep when the doorbell rang. He went immediately into the lounge, motioning Maine, who was standing motionless at the window, into the bedroom behind him and shouted 'Coming,' as he waited until the bedroom door had closed and hidden Maine from view. He opened the door to find the girl from the flat above with whom he had a passing acquaintance. 'Well, well,' she said in mock surprise, 'you haven't emigrated, after all. I'm sorry to bother you, but I hadn't seen you for weeks, and I was beginning to wonder if you were alright.' She smiled. 'That's very thoughtful of you, Sally,' Robin replied, remaining in the doorway, 'I'm fine, really, but I've had a friend to stay, and you know how it is. He's not very well, and he's just having a rest after lunch, otherwise I'd ask you in for a cup of tea, but you're well, I hope. I'd have expected you to be at work.' The girl called Sally nodded and kept smiling. 'No, I'm fine too,' she said, 'I have the afternoon off, and I just thought I'd check.' She turned away and made her way to the stairs leading to the next floor. 'Come up for a cup of tea, yourself, when you can,' she said, 'I do enjoy your company.' Robin smiled and closed his door gently, and Sally continued back to her room. She was right, she thought to herself, the blonde guy she'd seen from her window, coming and going from time to time, was a friend of Robin's. Funny; he didn't look his type.

Robin walked over to the bedroom door and opened it. Maine was sitting on the corner of his bed. 'It's OK,' he said, 'it was just the girl from the flat above. She hadn't seen me around for a couple of weeks and wanted to check that I was still alive!' He immediately regretted his choice of words, but Maine seemed not to notice, nodded and stood up, preparing to leave to return to the lounge. Robin sensed that the interruption had created a chance for them to get to the bottom of Maine's moodiness. 'I'll put the kettle on, Spencer,' he said, looking him in the eye, 'perhaps we could have a chat.' It wasn't a question, and he didn't expect an answer.

The two men sat opposite each other in the lounge, hot mugs of tea in their hands. 'So what's got into you, Spencer?' Robin asked. 'Ever since you got back from London, you've been like a bear with a sore head.' He took a sip from his mug, his gaze fixed on Maine, and waited. 'I'm screwed,' said Maine. 'I put a lot of money into the deposit for the house in Clapham, and I've lost it all. I should never have bought. I should have saved the money and rented, but I was too bloody sure of myself. I did keep some by for a rainy day, but a lot of that will go on the new documents, if I ever get them. It has left me short, and I'm not sure what I'm going to be able to do, even though I'll have a new name. I know as well as you do that I can't stay here for very much longer.' Robin waited, but Maine had said all he was going to say. 'I wish I could help you, buddy,' he said, 'but I don't have much put by myself.' Maine shook his head, staring down at the carpet. 'No, mate,' he said, 'I don't want your money; this is all my bloody fault, not yours.' Little did Robin know that the parting sentence was only partially true. It was certainly Maine's own fault, but he had already developed an obsession with the contents of the locked briefcase under Robin's bed, which, although hidden from him, had come to represent the solution to his problem. He had convinced himself that there was money to be found inside, and he had already decided how and when he would go about getting his hands on it. 'I'll try to find out how much longer you might have to wait for the documents,' said Robin. 'Thanks,' said Maine, 'I think I'll go out for some exercise. I may not be back before you leave for work.'

Chapter 68

The telephone on DI Knight's desk buzzed. He glanced across, picked up the handset and answered in his customary way. Then, after listening intently he got up, moved across to the door to his office, kicked it shut and perched on the corner of the desk. 'I see,' he said, 'don't worry; we're taking things very gently with the woman called Shandy, but I'll put the brakes on.' He listened again and then nodded. 'Of course,' he said, 'and we'll let you know if we learn anything more ourselves; thank you.' He opened his door and went into the adjoining room. 'Anyone know where Wes is?' he asked. The two detective constables in the room were preparing to go home but shook their heads. 'One of you get him on his mobile and patch him through to me, and afterwards tell DS Bradley and Carter that I want them in my office at 9.30 tomorrow morning.' He went back into his office, closed the door behind him and returned to the chair behind his desk. He didn't have long to wait before the phone buzzed again and it was Wes Brown on the line. Something was up because it was very unusual for DI Knight to summon him this way. He listened intently. 'Wes, have you had any further contact with the lady in Old Market since our meeting today?' Knight asked. 'No, boss, is there a problem?' answered Brown. 'We have to play very carefully,' was the answer. 'Report to me immediately, if she gives you any more information, but make no contact with her yourself. I'm setting up a meeting here tomorrow morning at 9.30. I know it's a Saturday, but I'll explain what's developed then.' Knight had put the telephone down before Wes had time to acknowledge the instruction he'd received. He pulled away from the side of the road and continued on his way home; he was still none the wiser.

∞∞∞∞∞∞∞∞

'I'm sorry to bring you in today,' Knight said unconvincingly as he looked at the three detective sergeants sitting in his office the following morning, but you'll probably be able to get away early.' He smiled briefly and continued. 'I had a telephone call last evening from our contact in the Met. They want us to hold fire, back off, our relationship with Shandy for the moment. They don't want us setting any hares running, particularly Mr Spencer Maine. It seems they may already know where he's living in Earls Court, although they didn't know who he was until after I'd spoken to them yesterday lunchtime, and they were able to put two and two together. It seems that they're watching someone else, someone who they suspect of running a very successful business supplying fake identity documents, and they feel they're very close to making an arrest, but they want to catch him red-handed, and it may be that our man might provide them with the chance they need. If he does, they'll 'kill two birds with one stone', as it were.'

DS Brown was the first to speak. 'The question is, should we just leave Shandy to her own devices or should we tell her to back off? She believes it's in our mutual interest to determine where Robin's flat is, and, if they speak again, she's likely to look for an opportunity to ask. That could put the frighteners on Robin. Alternatively, if we tell her to back off, she'll probably deduce that we know his address. I can't see any problem with that as long as she doesn't know anything more, but if she somehow tried to protect Robin by tipping him off, that could be difficult.' Knight nodded. 'Any other points?' he said, looking at the others. 'How well do you think you know, Shandy?' asked DS Bradley, looking at her colleague. 'I've only met her twice,' answered DS Brown, 'she doesn't care a damn about our suspect, but she clearly feels very protective towards Robin. My instinct tells me not to give her any reason to think we, or at least the Met, know where he lives.' Knight turned to DS Carter. 'Max?' he said. 'I go along with Wes, boss,' he answered, 'this may not have long to run now. Softly, softly is what I think.' Knight nodded to acknowledge the views that had been expressed and to indicate his agreement. He turned to DS Brown again and asked, 'before we knew what we know now, and if you hadn't heard from Shandy, how long would you have waited before contacting her again? DS Brown shrugged. 'I reckon I would have given her two or three days,' he said. 'Right, make that three days if there are no developments. Don't contact her again before Monday afternoon and check with me before you do. Softly, softly it is, but before you all go, Jess, have you had any success in finding out where our suspect has been getting his medication from in London since he's been there?' DS Bradley shook her head. 'Not yet, Boss,' she answered, 'but I think we're narrowing the field. I've given priority to his true name of Spencer Maine, rather than to Simon Lee because I couldn't see how he'd be able to change the name on his medical records without doing it legally. I hope I'm right. As soon as I've got something, I'll tell you.'

∞∞∞∞∞∞∞∞

In Earls Court, Maine was making himself breakfast when the meeting in Bristol started, and by the time it had ended, he was sitting down to eat beans on toast. There had been no note left on the kitchen table by Robin on his return in the early hours of the morning, and Maine concluded that there was no progress to report. He prepared himself for another day of reading and watching TV and brooding on what might have been. He had returned late the previous afternoon with a hacksaw and some spare blades. He had considered buying a hammer and cold chisel, but he had realised that any undue noise while Robin was out could attract the attention of the girl upstairs. He would keep the saw hidden until the very last moment, until he had a meeting with "Henry". He had decided that he would either break into Robin's briefcase before leaving for his next meeting with "Henry" or he would simply take it with him and break into it later, depending on the time of the meeting. He had made his mind up, anyway, to leave with his own suitcase, too, and not to return to Robin's flat.

Chapter 69

The weekend passed without incident or development, but there was a note on the table when Maine rose on the Monday morning. It read: 'Good news! You are to meet with 'H' in the forecourt of Paddington station at 8.30pm on Tuesday. I have more instructions for you, but I can give you them tomorrow afternoon.' Maine felt his pulse quicken. The timing of the proposed meeting was just right. He knew that it wouldn't take more than half an hour to get to the library from Robin's flat, and even though he would get there good and early, as usual, he would be leaving well after Robin left for work. That meant he would be able to get into the bedroom and remove Robin's briefcase. He would take it with him, with his own suitcase, and Robin wouldn't discover his loss until, at the earliest, he came home in the early hours of Wednesday morning. By then, Maine would be on a train to Manchester, or perhaps he'd already be there with his new identity.

There was no shortage of internet cafés in Earls Court, he had walked past two on his previous outings, and he would have plenty of time to get out to one that morning. He couldn't make a booking on line because he couldn't use his credit card. The police, he was sure, would have asked the credit card company to alert them if it was used, and it was probably best simply to throw it away. He knew that, once in Manchester, a city he had never visited in his life, it wouldn't be easy. However, it was a big place in which he could easily disappear, and he would again rely on his instinct and natural talent to get a job, earn some money and get a new bank account. The one problem that he hadn't really addressed, and which continued to nag at the back of his mind, was the need to renew his supply of prescribed antiretroviral medication because he only had enough tablets and capsules to last another month. He'd thought of going back to the clinic in the London hospital, where he had become a routine visitor over the past five years, but he had rejected the idea as too risky. It had proved to be the one aspect of his fraudulent life as Simon Lee that he had never changed. Had he altered his name legally, he imagined it would be possible to have his new name appended to his medical records, but that was impossible, impractical or downright dangerous in his situation. He knew he would have to tackle the problem very soon after reaching Manchester.

He prepared himself a quick breakfast and then put on the coat and hat, which had become his outdoor uniform, quietly, let himself out and then made his way briskly to the nearest internet café he had seen. He was preoccupied with his new plans, no matter how sketchy they might have been, and he paid little attention to his surroundings as he walked. He probably wouldn't have noticed the 'twenty-something' girl studying a London A-Z on the corner opposite, in any case, but he certainly didn't see her take up position some fifty yards behind him. She didn't follow him in, but a couple of minutes later a young man in denim jeans did and buried his nose in a computer at the other end of the room.

He was back in the flat before Robin's door had opened, with seven telephone numbers of flats and bedsits in Manchester that he had selected from the hundreds available on line. On the way back, he'd purchased the cheapest mobile phone he could find and a pay-as-you-go sim card. He couldn't make any reservations for accommodation until he knew what his new identity would be, and he wouldn't know that until he had received the new papers from 'Henry'. He would therefore make the calls on the way north, from the train. He made himself a mug of instant coffee and sat down to think things over again. What if there was no money in the briefcase after all? Things would be hard. Once he had paid the balance owing to 'Henry', he would still have enough for the train ticket, for a deposit on the flat and for the first round of bills, but there wouldn't be a great deal of change left over, and he would have to find a job fast. What if 'Henry' was alone? Could he snatch the documents and run? Probably, but there was the danger that there would be some 'muscle' lurking somewhere, and, in any case, even if he got away, and no-one knew that he was leaving for Manchester that very night, 'Henry' knew what his new name would be. All it would take was an anonymous telephone call to the police. No, it was best to grit his teeth and pay over the money and hope that, when he was able to saw the lid off the briefcase, he wouldn't be disappointed. Surely there was money in it; there was no other lock-up in the flat.

∞∞∞∞∞∞∞

'You could be at Paddington easily in half an hour,' said Robin an hour or so later. He had still to shave, but it was clear to him that Maine was impatient to learn the arrangements. I've been told to tell you that 'H' will not want to talk. He will be browsing the magazines in W H Smith. You are to do the same. He will come alongside you. You should not acknowledge him. He will place an envelope in the magazine he's looking at and will replace it in the rack and move away. You are to take the magazine, open it, remove the contents from the envelope, put the balance of what you owe him in the envelope, replace it in the magazine and replace the magazine on the shelf. Then you are to move away and leave. Don't hang around is what I've been told to tell you; just walk away and don't look back. It sounds straightforward to me. Do you feel better now?' Maine went over the arrangements in his mind and nodded. 'I'm going to have a shower and a shave,' continued Robin, 'and the good news is that I've got the night off tonight. It'll be my first one in two weeks, so why don't we go out for a drink?' With that and a brief smile, Robin disappeared into the lavatory and closed the door, leaving Maine thinking furiously. A night off tonight would mean that Robin wouldn't be leaving at six, in the usual way, and he wouldn't be coming home in the early hours of the morning and sleeping in until lunchtime on the Tuesday. He would, though, still be going out to work at six pm on Tuesday, which would give Maine all the time he needed to pack, take Robin's briefcase, and depart in ample time to meet 'Henry' at Paddington.

Chapter 70

The telephone rang for some time on the Monday evening before it was answered. 'Hi,' said Brown when he recognised Shandy's voice, 'it's DS Brown. Can you talk?' Shandy sat down at the desk she'd just hurried to from a room down the corridor. 'Yes,' she said, 'but unless you've got something to tell me, it'll be a short conversation; I don't have anything new for you.' DS Brown smiled. 'No,' he said, 'I don't have anything new, either, and you've already answered the question I was going to ask. I'll call again in a couple of days unless I hear from you beforehand.' Shandy answered with a brief 'fine' and put the phone back on its cradle. She looked at her watch; it was 6.15 pm on the Monday. She didn't want to put any pressure on Robin, but if she hadn't heard any more from him by Wednesday, she'd probably ring him to see that everything was still alright.

DI Knight was still at his desk when Wes Brown paused outside his office door on his way out and home. 'Nothing to report from Shandy, sir; I've just had a brief word with her. I've said I'll check with her on Wednesday unless I hear from her.' Knight was just about to acknowledge when his telephone buzzed, and he waved his left hand as if to say, 'off you go,' as he reached for the receiver with his right. He answered and listened to the brief message that came through from his point of contact in the Met. 'Thank you for letting me know,' he said. 'If I hear anything that might be helpful at this end, you'll be the first to know.' He sat back, reached across to the phone again and rang through to

Sandra, DSI Nolan's PA. If she'd gone home, the line would go direct to her boss, but it rang seven times. DSI Nolan wasn't in either. Knight put the receiver down and typed a quick internal email to say that the Met had cause to believe that the suspect, Spencer Maine, was planning to leave London for Manchester. They didn't know when, but they knew where he was living in Earls Court and were keeping an eye on him. They wanted to get both him and 'Henry' at the same time and were prepared to wait. Knight sent the message, tidied up his desk, took his suit jacket from the hook at the back of the door and left for home.

In the internet café in Earls Court, the desk in the cubicle that Maine had occupied that morning was bare. The laptop he had used had been disconnected and confiscated by the young man in jeans immediately after Maine had left, and it hadn't been replaced. It had already revealed to the Met the websites Maine had accessed. The girl who had followed him to the premises had been waiting outside and had followed him back to the flat. By the time Maine and Robin emerged at about 6.45 pm, with the intention of having a quiet drink together in a not-too-busy pub, she had been relieved, but her successor followed them discreetly on the opposite side of the road, speaking quickly into his phone. In the pub, they were watched by two pairs of eyes as they drank together in a quiet corner, and they were discreetly followed back to the flat two hours later.

Robin not being at work that night seemed strange to both men, but, having been out to the pub together, both men felt much more at ease. In a way, they both acknowledged that an end to the awkward existence that they'd navigated through since Spencer Maine had arrived almost two weeks before was in sight. Robin didn't expect that Maine would stay any longer than he could avoid once he'd got his new identity, and he was looking forward to having his flat all to himself soon, but he would never have guessed that it was Maine's intention not to return the following night. They had talked over their glasses of beer, but it was light-hearted stuff, and both had deliberately avoided discussing Maine's plans. The subject of money didn't come up again, and Robin quietly noted that Maine no longer seemed to be brooding about his financial situation. He seemed, thought Robin, to have come to terms with it, and he had also received Robin's news that he would be out most of the next morning doing 'personal admin', with equanimity.

Chapter 71

Even though rain was expected by mid-afternoon, Tuesday 28th June started with great promise, the sun appearing above the skyline to the east of the flat without any challenge at all from cloud. Maine watched from the window over the street below as the sky brightened, a mug of coffee in his right hand, his left in his trouser pocket. He had woken much earlier but had remained in his makeshift bed, staring at the ceiling and going over the events of the day ahead. He had been relieved to hear Robin say the previous night that he would be out for the first part of the day because he knew he would be in no mood to make small-talk as the time approached for him to make his departure from the flat. He would have a lot of time to kill that day and very little to do, and he knew that the hours would drag by. He had initially decided to leave the flat before Robin returned, even if that meant departing at midday, and killing time elsewhere, but then he had asked himself what would happen if Robin noticed the absence of his briefcase before leaving for work that evening. As Robin knew where and when he was meeting with 'Henry', Maine decided it was a risk he could not take, and he therefore decided to depart as soon after Robin had left as was safe. He simply had to pack his suitcase, unlock Robin's bedroom, remove the briefcase, lock up again and leave, and he would still have more than ample time to get to Paddington for his rendezvous. From there, his next stop would be Euston

Station, and, by early morning on Wednesday, he would be in Manchester.

The two breakfasted together, and Robin left to do what he had to do a little before ten, indicating that he expected to be back in the early afternoon. He hadn't been gone half an hour before Maine carefully unlocked his bedroom door. He had tried to resist doing so because the makeshift plastic key could only safely be used a few times before breaking, but he couldn't resist the urge to check that the briefcase, which he had now convinced himself represented the answer to his shortage of funds, was where it should be. He crouched down beside Robin's bed, lifted the duvet and breathed a sigh of relief as he saw the briefcase was still there. Turning round, he made his way quickly to the door, carefully locked it again and set about what preliminary packing he could do without alerting Robin to his intentions. By 11.30 am, he had done what he could and couldn't bear being indoors any longer. He checked his watch again, donned his hat and coat and went out for some fresh air and freedom. He walked what had become a fairly familiar beat to him since he'd had the confidence to venture out on his own, idly looking in shop windows to pass the time. He wasn't difficult to follow, and the detective in nondescript civilian clothing only had to react quickly when Maine crossed the road at the furthest reach of his outing and started back on the same side as he was. The detective ducked into a newsagent's and stood looking through the magazines on display until it was safe to resume his position behind, but not too close behind, his quarry. It was 2.15 pm when he stood at the corner of the street and watched Maine let himself into the building which housed Robin's flat. Forty five minutes later, he shrank into a convenient doorway as Robin appeared at the corner and followed Maine into the building and up to his flat.

Maine was lying on the couch, staring at the ceiling, when Robin let himself in. The two exchanged short but polite greetings, but it was clear that Maine didn't really want to talk; so Robin unlocked his bedroom door and busied himself inside, leaving the door ajar. When he could do no more, he emerged into the kitchen and announced he was making a pot of tea. He emerged with a mug in each hand and moved across to the centre of the lounge, placing one on the table beside the couch on which Maine still lay and sitting down with the other in the adjacent easy chair, looking across at Maine and inviting him to say something. 'Thanks,' said Maine, as he eased himself into a sitting position and reached for the mug of tea. They sat in silence for some minutes, before Robin broke the ice. 'You're not a happy chappie, Spencer?' he offered rhetorically. 'I'm sorry, mate,' was the almost grudging reply, 'I'll be glad when tonight is all over; that's all.' Robin nodded and took a sip from his mug. 'Yeah, I can imagine,' he said, not appreciating the full extent of what Maine had just said. 'It'll all be over by this time tomorrow, old son. I'll be leaving at six this evening, as usual, but if you want me to wake you when I get home, so that you can tell me how it went, that's fine.' Maine looked up and smiled. 'Thanks. I'll leave you a note.'

Chapter 72

The rest of the afternoon passed painfully slowly, and both men were relieved when time came for Robin's departure. Maine stood at the window and watched as Robin walked to the main road and disappeared around the corner. He waited a further five minutes just to be absolutely sure that Robin wasn't coming back for something he'd forgotten, and then he set about packing his suitcase. It didn't take long. Then there was only one thing to do before leaving. He placed his plastic skeleton key in the bedroom door lock for the last time and turned it slowly. He felt the plastic bend slightly as he applied pressure, and he paused for a moment, holding his breath, before continuing the anticlockwise motion. The lock clicked open, and Maine exhaled with relief. He returned the plastic key to his pocket, opened the door and stepped into the room, but was taken aback to see the briefcase on, rather than underneath, Robin's bed. It was locked, as it had been on the previous occasions, and Maine lifted it up with both hands, assessing the weight. He shook it. Nothing seemed to have changed. There were definitely papers of some sort inside. Robin must simply have forgotten to put it back beneath the bed, Maine told himself as he turned back towards the door. He went through into the lounge, closing but not locking the bedroom door, put on his coat and hat, took his suitcase in one hand and the briefcase in the other and let himself out. He paused only to put the spare front door key Robin had loaned him back through the door in what was a gesture of finality – there was no way back now - and then he went briskly down the stairs, through the front door and out onto the short path that led to the pavement. He extended the arm on the suitcase and set off in the direction of Earl's Court tube station, wheeling the suitcase behind him. The detective who had seen him emerge was talking animatedly on his phone as he took up his usual position, fifty to seventy yards behind him. It was 6.45 pm.

The choice of rendezvous was almost perfect, thought Maine as, trundling his suitcase along the pavement, he approached Earls Court tube station. Yes, he would have to go on from Paddington to Euston to catch his train to Manchester, but that would take less than half an hour, and meeting with 'Henry' at a railway station was ideal. He and his suitcase would simply blend into the background there, and it wouldn't matter if he arrived very early (as he preferred to do) because he would look like any one of hundreds of people, many with luggage, glancing at the departure board or waiting in one of the many cafés and bars for their platform to open. He took the escalator down to the platforms, having a choice between District and Circle lines, and decided to take the first train that came along. The detective behind him walked a few paces down the moving escalator to get a little closer because he didn't want to run the risk of his quarry boarding a train that might already be waiting at one of the platforms and seeing its doors closing before he could get to it. His precaution, although well-founded, proved unnecessary, and he loitered, like many others, waiting for the first train to arrive. When it did, he lingered at the back of the platform until he'd seen Maine board, and he chose the adjacent carriage, sitting near the door in a position that would enable him to see Maine when he prepared to disembark. Maine did so when the train arrived at Paddington, and his follower waited until he was half way to the exit from the platform before he, too, stepped from the train and continued after him, matching his pace. At the foot of the escalator, with Maine three quarters of the way up, he did what he'd done on the way down the escalator at Earls Court, walking briskly up the left hand side, passing the two stationary passengers who stood between him and Maine, until he had reduced the gap between them to about thirty yards. He didn't know where Maine intended to go after he left the station, and he hadn't been able to call his controller since descending below ground at Earls Court, but he was in good contact as Maine passed through the ticket barrier on his way out and set course for the main above-ground railway station. He watched as Maine walked past WH Smiths, pausing momentarily to survey the layout and identify the whereabouts of the magazines, before placing his suitcase beside a free table at the first café he came to and queuing to place an order. Maine looked at his watch, and the detective did the same. It was 7.20 pm. The detective continued past the café before moving across to the side-wall, placing his phone to his ear.

Chapter 73

Maine placed a tray containing coffee and a burger and chips on the table he had selected and sat down facing the concourse. He had over an hour to wait, but now that he was only yards from the planned rendezvous, he felt strangely calm. He went over in his mind the instructions Robin had relayed to him earlier in the week, although it now seemed much longer ago than that. He was to look for 'Henry', who would be browsing the magazines on display at the stationers; he was to do the same and then retrieve the envelope from between the pages of the magazine that 'Henry' had replaced; he was to remove from the envelope the papers he had purchased, and, having inserted the balance that was owing, he was to replace the magazine and the envelope it contained and walk away. He put a hand to his breast pocket, where the balance payment was tucked away, and reassured that it was still there, he picked up the free newspaper from the adjacent unoccupied table and, placing it to one side, read it as he ate his meal. From a distance, the detective who had followed him from Robin's flat watched out of the corner of his eye as he, too, studied a newspaper. He was joined some fifteen minutes later by the young woman who had last seen Maine enter and leave the internet café in Earls Court. After a brief discussion, she walked casually away and took up a position below the huge departure board further along the concourse.

At 8.25 pm, Maine stood up, stacked his tray and its contents in the usual way, and, with a measured pace trundled his suitcase out onto the forecourt, the briefcase in his left hand. He stood looking into the stationers for half a minute and then continued to where the magazines were on display. The only other person browsing the magazines was a short, rotund woman in an olive green calf-length skirt, dark tights and flat, 'sensible', shoes. Her greying hair was swept back into a bun, and she wore a three-quarter length shower-proof coat. Maine reached for a magazine and stood idly flicking through it, while keeping his eyes on his exposed wristwatch. At 8.29 pm he replaced the magazine and, while scanning the rest, took the opportunity to look left and right. He caught a brief glimpse to his left of a young woman on the concourse on her phone. She seemed vaguely familiar but then turned away as she continued speaking. He was momentarily puzzled and was wondering where he might have seen her before, when he became aware of someone close to him on his right. He turned his head to see that the grey-haired woman was returning a magazine to the shelf. Having done so, she turned very briefly towards him and smiled an apology. It was her uneven teeth that in the fraction of a second before she inclined to her right, gave her away. It was 'Henry'! For a brief moment, Maine was taken aback by the convincing disguise, but he managed quickly to regain control and reached for the magazine that still jutted out from the ones on either side of it. It fell open naturally where the white A5 envelope had been inserted, and Maine was able quickly and easily to slide the contents into his left-hand before extracting the wad of notes from his left-hand breast pocket with his right hand and inserting them into the envelope. He returned it to the magazine and returned the magazine to the shelf. His instruction was then to turn and walk away, but he couldn't bring himself to do so. What if someone else inadvertently picked out the magazine? He stepped back and waited as the disguised 'Henry' moved back and reached across, but at that moment, a two-tone siren sounded from all the speakers across the station and a disembodied, almost mechanical voice, announced: 'Security Alert, Security Alert. Evacuate, Evacuate. This is a General Evacuation. All staff and members of the public should follow the instructions of the appointed marshals to reach safe areas.'

Chapter 74

The message was loud and unmistakable in its urgency and was repeated. The immediate initial reaction of the people on the forecourt was to stop and listen, but this quickly gave way to movement. Marshals, identifiable by their yellow vests, were directing people to the right, towards the access road adjacent to the steps down to the tube station, and people were soon walking briskly or running. Maine joined the throng moving to his right, but as he did so, something odd caught his attention. It was that woman again, and she was still on her phone, but unlike everyone around her, she was stationary, and she was looking directly at him. And then he knew he'd seen her before. She had been outside the internet café when he had left after looking for accommodation in Manchester! Was this coincidence or had she been following him? Was she police? As he hurried along in the crowd, trying to avoid tripping people up with the suitcase trailing behind him, he kept the girl in sight. There was no doubt that she was working her way across the moving phalanx of bodies; she had her gaze fixed on him and seemed to be trying to intercept him before he reached the rear entrance to the tube station. He looked to the right, up the access road that led to Praed Street; it was also full of people, but at least they were all moving away. He inclined to the right, but saw two armed police moving up the access road towards him, the crowd breaking to allow them through, and he quickly corrected. Although they were probably more interested in whatever had necessitated the evacuation, he couldn't take any chances with them. He realised he would have to deal with the plain clothes officer, if that is what she was, and try to get lost in the throng heading down to the tube station. He reached the entrance to the underground marginally before she did, paused momentarily to create space between him and the backs of the people immediately ahead, and swung his suitcase in a low arc across his body with his right arm. He let go of the suitcase as it impacted with her solar plexus and fought his way down the short flight of stairs as she fell back into, and was swallowed up by, the sea of people being pushed on by those behind them and finding themselves unable to stop themselves tripping over and trampling on her.

He elbowed his way along the corridor to the ticket barriers, which had either been opened or been forced open by the crowds. He was oblivious to the sensitivities of the people he thrust aside, and glanced over his shoulder as he started down the escalator but saw no one pursuing him. He initially tried to weave in and out of those standing on both sides of the moving staircase, but they were so tightly packed that he gained little advantage and decided, instead, to make himself as invisible as possible. There would be a choice of platforms at the bottom, and that would give him the edge. Still holding-on tightly to the briefcase, he opted for the platform on his left and resumed his weaving, pushing, and elbowing to put as much distance between him and any pursuer as he could and to get near enough to the edge of the platform to be able to board the first train to arrive. As he turned into the platform, he glanced back and up to the top of the escalator, where an armed policeman in full body armour was doing his best to make his way down, and in his wake was the a dishevelled but determined plain clothes policewoman. He doubted that they could see him as easily as he had been able to spot them, and he redoubled his efforts to get closer to the edge of the platform, spurred on by the customary breeze from the tunnel on his left, which heralded the imminent arrival of a train.

Clutching, elbowing and thrusting himself forward, his behaviour was too much to tolerate for one tall, middle aged, man in a suit who'd already had his travel plans completely ruined by the emergency evacuation. His response to Maine's aggression was to cast all normal propriety aside and grab him by the shoulder with his left hand while placing his foot in his rear and pushing violently. Unfortunately, he did so just as the person between Maine and the platform edge stepped to one side, and with nothing to stop him, Maine flew off the platform.

He was still clutching the briefcase as the train hit him, and the last image that registered in his brain before the impact was the shocked face of the driver, only two feet away. His watch stopped at 8.43 pm.

Chapter 75

The account of the evacuation from Paddington Station and the death on the underground that followed formed the first item on the television news bulletins that evening. It was reported that the evacuation had been initiated after the receipt of a 'credible' telephoned warning of a bomb on the concourse, but that the warning had turned out to be a hoax. There had been no other statement from the Metropolitan Police at that early stage; the identity of the man who had fallen in front of the train on the District and Circle line from an overcrowded platform had not been established. DI Knight watched the news bulletin from the comfort of his couch with his wife, Molly, curled up at his side, and thought little more about it that night. However, he hadn't been in his office for more than five minutes the next morning when the phone on his desk buzzed, and he was connected to his opposite number in Scotland Yard. When Detective Sergeants Brown, Bradbury and Carter had all trickled in, some half an hour later, he called them into his office.

'Guess who the guy was who fell under the tube train at Paddington last night,' he asked, looking round at them, unable to keep a half smile off his lips. He rightly assumed they had all picked the news up from somewhere. There was a pause before Jess Bradbury hazarded a cautious guess. 'Was it our man, boss?' she asked. 'It certainly was,' he answered. 'He managed to get down to the underground with lots of others before any barrier could be placed across

339

the access from the main line station and before the underground trains had been stopped. It seems that his fall from the platform was accidental, but we'll probably never know for sure because the coppers who went down after him didn't get to the platform in time to see it happen. He'd already used his suitcase to stop one of them nabbing him above ground, but he still had a locked briefcase with him when he fell, and unlike him, it survived the fall. It turned out to hold papers relating to a Mr Robert Hood, but in his inside coat pocket was a driving licence and other documents in the name of Peter Andrews. The driving licence in his wallet identified him as Simon Lee, but we all know who he really was.

The Met picked his mate, Robin, up shortly after he got home to Earls Court in the early hours of this morning. He says he knew Maine was meeting someone at Paddington last night but that he expected to find him in the flat when he got home. The suspicion is that Maine met the guy they've been after, that the meeting took place in Paddington and that Maine collected and paid for the new identity of Peter Andrews before the hoax bomb alert. They won't be sure until they've analysed the CCTV records, and that will take some time. It seems that 'Robin' initially professed ignorance about the briefcase but has since revealed that it was, indeed, his and that his true identity is Robert Hood. He kept the briefcase locked and hidden under his bed and claims that his bedroom door was also locked when he left Maine in his flat and went to work that evening. However, said door was unlocked and ajar when he and the police who detained him entered his flat. The Met are working on the theory that the hoax bomb alert was linked to the meeting; that it was intended to generate sufficient confusion to allow both men to get away. It was certainly successful for one of them and, had our man Maine boarded the tube at Paddington, it could have worked for both, but there was enough of him left on the track for the coppers who were first on the scene to be pretty sure it was our man who fell. It was the blonde hair that did it, but they've since used his fingerprints to establish his identity for certain.'

'So,' asked DS Brown, 'the guy they were really after, the guy called 'Henry', got away?' 'He did,' Knight replied, 'and the Met aren't happy about that at all, but it turns out that the briefcase Maine was carrying revealed something more, something that has particularly interested our friends at Scotland Yard. In addition to the papers relating to Robert Hood, there was also a package of lost and stolen passports and some offshore bank account statements that suggest 'Robin', or to be more accurate, Robert Hood, had stashed a very tidy sum away. It seems that he might have a lot of questions to answer about his dealings with the elusive 'Henry' and might just be able to tell the Met where to look for him.'

Knight paused as he looked around the senior members of his team. He couldn't help but feel very satisfied at the way things had turned out. 'I'm going up to have a word with the

Superintendent,' he said. 'Please pass on my thanks to Tom and Nicola for all their hard work. Wes, I know Shandy's information was very timely and helpful, but, the way things have turned out, it might be best if you didn't say anything more to her. However, you, Jess, could perhaps let Mr Carver know the outcome, and Gloria, too, for that matter. Max, you might thank Mrs Peabody for us, too. It won't be long before the papers get hold of the story, and I think we owe it to those who have genuinely helped the inquiry to get in first.' He looked around the room. 'Any questions?' he asked. There was none.

∞∞∞∞∞∞∞∞

18425256R00189

Printed in Great Britain
by Amazon